Novels by Sherman Sm

The Honeysuckle R
Silencing The Blues Man
Sausalito Night Music
Golden City On Fire

For information on the author and all his writings go to:

SHERMANSMITHAUTHOR.COM

This book is a work of fiction. Any references to historical events, real people, or real places are used fictionally. Other names, characters, places and events are products of the author's imagination, and any resemblance to actual events or persons, living or dead, are entirely coincidental.

POETS CAN'T SING

BY SHERMAN SMITH

CPSIA information can be obtained
at www.ICGtesting.com
Printed in the USA
FSHW020914030219
55449FS

9 780578 4129

POET'S CAN'T SING

Stella was a petite bottle blond, deliciously curvy, with a haughty, sultry, heart shaped face, who looked much younger than her thirty-seven years. In her rose- colored evening dress, she was a knock out. She sat in the empty bar with her chin nested in her hands and stared at the piano. It wasn't a Steinway, far from it, it was a bro-ken-down old clunker which she had paid six bucks for at an estate sale. With three keys missing on the piano, the estate agent should have paid her for taking it off their hands. Now she hoped that it would be the best six bucks she had ever spent.

In a moment of profound feminine insight, or stupidity, she had foolishly bought a shuttered night club out in the fog smothered avenues of San Francisco as a gift for Earl and Brooks, her fellas. The club, like the piano, was over-due for life support and could aptly be named *"The Dearly Departed"*. Foolish? Yes, and then some. For the time being it would remain nameless. She was a nurse. What business did she have owning a bar? Buying the bar had been a last desperate bid to keep Earl and Brooks together, which is not easy when you have two blind men who can't stand the sight of each other. She loved these two cantan-kerous men, and it tore at her heart when they argued like two school boys caught in a testosterone haze. She lifted her chin and crossed her fingers. "Please, not for me, but for them," she begged all the gods and lucky charms that could be called upon. Tonight, she would need more than luck. She needed some good old-fashioned magic. New Year's Eve, 1948, was coming at her like a runaway locomotive on greased tracks.

New Year's Eve and the wall clock said that she had fifty-eight minutes until the doors were to be opened. No, make that fifty-seven minutes. She had called in all her I.O.U's and made a few herself. Now there was nothing to do but wait. Ivory, Stubs, and Henry, her waiters and friends, busied themselves stocking the bar as she sat at the piano, tapped a key or two, and sang low and soft to herself.

The doors opened. Show time.

She and Earl sat near the piano. She smiled at Earl as she slipped her hand from his. She nervously lit another cigarette, inhaled, then blew out a blue smoke ring. The place was busting at the seams, tables full, with customers waiting at the door. The air was already thick with pungent tobacco smoke. Noisy. She could barely hear herself think. Earl found and patted her hand.

Stub slopped drinks from behind the bar while Ivory frantically worked the floor, seating guests and serving the drinks. She wanted to jump into the fray and lend a hand, but she couldn't leave Earl. Henry had stepped out and would deliver Brooks at eight which was in little less than an hour. if it hadn't been for Henry none of this would have happened.

The worst thing she could imagine was Brooks walking in the door right now. This was Earl's moment, and she knew he wasn't about to share it, especially with Brooks. She looked at the clock and made a mental note *to* throw the damn thing out later.

Earl was blind. He sat beside her, nursing a Manhattan, running his music through his head, as he waited for his moment. He was of medium build, average height, with salt and pepper hair, more salt than pepper. He was considered by many of her female competitors to be a handsome man. Tonight, he wore the white tux and top hat that she had given him. The red and purple spider web scars that crept out from behind his dark glasses added character. At thirty-six he had the beginnings of a drinker's double chin. His dark blue bow tie was askew. She had given up trying to keep that straight. He was a piece of work, complex and as difficult as the day is long. She wouldn't have him any other way.

Earl listened to the murmur of conversations, laughter, an occasional cough, the clink, and clack of bottle glass. "Stella," he asked, "the piano, it has been fixed? It has all its keys and is tuned?"

"You ask me again and I'll scream." She answered. His question had become ad nauseam.

Earl nodded, then finished his drink. When he first got out of the Veteran's Hospital he had played for tips and chump change at a small piano bar. The owner had insisted that he only play mellow night music. He had protested *that it was a god damned piano bar. Nobody wants to sing along with 'Sleepy Time Down South."* That got him nowhere. He ramped it up. They came to an agreement, and he was given his walking papers. Tonight, was his night, and he was going to play and sing the blues as only a blind white man who happens to be terrified of the dark can. He stood and held his arm out for guidance. "I'm ready."

Stella escorted him to the piano. She made sure the piano bench was positioned right where he needed it before he sat down. She started to reach for his tie to straighten it but opted not to. Table candles reflected in his dark glasses as she whispered in his ear. "This is your moment in the sun, love." She kissed him warmly on the cheek. "Would you please share just a little of it when Brooks gets here? For me."

He leaned into her kiss, making no promises in return. He sat motionless as Stella introduced him. "Thank you, ladies and gentlemen, friends, for coming tonight to this... this place without a name." Her laugh sounded nervous and put on. "I'm looking for the right inspiration. Ideas, anyone?" The laughter returned was genuine. "Please welcome my inspiration, Mister Earl Crier."

Earl flexed his fingers then struck a few experimental notes. He swept into a tune so gently the audience listened before they knew that it had even begun. His voice had a deep rich bluesy roadhouse quality etched with a touch of irony. He sang straight down the middle of the note and understood the emotions in a way that made you feel as if he was letting you in on a story he had just made up.

Stella stepped back to the bar and took a gin and tonic from Henry. Her eyes searched the crowd as she tracked the facial expressions around the room. Earl was in top form, his music as lovely as a warm wind in the shade. The crowd quieted as they too fell in love with her guy. She tapped out her cigarette then raised her glass towards the audience, then clicked a finger nail several times on the glass as she turned towards Earl.

Earl heard the click and the crackle of ice in Stella's glass; a crystal chime. "Here's to our Stella," he spoke into the microphone. His voice a portrait of his soul, as his fingers danced across the keyboard, and he began to sing.

The front door opened, followed by a disquieting murmur from the crowd. Stella turned. There in the doorway stood Brooks. Her moment in the starlight blew away like an old playbill on a cold winter's night. He had arrived early, and if anything, he knew how to make an entrance. *Oh Brooks, not now,* she thought. All eyes were riveted on him. He was reedy thin, and Abraham Lincoln tall. He was dressed in a black tux, white bow-tie, and a black top hat. The murmur of surprise that rippled across the room was drawn by Brook's most remarkable feature, a white silk cloth that had been made into mask that slipped over his head, the open end just touching his shoulders, with a hole for his mouth and a sewn on black sash that marked where his eyes should have been. Stella had made it replace the hideous bandage that covered the face he had lost when a Nazis V-2 Rocket had made a direct hit on his favorite pub in London. The room grew still in a mixture of curiosity, and anticipation. She noticed the tremor in her hand as she lit another cigarette and glanced nervously at Earl.

Earl could taste the change in weather but couldn't quite determine the storms direction. His voice softened, his fingers lighter on the keys, as he sang his song to her: 'I can See My Stella Beneath a Moonlit Sky." His laconic voice, raspy and emotional, spoke of how he could see the woman he loved, though he could see no other things, the moon a love-light in his mind's eye.

After a moment he stopped singing.

As the storm blew close he continued to play bits and pieces at random. The music moved like a spiderweb stirred by a sudden breeze, it changed like a leaf twisting as it fell to the ground. And fell silent.

Brooks held his hand out with cab fare for the cabby

who took a dollar ten, hesitated, then took a quarter more. Henry stood aside, exchanging a warm loving wink with Stella.

Brooks stood silent as he too tried to sense the weather. And his timing. His snow bright cane came down with a thunderclap on the wooden floor. *KNOCK! KNOCK!* He pounded his cane on the floor.

A dark cloud crossed Earl's mind, and he remained silent, with a scowl he could not hide.

"And you Stella mean everything to me." Brooks said with a poet's voice as he raised his cane high, a romantic figure behind a mysterious mask. "Where are you my dear?"

Stella stepped forward and stopped when there was a straight path between the tables for him to follow her voice. "Right here," she said as she let out a dramatic sigh. Brooks, using his cane, stepped forward. "Say again please." He followed her voice, his slow deliberate steps seductive and hypnotic. He held his head high with surprising self-confidence.

A woman seated at the nearest table to his left took in a short breath as he drew near. He paused, turned and bowed. The woman could just make out a thin smile beneath the solitary hole in his mask. The silk edges fluttered lightly with his words. "I can assure you madam that the mystery of what beauty lies beneath your intoxicating perfume is as curious to me as what lies behind this mask to you." He tapped his cane twice lightly. "I'm over here," he heard Stella say as he turned back towards her. There was a half breath of silence around the room followed by a torrent of applause, pounding rain beating down. driving the stifling heat of the day away.

Earl played the first stanza of '*When Fools Rush in.*' a favorite Johnny Mercer tune.'

Stella cast a punishing evil eye, she only wished he could see.

Earl leaned into the mike. "Ladies and gentlemen, we have a poet in the house. Brooks Weingarden, the third. A poet, you see, is a musician who can't sing; Brooks has a slightly reckless alto voice which always wanders off looking for notes in all the wrong places. How can you sing if you can't remember the words? Words need to find a man's heart and some men's minds are hopelessly small targets. The scarecrow in the Wizard of Oz needed a brain, and the tin man a heart. Brooks here, would be grateful for either. Poets? Hah!" As easy as flipping a coin Earl changed his tone and sang to Stella's song with intoxicating charm.

Brooks held onto Stella's arm as they approached the piano wordlessly. A hush fell across the room so profound that even Earl fell silent as some of his self-importance leaked out of him. Brooks let Stella's arm slip away as his whole body drew up into a tight knot of anger. He shook with it as he drew back his arm, fist clinched, wanting to strike out. Stella stepped back unable to find any words to ease his anger. A single cough broke the quiet.

Earl's right hand, as still as a willow's branch on a windless day, jumped, then dropped, striking a solitary key. The *F Sharp,* a lightning bolt, that took the breath from the room.

"Brooks…" Stella whispered. "Please. Don't."

Brooks shrugged, bringing his shoulder almost to his ears and back down. His silken mask fluttered as it settled back into place.

Earl slowly pulled his hands away from the keyboard and let them drop into his lap. "Stella...", he said in a weak attempt to regain control of the moment.

"And you, Sir," Brooks said as if addressing a student who had just been caught cheating on an exam, "are a clown in a world sadly lacking in smiles."

Stella squeezed Brook's shoulder. "Enough, please." She stepped behind Earl and put a hand on each of his shoulders giving a light massage as she whispered in his ear. "This is my place sweetheart, and like it or not I've got the final word on who stays and who plays." Earl opened and closed his mouth a few times, at a loss for words. He made a conciliatory gesture with one hand and smiled a tight smile. "That's better. You are going to have to share the piano with Brooks. You are going to have to share the stage. I love you both — but in different ways. Brooks will never share my bed. So, move over lover and share what you can."

Earl shared the piano stool with Brooks in an uneasy truce. "How are you at chop sticks?" Earl asked, pandering to the audience.

"Careful," Stella whispered from behind them with an indulgent tone that mothers use on children and bartenders use on drunks.

"Lousy," responded Brooks. "When was the last time you saw a blind man eat Chinese?" There was a half-breath of silence followed by an explosion of laughter.

The Storm clouds passed to Stella's relief. She stepped back to retrieve her drink.

Earl knew that he could out play and sing circles around Brooks. He also knew that he would not sing down to Brook's level. He was too good for that. Since losing his sight music had become his life. Now he was caught between a rock and a hard place. He ran his options through his mind. *Stella had given him a short list: Either find a way to work with Brooks, treat him as your equal, or ship out. Bull shit! It'll be a cold day in hell when that no talent egotistical bum is my equal. Why I'd rather... lose Stella? No...* He flexed and toughed his fingers together, then played a few mystical notes on his chin. *Give up music. Neither is an option. Wait a minute, there is something that Brooks can do better than anyone I've ever heard. How far can he take it? Shit let's find out.*

"Brooks, back at the Veteran's Hospital I once heard you whistling something in the shower." He began to play a Duke Ellington piece.

"You want to whistle us up a tune?" His fingers dusted magic on the keys. "I'll just tag along."

Brooks began to play, his long sensuous fingers gliding across the key board. He wasn't as good as Earl and felt the pressure of trying to keep up. "There, I think you've got it," he said as he gave Earl the piano, rose, and fumbled for the mike. He stood, dark, mysterious, and elegant. The music within him, blowing out of his white silk mask, topped with his black top hat, was deep and wide as a clear glacier fed stream. Earl played alongside. Neither performing down to the other. Their music sounding like the best of old friends. Next, they slipped into *Jazz Me Blues*, with a few original twists. This time Earl had trouble keeping up with Brook's whistling genius. Brooks brought the crowd to a standing ovation with *Peer GYNT, Theme of Grieg. That one was solo.* Earl didn't do classical. Brooks did.

Henry stepped edged his way through the tables with his

clarinet and joined them. He was out whistled, soon stepping aside. Earl leaned in towards the mike Brooks held. "Stella this is for you." Henry played a long haunting note as the trio played Stella's song... The last stanza Brooks whistled solo.

"Ladies and Gentlemen, Brooks Weingarden, our resident poet," Earl said. "Poets can't sing but man — oh man — he sure can whistle."

Stella cried happy tears. Her laughter the best music of the evening.

1

THE BLIND MAN'S DRAGON

The scream came suddenly in the night.

Stella peered over a patient's chart towards the door at the far end of the dimly lit ward. This scream she knew, and her heart always seemed to skip a beat when Earl Crier screamed. His was an expression of the wildest, deepest, anguish of the human soul. She brushed her dark auburn hair away from her emerald green eyes and stared intently towards the open ward doors from where Earl's cry had come.

There was a time when Stella had thought she could get used to night terrors. She knew that the veterans' hospital was never silent. She heard her patients' anguish every night as they struggled with their vivid memories of places they'd been and things they could never forget. She understood what war had done to them and gave comfort where she could. Men screamed with primal fear and anguish when they were closest to the horrendous memories they had buried deeply, but not deeply enough.

Many of the patients in her ward were there because they were beyond healing, stored where they received only the basic necessary care. Here they were purposefully kept out of sight, tucked discreetly away from a post-war America that did not want these living reminders of man's capacity for heinous cruelty and violence visible and blaming.

Earl's cry was not a whimper, a cry of desperation, or of surrender.It was a plea for sanctuary. Unlike the others Earl was not a wait-and-see patient. He was not disposable. He was blind, otherwise sound of mind and body. Well, mostly. Earl touched Stella's heart where the others couldn't. Like the rest, he had his nightmares, only it was not these dark dreams that troubled him. His dream always began and ended the same way: he was trapped in the pitch-black hold of an ammunition transport as it was sinking in the frigid Murmansk Sea.

* * * *

He was alone; the Master Chief, dead nearby. Tons of explosive shells spun around him like crazed bowling balls. His leg was broken. He could hear the groans of the ship as it settled down into the dark depths of a bitterly cold sea. Without hope, he prayed for an explosion and a quick death.

The explosion came. Deafening. Ferocious. When his vision cleared he could see through a great hole, where the ship had been torn in half, a million stars twinkling in the night sky. Fifteen-foot, brooding gray waves slammed the aft section of the ship as it slipped beneath the angry sea. It appeared as if Hell had indeed frozen over as the sea rushed in.

* * * *

That was when he would wake, and that was when he screamed. It was in that waking moment that he knew that the dark was eternal, that he was in the serpent's lair. The memory of light and sometimes color in his dreams, no matter how terrifying, was his sanctuary, but when he woke his blindness became his all-consuming reality. Here the dark was deep, real, and terrifying.

Stella sighed and shook her head. She knew that Earl was terrified of the dark. When he was a child his mother had left a candle lit by the side of his bed to protect him from the dark creatures that lived in his imagination. Here there was no escape. No sanctuary. He would wake. He would scream. Then he would try to find some sanity, something right in a world that had gone suddenly dark and terribly wrong. It had taken time, but somewhere along the way he found refuge within himself. Now when he woke, he still screamed, but then he would sing, his rich voice haunting as he sought to master his blindness and the beast that lurked within.

Stella waited for his song.

His pillow damp with sweat, mouth dry and dusty, Earl rose, determined not to spend one more eternal moment in bed. He listened to sounds in the cavernous hospital which was now his home, the same sounds he heard each night an hour or so after midnight. The murmur of voices of the orderlies and the screams from patients whose personal banshees startled the very air. He had to rise, to get to his feet, to stand strong, to raise his voice in song, to let his dragon know that he would not go gently into this unforgiving dark. The fingers on his left hand balled into a tight fist as he heard a cruel whack on human flesh, followed by a cry, as Elroy Hawk, a vindictive hospital orderly, slapped a helpless patient out of his night terrors. *Elroy*, he thought, *you mean miserable son-of-a-bitch. There is a difference between justice and retribution. The day will come when you'll get your due.*

He slipped into his hospital robe and slippers, then with

a slow stiff limp he counted his steps, seventy-one in all, to the day room where there was a piano. There he would rage and sing his blues until in the wee hours of the morning he would fall into an exhausted lethargy with his fingers still on the keyboard.

Stella listened as Earl's music slowed to a gentle refrain. She looked at the clock, which ticked a little after five in the morning. Earl had labored over the ivories a little longer than normal, she thought; perhaps this morning he might sleep a while. Earl napped, rarely slept; it was easier that way. Often before getting off duty, Stella would slip into the day room, gently wake him and massage his neck. A peaceful moment she shared with no other patient.

She stiffened when she heard the distinctive clack of Elroy's shoes in the outside corridor. When Elroy was up to no good he walked hard, a sound always followed by trouble.

Elroy wore his usual Cheshire Cat grin as he leaned against the wall just outside the day room. He lit a cigarette and waited. Standing six-foot-one, he was all brawn, with an abnormally large blue vein that dominated the left side of his huge cordwood neck. His hair, an unnatural duck down yellow, was cropped short, which drew attention to his dark-brown ferret eyes. By all measures Elroy Hawks was an intimidating man.

He drew on his cigarette as he waited and listened to Earl's music as it moved from a frantic dance to a gentle waltz. The blind fool's caterwauling irritated the hell out of him and he got a perverse kick when he got a chance to wake the clown up by slamming his fist down on the piano keys an inch or two from his head. He chuckled an unusually perverse laugh.

"Not this morning, you son-of-a-bitch," Stella said as she set a bed pan down and set her sight straight on Elroy. All of five-foot four, Stella, as head nurse, rarely took any guff from anyone, especially Elroy Hawks. If he weren't the hospital administrator's personal goon she would have seen to his termination the same day she had come on board.

Elroy tapped out the cigarette on the bottom of his shoe, stuck the long butt in his shirt pocket, and walked calmly over to the elevator. Once inside, he turned, with his middle finger extended in a profane salute. His grin broadened. "Your day will come." The door hissed closed.

2
WELCOME HOME, SON

Henry Akita, tired and heavy-hearted, fished in his pocket for a dime as he waited for the Geary Street trolley to pull up. It was raining cats and dogs, with a blustery wind. He had spent the day searching for a room and had been turned away from the YMCA, and the door had been slammed in his face at a dozen boarding houses.

His face and the color of his skin said that he was Japanese American — Nisei — and San Francisco was notorious for its prejudice against Asians. NO JAPS ALLOWED signs were still prominent throughout the city. The war had ended but not the bitterness of the experience.

The hair on the back of his neck prickled as he boarded the streetcar; every eye was on him, and none was friendly. He felt the awful weight of prejudice as he slipped the coin into the coin box. He pulled his hat down low on his forehead and grabbed a pole for support as the tram started up. He took an empty seat in the back behind two Negroes, kept his head low to avoid making any eye contact, and stared out the rain-splotched window.

Henry had fought for his country, the United States of America, and he had earned the right to call California his home. He had been born on a small farm near Salinas. That he had served his county with the 442nd Regimental Combat Team as a combat medic made little difference. His race usurped his experience.

He had a year of pre-med at Berkeley before the war and wanted to go to Stanford under the new G.I. Bill — a huge opportunity for thousands of returning veterans. It just took a little longer for the government to get around to you if you were Nisei. Because of his combat experience he had been able to land a job as a Grade II orderly at the Veteran's Hospital and was assigned to the long-term care ward where most of the patients' wounds, physical and otherwise, had been suffered in combat against the Japanese. These were the cards he had been dealt and the cards he would have to play. No one had said it would be easy.

Three days after being discharged he had gone home to the family farm near Salinas, where he found the once-thriving multicultural farms now empty of brown faces. None of the Japanese-Americans that had been shipped off to relocation camps in 1942 had returned home; at least not yet.

He remembered the postcard he had received in May 1945. The last line, in his mother's petite handwriting had simply said: *The camp will be closing soon, and your father is looking forward to us going back to the farm. We will not be able to go home until the war is over. The farm where we will be allowed to work is somewhere in Michigan. Where, we haven't been told.* It was the first mail he had received in three weeks and it came two days after they liberated Kaufering IV Houlach, a sub-camp of Dachau.

* * * *

Henry crouched low behind the first of a long chain of wooden railway cars that led towards the large wooden gate at the front of the concentration camp. The gate was open, with more cars blocking his view into the camp. An order had been given to try not to damage the train cars;

no one knew what might be in them. There were rumors: the most hopeful was that the cars were filled with Red Cross supplies of food and medicine intended for the prisoners and not yet delivered.

The sun was bright in a cloudless sky as brilliant searchlights still blazed across the gate and the glistening barbed wire. He could see armed guards with maddened guard dogs straining at their leash. The roar of tanks filled the air as the advance column approached the gates to one of the sub-camps of Dachau. He waited for the first shots and the battle for the camp to begin.

At the first sight of the American troops, the guards dropped their weapons and raised their hands. His platoon stepped out from behind the railway car and approached the camp with caution. The camp guards had thrown down their weapons but were gunned down without mercy. The dogs charged the advancing Americans only to be chewed up by machine gun bullets.

The first and the worst thing he noticed as they approached was the stench of rotting cadavers. There was a cry for a medic but the only casualties he could see so far were the Nazi guards. He rushed forward to where a soldier pointed. The door to a weathered railway car was wide open, the car filled with hundreds of dead bodies the retreating S.S. garrison had simply left to rot. A medic wasn't needed.

There were forty cars in all.

The scene near the entrance to the high barbed-wired fenced interior of the camp numbed his senses. Dante's Inferno seemed pale compared to the real hell of what lay before him. Inside the camp there were storage rooms filled with stacks of recently gassed prisoners; men, women, and children. A row of small cement structures near the prison entrance contained a coal-fired crematorium, a gas chamber, and rooms piled high with naked and emaciated human corpses. And piles upon piles of ashes, human ashes. He had to look away.

He looked out over the prison yard where he saw dozens of dead inmates lying where they had fallen in the last few hours or days before their liberation. Since all the bodies were in various stages of decomposition, the stench of death was overwhelming. He knelt, puked, and cried as he had never cried before. As he did so hundreds of emaciated prisoners staggered out of their crowded barracks and soon pressed at the confining barbed wire fence. They began to shout in unison, a blur of languages, which soon became a chilling roar. Most of the adult prisoners could not have weighed more than 80 pounds. He didn't know how some of them could still be alive.

He didn't know it then, but that stench of death would stay with him the rest of his life.

Amongst the dead he saw a hand move. The hand, skin clinging to bone, belonged to a man who should not have been alive but somehow managed to hang on to that last grasp of life. Henry knelt next to him, took his hand, found a pulse, and began to cry.

With a frail voice the man looked up at him. His eyes taking in Henry's face with profound curiosity. "Your eyes," he said in English with a pronounced Italian accent, "your face... are these the eyes of an angel?" He lay still as Henry once again struggled to find a pulse. He picked the man up, leaving some of his worn concentration camp gray-striped uniform stuck to the frozen ground. The man spoke to him in a whisper he could barely hear as he carried him towards a deserted guard's barracks in search of a bed and some warmth. "I don't think that you are an angel," he whispered. "I think you are mortal like me. I've been waiting for you. What took you so long?"

Henry slipped on the snow and fell to one knee. The frail little man looked at Henry's face and Asian eyes. "Perhaps one day I'll tell you about the angel's eyes. I'm going to see them now." That was the last man to die in Henry's arms, but not the last of death he would see in the war.

At Dachau he could not forget that his family was still interned in a relocation camp back in the good old United States of America, land of the free. The camps were not the same, but that did not ease the pain in his heart.

* * * *

A few blocks from his intended stop the street car jolted to a halt.

The doors opened with a hiss as four young punks dressed in worn San Francisco Don's varsity jackets boarded and made their way towards the back of the car.

A beefy pug slammed his fist forcefully down on the back of a seat jarring its occupant. "Look what we got here." He leaned down and stared into the black man's eyes looking for any sign of rebellion. The man never took his eyes off his own shoe laces. "I got no problem with niggers riding in the ass of the bus where they belong, but I'll be damned if I'll ride in the same car with a butter-head."

Henry looked up from beneath the brim of his hat. All eyes were on him except for the black men. The conductor jerked his thumb up pointing towards the door. The punks in their varsity jackets were not the sporting types, and they were out for blood. Henry rose and made for the door, careful not to turn his back towards them or to give them any further reason to attack. There were low whispers throughout the tram. "I didn't know there was a Jap on board. The nerve, and our boys just barely back home — those that made it." There were no sympathetic eyes.

The doors hissed closed behind him.

The rain had lessened but the wind still blew cold and raw. He hastened towards a side street without looking back. He did not need to, the hiss of the trolley's door a second and third time followed by the heavy sounds of running feet on the rain drenched street, told him all he needed to know. He had been taught self-defense in the Army and had been a boxer in high school, but he wasn't foolish enough to take these guys on. Right now, he needed to get off the street.

He ducked into the front door of a neighborhood bar: Adam's Place. It was early, the bar empty except for a man sweeping up peanut shells off the floor. The man was short, about Henry's height, with a belly worthy of any barkeeper. He had a full head of cloud white hair, with spectacles perched on a blue-veined nose set against a rose-flushed face.

"Good morning," the man said with a welcoming smile. "I'm not open for business yet, but you are welcome to some coffee on the house." He leaned the broom up against a table and peered through his glasses at Henry.

"Thanks," Henry said as he looked over his shoulder, then slid into a dimly lit booth in the back of the room.

The barkeeper seemed to notice Henry's edginess as he calmly walked over to the bar and pulled what appeared to be a sign from a drawer and hung it on the back of the cash register.

Through the corner of his eye Henry saw the barkeeper pull a baseball bat from its hideaway. Things are getting dicey, he thought as he retreated to the deepest corner of the booth. He felt beneath the table to see if there was room beneath. The table wasn't bolted down. It gave him an even chance to avoid the bat, if he could use the table as a shield. An old man with a bat he could handle, if the street thugs came in, he was toast.

He eyed the door, they were close.

The barkeeper wiped his hands on his apron. "No need to worry," he said in a non-threatening voice. "You stay put, out of sight and out of mind. I've dealt with hooligans like this before." He knew by the shouts exactly who he was about to deal with.

The beefy pug, with acne and a sweaty lock of hair drooped over one eye, burst into the bar as if he owned the place. His three pals skidded to a halt immediately behind him. They were jazzed, high on adrenaline and eager for a fight. One twirled a length of bicycle chain. The beefy pug screeched: "Hey, old man, you got a Jap in here?" Their eyes searched the bar.

"You see that?" The barkeeper brought down the bat with a resounding whack on the side of the bar, then pointed at the sign he had hung on the back of the cash register. NO JAPS ALLOWED! "I put it there December 8th, 1941. I don't cotton much to anyone who attacks my country — nor," he punctuated, "punks who act like storm troopers, without a brain or a grain of decency. My door is open for fresh air, not to punks like you." The bat slammed against the side of the bar. Whack! "Now get!"

The toughs saw the old man meant business. "Your

day will come, old man," the greasy pug hissed, his finger pointed menacingly. "Right now, we got a Jap that needs to join his ancestors." The bicycle chain whipped the back of a chair, stripping the paint. They left as abruptly as they had entered, their cries fading as they sought their prey elsewhere.

The barkeeper waited a moment then poured a cup of coffee. "Cream?" he asked as he turned towards where Henry sat.

Henry was lost for words, dumbstruck by this simple act of kindness.

"Cream?" The bartender asked again.

"No, sir. Cream? Ah... sure... No, black is fine."

"Well, when you make up your mind, come on over here to the bar where there's better light, those assholes won't be back."

A breeze blowing through the open door scattered peanut shells across the floor as Henry approached the bar. He stepped softy in a slight dance, not wanting to crush any of them; the old man was trying to sweep them up. He could not help but step on a few, and each crunch seemed as loud as an exploding artillery shell.

The barkeeper chuckled at his expense. "Are you working at the Vet's Hospital?"

"Yes, sir," Henry said. He looked at his watch. "First day. How did you know?"

"Your shoes are a dead give-away, son. You bought them at the hospital supply store?"

Henry nodded.

The man held out his hand. "Edward Gibson." He looked Henry over. "Nisei," he said with a little respect.

13

"You served with the 100th?"

Henry stood straight, proud to answer: "442nd Regimental Combat Team; Medic."

"Well, I'll be damned," Edward Gibson said as his eyes misted over. "I didn't catch your name, son? My friends call me Gibby. I'd be proud if you would do the same."

"Henry." Now he felt foolish for thinking Gibby an enemy when he had picked up the baseball bat. "Henry Akita," he finished, not afraid to use his Japanese name.

Gibby turned a light on behind the bar. "Henry, take a gander over here, I think it will explain a few things." A 'T-Patch' shoulder emblem from the 36th Army Infantry Division hung proudly in a glass frame. A framed picture of a young man in uniform sat on the counter immediately below. "This belonged to my son Adam." Gibby's eyes glistened with the memory. "The photo was taken just before he shipped out. He served with the lost battalion. Adam's platoon took ninety percent casualties. But of course, you would know about that wouldn't you?" Gibby held his gaze. "A Nisei medic saved his life. The day I got his letter is the same day I took this out of the window." Gibby pulled the sign NO JAPS ALLOWED! from the back of the cash register and tore it in half. Then half again. He held out his hand. "Welcome home, son."

3
WAIT AND SEE

The itch spread upwards from between Ivory Burch's toes; his skin begged for relief. His right foot ached, the way it had after the first ten miles of his forced march to the prison camp. His leg muscles twitched with the memory of working twelve hours underground digging tunnels before being forced to build a roadway through dense jungle. A hundred times he had tried to resist the urge to scratch. The relentless itch drove him nuts. He sat up, pulled his bed sheets back, reached down, and groped absently beneath his gray hospital pajamas - but there were no toes to scratch, no ankle or knee, or calf. Only the pain, masked by the unrelenting itch, the ghost of flesh gone bad.

When he had stumbled out of the jungle after four plus years as an honored guest of the Emperor of Japan, a lowly and forgotten prisoner of war, he had escaped with his life. Barely: his legs, as thin as cricket bats, were covered with weeping tropical ulcers. A deep sword wound on his right thigh had gone gangrenous and everything from there down had to be removed. The field amputation had been guillo-tines style. The skin and fascia cut at lower levels than the bone. The stump, left open to drain, had not been sutured or closed. It was covered with a dressing, traction applied to the skin of his lower thigh as he healed.

His healing was slow because of malnutrition, beriberi, malaria, and a host of complications. His one constant nightmare, the one that nibbled away at his will to live, was the faces, voices, of the men who had died there. It was harder to heal than the maladies that ravished his flesh.

He had been captured in China December 8th, 1941, the day after the bombing of Pearl Harbor, and remained in brutal and inhuman conditions until, after a desperate escape, he found his way back to friendly hands three days after the Emperor of Japan surrendered in total defeat.

He had not fired a shot during the entire war but had suffered shame and abuse every single day, each day, each hour his agony and desperation a brooding fever. In the end he was the only man to crawl out of that hell hole alive.

At Letterman General Hospital it was determined that not enough skin remained on his thigh to stretch over the truncated femurs. A second and third amputation would be needed to saw and shape the bone, grind down the stump, so the soft tissue could grow and harden.

There needed to be enough loose flaps of skin that could be pulled over it so that a pointed bone would not puncture the recovering flesh. This would take time and it could not be done until Ivory recovered the strength needed to endure the additional trauma of the surgeries.

There were too many patients to deal with, most with a better chance of going home. The doctors did not know if Ivory had enough fight left in him to survive. So, Ivory was tagged a "wait and see" patient and transferred to the Veterans Hospital in San Francisco, where they would wait and see if he would live or die. There was no medicine that could heal what Ivory needed to heal.

4
ANRUI

Henry tried but could not ignore the hostile looks, the anger and hatred that seemed to follow his every move during his first few days of orientation at the Veterans' Hospital. He thought that he had been prepared. Now he felt insecure, anything but prepared, naked beneath a hot and unforgiving sun. Prejudice is a living thing. You feed it and it multiples. You try to ignore it, and it will surprise you with its ferocity. To kill it you must cut off its food source; and he was that source. Like it or not, he had eight hours ahead of him in a ward filled with angry, dismembered veterans who had every reason to hate his very existence.

When he was first assigned to this ward, where men were still paying with their own flesh and blood for battles long lost or won, he wanted to turn and run. Every man has his breaking point and he knew that his was tracking his own shadow. If he bolted and ran now he would never get a scholarship to Stanford Medical School. He planned to study obstetrics, where he could bring life and hope into this world once so filled with death.

He stood at a window that overlooked a cold, wind-swept parking lot and the city beyond and watched as a wall of dense fog blew in from the ocean, obscuring the view one block at a time. He needed a warm, friendly sunset, not cold, gray gloom. Perhaps his father had been right: his dream of becoming a doctor was too lofty. Part of him wished that he could just go back home and grow artichokes alongside his dad. But the farm had been confiscated. While he had served his country, his family languished in the Tule Lake Internment Camp.

"You're looking chipper," the ward nurse said. She lit a cigarette and handed him a clipboard. "You ready for this?"

It was their first meeting. She had been off duty during his orientation. He glued a smile on his inscrutable face and looked straight into her cool, emerald-green eyes. "No, but I'll make do."

"Stella Tate." She held out her hand. Her smile was warm and sincere.

Henry took it in his as his heart fluttered a little. He had almost forgotten what the soft warmth of a woman's hand felt like. And she was white and willing to shake his hand.

"I've read your file." She gave a reassuring smile. A blue smoke circle danced between them as she exhaled. "You'll do fine."

"Thanks." He took a deep breath and looked at his first patient's chart. He did not need to read far before he knew there would be trouble.

Ivory Burch, age 28
Corporal, United States Marine Corps
1940-1946
P.O.W., Philippines. Escaped 1945
Dengue fever, malaria, etc., etc., etc.

If there was one patient in this entire hospital who would harbor a deep hatred of the Japanese, it would be Ivory Burch. *Great*, Henry thought, *hang me out to dry with a monsoon blowing up my ass.*

In the wee hours of the morning Henry woke a patient, lifted his head for a drink, and administered a sleeping pill. The night shift had been quiet except for the mumbles, screams of terror, and whimpers that came every night.

He suspected that in time he would get used to the night sounds, the sudden, startling cries in the dimly lit ward.

He had heard too many men cry out from where they had fallen on the battlefield. This was different. He felt useless. He busied himself reading the patient clipboards, familiarizing himself with every Tom, Dick and Harry. Their medical records said little about the real men who languished in the beds surrounding him. He walked on pins and needles to avoid conflict, knowing that his mere presence added to their pain. He did not want a confrontation and hoped for the best for the wounded veterans surrounding him.

Henry looked from the clipboard to Ivory as Ivory tossed fitfully in his sleep. Ivory was emaciated and looked a couple of decades older than his twenty-eight years. As a prisoner of war, he had suffered severe weight loss, physical, mental, and spiritual deterioration.

His mental health was as much a cause of his infection as the multiple jungle parasites that plagued him. Ivory needed to have his stump ground to fit a prosthesis. If they waited much longer they would have to take more of the leg. Henry sighed, whispering aloud, "Anrui."

"Pardon me?" Stella asked. She had come into the ward as quiet as an early spring breeze.

Henry bowed slightly, looking contrite, saying nothing at first. Stella held her gaze on him until he answered. "Anrui," he said in a low whisper, afraid that one of the patients might hear, "is a Japanese word that is difficult to translate." His eyes roamed the room as he checked to see that they were not being overheard. "Anrui is the kind of sorrow and pain that can't be seen, a desperate anguish that takes away the will to live." He held his hands up framing his face. "You see this face? It is the same color as the bastards who tortured and did everything short of killing this man. What do you think Ivory Burch is going to do when he sees me?" He looked Stella straight in the eye, "Please, I'm begging you." This time he was too loud. He hung the clipboard with Ivory's charts at the end of his bed, changing his voice quickly back to a whisper. "Not this one, please. Move him to a different ward. Move me to a different ward."

They stepped out of the ward where they could talk easier.

"Doctor Garitty thought you might feel that way." Stella said. "The answer is no. Henry, when you applied for the position you knew there were going be men here who have good reason to hate the Japanese. Men fed a diet of hate and violence don't change easily. The politicians may have signed papers that says the war is over; meanwhile, men like Ivory Burch are thrown into a place like this because there isn't any place else for them to go.

"If Ivory can't find a way to confront his demons here - he never will. And if he doesn't it will kill him. You better than anyone else can help him get back what's left of his life."

She knew she was coming across too hard and softened her voice. "Henry, you have held men in your arms on the battlefield who just wanted to know why they were dying. You've seen the look of raw hatred in their eyes when they killed the enemy close, or saw a buddy blown to bits. Hate and anger are two of the most debilitating wounds many of these men carry. How many Nisei have the same wounds and are unwilling to forgive the prison camps and the blind prejudice they and their families have lived through?" She searched his eyes with hers looking for an answer.

"Jesus, why do I feel like I'm a clay pigeon in a shooting gallery?" Henry's eyes widened as someone in the ward screamed louder and longer than the others.

"Henry, you're being summoned," Stella said. "It's Ivory. He's asking for your help the only way he can."

5
IT'S ONLY A DREAM

Ivory could not remember the last time he had slept well. When he slept he woke up more exhausted; his mind seemed always to be in a blurry fog. His body had been through hell's grinder and needed rest; his spirit knew of worse places. He just wanted to be left alone, to close his eyes, and finally get some peace.

He had one constant nightmare; everything else that he had experienced as a prisoner of war was lost in a deep, protecting haze. He had escaped from the Japanese prison camp, but he could not escape its nightmare. He told the doctors all he needed was a few short naps and he'd be fine. Take two of these and you'll sleep like a baby was their usual answer. No, the drugs would just take him exactly where he did not want to go. He tossed and turned, then he tried to get out of bed, his one good leg betraying him. The medication proved to be stronger than his will, and he fell back onto his bed in a deep, troubled sleep.

His nightmare always began the same way: waking on a hard-earthen floor, drenched in a fever sweat, exhausted, his joints aflame, his skin screaming from the fire ants that fed on the lice that swarmed across his flesh. This is the way he had woken every day he had been a prisoner of the Japanese.

He woke never knowing if he had slept.

* * * *

The morning was hot; the sun was not yet over the jungle canopy; the air was combustible, a miasma of jungle rot mixed with the stench of death palatable to all his senses. His latest bout of malaria had left him flushed and fuzzy; infected sores and tropical ulcers plagued his wasted flesh. The tattered remains of his uniform crusted with filth hung like strips of carrion. His extended gut ached with hunger; his tongue was swollen and raw.

This morning he had not been able to eat his meager ration of rice.

Despite the heat and stifling jungle humidity his body shook with chills. He rose, fearing a beating if he did not, and stumbled out to his work detail. His limbs swollen with symptoms of beriberi made his walk a stumbling gait as he caught up with Sergeant Ware.

"How many?" Sergeant Ware asked without turning to look at Ivory. The sergeant wore only a loincloth made of what was left of his uniform. His hair was long and matted with mud, dried excrement, and crud. His beard carried thirteen months of the same.

"Too many." Ivory answered his voice weak and lethargic. He and the sergeant were on burial detail. Nine prisoners who had died in the tunnels overnight lay stacked like cordwood at the entrance. Five other prisoners had died in the camp from disease, abuse, or despair. Ivory and the sergeant waited, eyes to the ground, as a guard beat a malingerer with a bukuto — a wooden practice sword. When he finished they went to collect his body, his body

weighed next to nothing as they struggled to lift him.

"Six," the sergeant groused. "If this keeps up there won't be enough of us left to finish the tunnels."

"He's alive," Ivory said. The beaten man's lungs rose and fell in\his pitifully shrunken chest.

The sergeant shook his head. "No, he's dead, all right. God just ain't found him yet. That's just his spirit, tired and broken, pleading to be taken from this hell."

They carried the body to the edge of a cliff, the rocky river bed sixty feet below an open graveyard, then swung him over the side as they had the bodies of the men who had died the day before and the day before that.

"I gave him my word." Ivory said. His body shook with malarial chills as sweat beaded on his forehead.

The sergeant reached out to steady him. If he were to collapse, and be seen by a guard, he would be gutted with a bayonet and thrown over the side. There were no replacements available and the sergeant knew that he couldn't do the job on his own.

"I promised to visit his folks if I made it out of here and he didn't." He looked down at the horrid stack of cadavers. The sergeant could barely hold him upright as Ivory looked at him with a pained expression. "I... I can't remember who he was."

They turned back towards the stack of cadavers outside the tunnel entrance. One lone tear seeped out and evaporated leaving a short salty grimy trail. "Sarge, who was he?"

The sergeant pinched what was left of the flesh on Ivory's forearm, trying not to draw blood because nothing healed, and the slightest wound invited infection. Regardless a small spot of blood oozed forth. He nodded, then spat from a dry mouth. "It doesn't matter," Sergeant Ware said. "If we don't get out of here we'll be joining them soon enough." He looked at Ivory, weighed what he saw, then took a good measure of himself. "I figure it might be two, three days at the most before they slaughter the lot of us. The Japs don't want no witnesses to what they're burying in the tunnels. They're in a hurry to get out of here themselves and want no trace left behind."

He stopped talking while they loaded three bodies into a wobbly wheelbarrow and moved awkwardly back towards the cliff, where they stopped three yards short of the cliff's edge. Sergeant Ware squatted in the hot sun, his hands still on the handles of the death cart for support. "You and I are China Marines, most likely the last of our outfit still standing. If we die here no one will know what happened to some of the best men the Marine Corps ever produced." He rubbed his cheek, grimaced, then pulled a rotten tooth from his mouth, which he bounced a couple of times in his hand before giving it a gentle toss towards the cliff's edge. He spat a bloody spot of phlegm a he glanced cautiously around to see if any of the guards were paying attention.

The sun was at its height, and when it beat straight down the guards sought shelter in the entryway of the tunnels to keep cool. The camp appeared empty of life except for the two wretched souls who struggled with the death cart in the blazing sun. "Doubt we'll get any better shot at getting out than right now. You with me? There's an animal track along the cliff about thirty yards out at the bend in the river. It's too steep to take us down all the way, but it looks like the pool at the river's edge might be deep enough to make a jump for it."

Ivory shook his head, confused. He knew that the Japs

25

guarded the narrow trek, the only path in or out. They had carved it through the hardwood and sucker vines. There was no need for a fence. Escape in this jungle was suicide, especially in their condition. The Japs had a standing order that for every man who tried to escape they would execute twelve. The last man who had tried had been captured and burned alive, after he had witnessed the executions of twelve of his fellow prisoners.

Sergeant Ware, his body shaking with malarial chills and fear, cocked his head. "You are thinkin', why try, it doesn't matter? Every man jack here is dead. You. Me. We stay here we're dead, and that is God's truth." He tried to spit and came up dry. His voice crackled from lack of moisture. "Only there ain't no God." He looked out at the vast green canopy that ate the horizon. His Adam's apple worked its way up his emaciated neck. "If you are worried about twelve good men – don't. At this point the japs can't afford to lose them and get their damn tunnels done. The jungle isn't going to give us much more of a chance, but it's all we got. You with me?"

The sun beat down. Ivory's head pounded with a relentless headache. Every single bone, each muscle, every inch of skin ached. There wasn't much left of him that cared anymore. "I'm... I'm..." A spasm in his gut caused him to winch as his dysentery ran another lap. He couldn't answer. He squeezed his eyes shut as he tried to shake off the fog. He was sick in so many ways and just wanted to lie down in the cool shade and let it all go. There was shade, but none cool; the air was hot and hard to breathe. He gathered the last reserves of his strength and opened his eyes only to find that he was staring into the sightless eyes of one of the carcasses in the wheelbarrow. Sergeant Ware was gone.

"Wait." He had no choice but to follow.

The jungle crowded the cliff's edge where thick, moss-covered branches hung low. Sharp thorny vines tore at his skin. Insects buzzed, swarmed, and he waved his hands to protect his eyes. He strained to breathe, the air a thick, hot porridge smelling of jungle rot mingled with the odors of the graveyard below. The river was an illusion beneath a pall of steaming humidity. Frantic, he spun around and tried to follow the sergeant's tracks, while at the same time searching desperately for the telltale flash of sun off the muzzle of a Jap rifle raised in his direction. Dysentery doubled him up with a mind-numbing spasm. His vision swam dizzily as his strength failed him.

He heard a splash as somewhere ahead Sergeant Ware took his leap for freedom. His bowels released, and he fell forward, his energy sapped. He was unable to move; the heat, stench and fear formed a rolling fog in his muddled mind. He wasn't afraid of dying. It was the terror of being caught by the Japanese that screamed at him to get up, to keep moving.

Sergeant Ware froze. The trail was steep and narrow, the earth beneath his feet loose and crumbly. He wasn't close enough to jump but couldn't get any closer: he glimpsed a nine-man Japanese patrol through a break in the jungle across the river below. He was a sitting duck.

Small stones and loose earth slipped out from beneath his feet, a small landslide that in moments would cascade into the quiet river below. All they had to do was look up. The trail gave way. He flung himself towards a small ledge that he hoped might conceal him from hostile eyes below. He landed with an audible UMMMPH. A rib snapped, driving the air painfully from his chest. He rolled, frantic for a handhold. It sounded as if half the mountain had splashed into the river below.

The first shot drove a million birds screeching from the jungle canopy. The echo of the rifle shot died in the chorus of startled birds as they lifted from the trees filling the skies with their rush of wings and sharp cries.

Ivory had not heard the shot nor the riotous cries of the jungle. He had lost consciousness. His body was hidden in dark shadows. There were more shots. He remained hidden until the heat of the sun dropped below a neighboring mountain peak.

He woke. A leech clung to an infected jungle-rot sore on his green moss-stained cheek. He tried to grasp his sur-roundings. The jungle floor grew dark with murky shadows. If he stayed where he was, the Japs would find only his bones in the morning. He remembered the wheelbarrow and the dead man's face — a hundred faces — ghosts urging him on. The sergeant had gone without him and he hadn't the strength to follow. He thought of the river, the cool shallow water below. A peaceful way to die. So many waited for him there.

Ivory heard the camp scream to life: "TENKO! TENKO!" The alarm had been raised. The camp was just on the other side of the trees. The Japs were tense; the camp commander was screaming for a roll call, the fifth for the day.

"SPEEDO!" The guards were afraid, for if there was a successful escape one of them would face the wrath of their Commander. People would die for the Sergeant Ware's foolish flight.

"SPEEDO!"

Ivory winced as he pulled the leech from his cheek and

slowly chewed it for the protein. His throat was so dry that the moisture from the leech was barely enough to allow him to swallow it. He continued to chew as he reached up into the mossy undergrowth and began to climb up into the dark.

Guards screamed and beat the path near the cliff's edge, stabbing into the thick foliage with their rifles and long bayonets. None looked up; their screams masked any sounds from his escape. The dark curtain of night that was falling swiftly across the jungle would render their search short. The Japs were as afraid as he was of what lurked in the jungle at night. Ivory climbed into the dark as high as he could; then he stripped off his rags and tied himself to the branches lest he fall.

From the height at which Ivory was hanging, there was no dawn, nothing so merciful. Instead there was an explosion, a searing nova that struck his exhausted eyes like red-hot needles. He had not slept as he hung suspended in the night. His malarial chills had returned, and it had taken all his will-power to keep his teeth from clattering and his shaking from giving away his hiding perch.

Without mercy the sun moved from warm to cruel heat and began to scorch the jungle with a blinding yellowish-white glare highlighting Ivory's pale, ashen flesh against the deep green foliage. From his perch he could see down into the camp where the prisoners had stood all night as the Japs demanded one roll call after another. Three bodies lay in a pool of gore where they had been beheaded. Another three were kneeling at the edge of the execution pit.

Panic stole reason, and Ivory tried to untie the frail cloth that bound him to the tree. He was in plain sight, hard to miss. A guard had only to look up and that would be the end. The branches cracked with protest as he struggled with the knotted cloth. He froze as he saw the eyes of several of the prisoners gaze up at him. His fingers, swollen, tore at the cloth in desperation as the eyes of the Japanese Commanding Officer followed their gaze. *"Soooo!!"* He raised and pointed his sword at Ivory's naked form twisting and turning in the tree branches.

"Ketojin!" the officer screamed.

A soldier raised his rife and fired.

The cloth tore just as the bullet sheared a small branch inches from Ivory's shoulder. He fell, caught a branch, fell again, grasped one that held and hung on for dear life. Shots, too many, too close. He could hear the Japs crashing through the undergrowth. The branch snapped, and he dropped. His hands were scraped raw as he reached out.

He screamed as he landed squarely on the back of a Jap soldier. They rolled near the cliff's edge. The Jap, outraged, smaller, though stronger than he, pinned him to the ground with one arm and raised his bayonet with the other.

* * * *

Ivory thrashed wildly in his bedding. "Wake up! It's only a dream," someone said. "Wake up!" Strong hands held him down as he fought for his life. The bayonet raised and started to fall. He tried to run, his amputated leg useless as he opened his eyes, his terror beyond measure.

"Easy, fella, it's only a dream. I've got you." Henry Akita said.

Ivory's eyes went wide as he shrieked at the sight of his

Nisei face.

"Easy Ivory, it's only a dream."

The terror slowly faded from Ivory's eyes. The only sounds Ivory heard were the words "it's only a dream," the pounding of his own heart, and in the distance someone singing sweet and low with a piano whose music sounded as soothing as a waterfall in springtime.

6
ELROY

Elroy lurked near the doorway, a silent predator, and stared with cold, feral eyes at the new orderly. He didn't care if Henry was a so-called Nisei, a war hero. Hell, he was a Jap and didn't belong here.

Elroy wanted to nail the bastard, to get something on him he could use for blackmail or better yet to get him fired. If he could get away with it, he would kill the slant-eyed son of bitch. He stared at Henry with a self-satisfying hatred. Truth was, Elroy really did not give a rip if Henry was Nisei. Elroy did not like or trust anyone, the color of their skin be damned. It wouldn't't hurt business any to scorn a Jap, not in this place.

Stella was the one person he could not manipulate, and that festered in his soul; as if he had one. The fact she had taken Henry under her wing only put an extra target on Henry's back. The patients at the hospital had been easy pickings until she came on board. When any of the patients needed booze, smokes, girly magazines, something other than hospital chow, Elroy was open for business on a cash-only basis. If any of the staff wanted time off, switch a shift, or had a complaint, they paid for it or it did not go upstairs. The doctors were the most profitable. When the high and mighty bastards screwed up — and they did — they paid.That was until Stella showed up. Under her watchful eye, the docs did better, and that had cost him a bundle. If it had been up to him alone he would have taken care of her, but not before she paid with a pound of female flesh.

He shifted his eyes to where he couldn't't quite see her as he felt the blood-lust throb in his corded neck, and below. If it wasn't for Victor Mann, the hospital administrator, he might have already satisfied the urge.

Mann protected his back and Elroy returned the favor. Victor Mann was a useful puppet for the moment. Fools had limited value. Stella and Henry were two of a kind: dangerous and not to be underestimated. Both to be eliminated. Mann did not like to dirty his hands with staff issues and had left enforcement to him. That was until Stella had come on board. Try as he might, he had not been able to get anything on the bitch, and now he was about to play hardball.

No, sir, they are not going to screw up a sweet deal, he thought as he watched Henry coddle a patient. *Given the chance, every man jack in the ward would gladly carve out his Jap guts with a knife*. Elroy held onto that thought. *Nahhh, too risky.*

7

AN AIR OF POMPOSITY

Henry heard someone run fingers across the keyboard of the piano in the day room. It was Earl, and his voice was one of the few beautiful sounds in an ugly place. Perhaps it was time to meet the man. He was drawn towards the voice like a moth to a flame. Inside the day room he found a blind man who played the piano better than anyone he had ever heard. He was no Sinatra, his voice was too deep, raspy with a tough of stream-washed gravel, but the man could sing, no doubt about it. A regular pied piper. He stopped at the door and listened. The hospital had a dark sad air as too many men agonized over so much they had lost – hope a passing dream. Earl's music brought light and promise, the notes building castles in the air.

Earl cocked his head and continued to play. Interrupting the lyrics, he spoke. "If you are one of the walking wounded, come on in. I don't own the place. Just passing through, same as you." He listened to the footsteps. He could usually tell when it was one of the patients; they had their own sound and smell. These steps were too steady for a patient. Not a nurse; their shoes had hard rubber heels.

"One more time... Ahhh, you must be the new orderly. I didn't catch your name. Earl Crier is mine."

"Henry." He held out his hand. "Henry Akita."

Earl continued to play.

Henry brought his hand slowly back. "Man, I could listen to you all day and all night. Where did a white man like you get that much soul? I thought Bing Crosby had a lock on it."

Earl beamed at the compliment and it instantly sounded in his playing. "I've always sung, played the piano a bit, everything seemed to come together after I lost my sight. Something about heightening of the senses."

Earl stepped up the tempo, adding a little spontaneous interpretation. Henry could see that he was pure music from the way he held his head, the flex of his shoulders, the way his fingers danced across the ivories.

"Your vision is it a total loss?" Henry asked.

Earl nodded.

"How did it happen, may I ask?"

Damn!" Earl swore after hitting a clinker. "That happens when I don't pay attention. It's kind of like walking and chewing gum at the same time." He didn't hit many but when he did he always felt a little embarrassed. He ran his fingers across the length of the keyboard until he found the key that betrayed him, then replayed the same notes two and three times over until he had it right.

"No problem. A fellow gets asked a heap of questions in a place like this; mostly by the doctors — same questions, same answers. The sight I have left is in my dreams. Beyond that all I can give you is my name, rank and serial number. Earl Crier, Merchant Marine, Ship's Cook, no serial number, just my date of birth, if you have a need to know." He leaned forward and put a finger to his lips. "The rest is classified." He was in a good mood, not often that he had someone new to show off to. "Hurrah!" He sat back, stretched his fingers, and began to play. "Here's a little number I learned while waylaid in Iceland." He launched into a frivolous tune about a man's proposal being returned by a rude middle finger.

Henry laughed. Music! He had almost forgotten how much he had missed it. He watched Earl's fingers as they danced across the keys, a taste of cool water in a drought-stricken land. He had heard from Stella that Earl pounded the ivories most nights and wondered if he might bring in his clarinet. He hadn't played in a month of Sundays and knew instinctively that he would never be able to keep up with the one and only Earl Crier.

He already had a sense of the man's genius. Before the war, he had played with a small bebop band made up of Nisei farm boys like himself. It had strictly been a kitchen band — he simmered pleasantly in the memory of that and baseball. Ahhh, to be young again. He thought for a moment about the years between, the dark memories, friends lost, and five years weighed back on him.

"Well, time to make the rounds," Henry said, already looking forward to the next time he could catch Earl at play.

Earl played until his fingers grew tired and stiff. Enough for now, he thought, as he rubbed and stretched his fingers. He suspected that the frigid temperatures in the Murmansk Sea were the cause of the arthritis that was just beginning to slow him down.

He massaged his fingers as he counted the steps back to his room. For the last few weeks it had been his private suite. Stella had moved him there because of his singing at all hours of the night. It wasn't his fault that he couldn't tell the difference between night and day. The singing was something he had to do. When he had been a boy he had fallen into an abandoned well and has been scared stiff of the dark since. He had sung in that hole to keep from screaming. He sang now for the same reason.

The room had four beds and a private privy; officer's quarters. Seventy-six steps give a step or two, from the piano to his room. He reached for the door handle. It was open. If it was housekeeping, there would be a cart out front. Theft was common. "Blind man coming in," he said. "I've only got these here cheap dark glasses if you're intent on stealing something of value?"

"Oh, there you are Earl," Stella said, the smile evident in her voice. Earl's voice always brought a slight flush to her cheeks.

"Stella, you are my rose in Spring." Earl sang. "If I have but one regret it is that I cannot see the woman behind that voice. I'm told beauty is in the eye of the beholder, in which case step over here where I can hold you close." He sensed that someone else was in the room. "A little late for rounds?"

"I should have gotten off duty forty minutes ago," she said. "Oak Knoll shipped in six new patients for extended care. Meet your new roommate, Captain Brooks Weingarden."

"Roommate? The hell you say. I'm doing just fine without having to worry about tripping over someone else's dirty laundry. Find him a room elsewhere." Earl swiped his cane across the surface of his bed to make sure no one was on it.

Stella hadn't expected his sudden flash of anger.

"Brooks, what kind of cock-eyed name is that?"

"Captain Brooks Breedloff Weingarden, the Third." His new roommate said with an air of pomposity. "And unless you are of senior or of higher rank, you had better put a

'Sir' on that."

"Jesus, just what I need: an officer with a holier-than-thou attitude with a stick up his ass. I've got news for you, pal. Here, I outrank you. I'm a civilian. Get him the hell out of here Stella."

"The Captain stays." She used an indulgent tone that mothers use on children and bartenders on drunks.

"The hell you say," Earl grumbled. He didn't like her tone. It was the first time she had spoken to him that way. That he was now in the doghouse with Stella was another reason to dislike the frigging officer that had just been forced upon him.

Stella left, her last words grating on him. He stood with his back towards where the Captain's voice come from. Both men remained silent for a long moment. Earl passed wind, the cabbage soup he had for dinner, true to course, then stepped forward just enough to avoid the unpleasantry. He smiled as he released one last parting message.

"You are one big pain in the ass, and don't mince words about it, do you?" Brooks said. "That makes two of us. It's a shame the nurse had to leave." Brooks said reluctantly. "We must be quite a sight. Two blind men in a stare-down."

Earl turned towards the sound of the Captain's voice. "Sorry, I didn't know."

"The nurse told me. She said we have two things in common, being blind, and music. It sounds to me that there are three — the third being the nurse. She sounds like quite a dish. Stella?"

"Why you son-of-a-bitch," Earl flared as he raised his cane, turned, and brought it down on the nearest target; his water glass. "If I ever..."

"Cool it, Mac, I can assure you, the dame won't give

me anything more than a nurse's professional attention," Captain Brooks Weingarten said. He touched the bandages that wrapped his entire head. The only openings were for his nostrils and mouth. "Humpty Dumpty had a great fall... I'm told I'm lucky to be alive. I've got a different opinion. I was hoisting a few pints in an RAF pub in

London when a Nazi V-2 rocket took out half the block and most of my face."

"Ouch," Earl said. He almost felt sorry for the guy. Almost.

"You're not just whistling Dixie." The Captain felt his way across the room. When he found Earl, he tapped his cane twice and held out his hand. "The name is Brooks. Here's my hand. If you ever call me 'sir' or 'captain' I'll take your cane and shove it where you don't want it to be."

"You think you're a pain in the ass, hah, you haven't seen anything. For the moment, we're stuck with each other. I don't like you, and you don't like me. Now that we understand each other, shut the hell up, and leave me alone."

"Glad to oblige. Brooks?"

"I've changed my mind. That's 'Captain' to you."

"Not a chance," Earl said with a grim chuckle. "If it will help, I could just lick your boots and call you your majesty."

"Let me think on that," Brooks said.

There must be a little give and take here, thought Earl. *I ain't leaving and he's staying, or so Stella says.* "Earl. If I don't answer to that, call me a foul-mouthed old fool. I'll know who you are talking about. You were a flyboy?" Earl asked, extending a wilted olive branch.

"Hummph." Brooks reacted to the change in tone. *I'll be*

damned, the dumb bastard gave that round to me. And he didn't have to — at least not yet. "No," he answered. "USO. I was a song and dance man, played a little piano."

Earl perked up. "You still play?"

"A few tunes I used to be able to play with my eyes shut. Anything else and my fingers trip over themselves." Brooks fumbled in his pocket. "Here, have a pull. It's not the best hooch around but it will do."

"Where did you get that?" Earl asked.

"An orderly who suggested that I could get anything I want for a price."

"His name wouldn't be Elroy by any chance?"

"One, and the same." Brooks said as he took more than a sip, then held it out for Earl tapping his thumbnail on the bottle.

"There are lots of ways to die in this place and that's one of them. Want some advice? Hell, I'll give it to you anyway, free of charge. Watch out for Elroy. He's a viper with a dangerous bite."

Brooks took another swig and then raised the bottle. "Elroy. My man... HOORAH!"

8

ON THE SAME NIGHT TRAIN

"You're looking chipper," Stella said to Henry. They were taking a break in the hallway near an open window. Their patients were sleeping quietly in the ward just beyond the double doors. She smoked. He didn't. No nightmares yet, but they would come. If there was one thing you could count on it was that the dark memories of war always surfaced.

"I got a good night's sleep." Henry's sigh implied the recollection of a golden moment. "I haven't slept that well since I had a week's R&R in Italy. The food and wine were fantastic. The women were not interested in us Nisei, and I slept like a baby for a week."

"You found a room?" Stella asked.

"Walking distance from here," he answered. "Adam's Place, a little bar around the corner from the trolley stop. I got an upstairs room with a private bath. On a sunny day, if I leaned out the window I might almost see San Francisco Bay. Gibby, the guy who owns the place, thinks I might have patched up his son Adam back in France." He shook his head. "I wouldn't have known Adam from a thousand other guys I worked on. Who knows? I got the room for a song." After a moment of silence Henry added: "Adam didn't make it. According to his pop, the poor guy bought it two days before the Germans surrendered. A Jeep accident. What a lousy time to have your number come up."

Stella blew out a blueish tobacco cloud. "I know the place. Gibby is the salt of the earth. How did you manage to connect with him?"

"That's a long story, I don't think you want to hear it."

"You might be surprised." Stella continued, "How Gibby managed to keep the place open during the war years I don't know. The heart went out of him when he got the letter about Adam. Fran, his wife, died two weeks from the day they received notice of Adam's death. Sadly, there were more than a few casualties during the war that were not on the battlefield." She glanced thoughtfully back towards the ward. *Tell me about it...*

The first notes of "Rose Marie" echoed through the empty hallway. A rich whistle almost tone perfect followed. "Brooks?" she asked.

"It isn't Fred Astaire," Henry laughed. "Brooks and Earl are two of the most unlikely roommates that ever existed. They're like school boy rivals negotiating for turf. They've got two things in common: their music, and the fact that they are two blind men who can't stand the sight of each other.

'Earl has been driving Brooks nuts with his night-time serenades. He wakes Brooks up four or five times a night. You know Earl, when the man has got to sing, he sings. Brooks huffs and puffs and blows up like a holier-than-thou peacock which only exasperates the situation. As soon as Earl nods off Brooks whistles. I figure they'll eventually wear themselves down to a truce."

"Perhaps a duet." Stella smiled, the way a woman with a good heart and a little understanding can.

"The man certainly can whistle." Henry said. "Earl is right. Brooks can sing — off key — and he can play the piano, but Earl can play circles around him with one hand tied behind his back."

"And childish tempers." Stella tapped out her cigarette, looked at her watch, then lit another. "Neither of them should be here," she said as if she was the sole holder of a vast secret. 'Technically Earl doesn't qualify for veteran's benefits. He was a ship's cook in the merchant marine. For some reason the Navy has given him a free pass. His file is sealed, classified 'Confidential'. He hasn't served one day in the Navy. I asked him." She shrugged her shoulders. "Medically there is nothing wrong with him. Being blind does not give you a long-term pass for a room and three-square meals here. The doctors don't even have him on their rounds. "Brooks," she continued, "does not have to be here either. I've done a little asking around. Brooks can afford a lot better care then he can ever get here. He comes from a well-heeled family in Connecticut. Old money. He didn't want to follow Dad into the family law firm, so he dropped out of Yale Law School and hit the road with a string of second-rate bands.

"A couple of years before the war he fell head over heels with a Hollywood platinum blonde. She helped him get into the movies. He got a few walk-on parts but never a speaking role. Hard to tell now, there was a time when he was a real Hollywood swell, a handsome man with a classy celluloid smile. He almost made it."

"What happened? The war? Henry asked.

"Gin and tonic," she answered ruefully. "Gin has made more than one prince a pauper. Brooks liked women, cheap sex, booze, being the center of attention, and throwing money around. One thing Brooks knew how to do was throw a party. Lots of people, plenty of booze, and you would have thought he'd be Hollywood's next heart-throb.

Unfortunately, Brooks became yesterday's has-been before he had a chance to show any real talent he might have had."

"Sounds to me like the guy has some dough, and plenty of connections. What the hell is he doing here?" Henry asked. "This place is for lost causes."

"His file is rather interesting. After Pearl Harbor most of his pals signed up with the Army Air Corps. Pilot wings were quite the ticket; since the Navy had been sunk at Pearl Harbor, the air boys and submariners were our last defense. After throwing a few farewell parties, he didn't want to look the coward, so he went down to the recruiting office with a poster girl on each arm. He wanted to be a pilot, but he wasn't officer material. His pride wouldn't allow him to be an enlisted man, so he joined the Army Air Special Services. He faked his resume, including graduation from Yale, graduating sixth in his class. Try two semesters."

"The two-bit bands he played with suddenly became the Red Nickels Band, Bob Crosby, Red Norvo and a host of others. Brooks got his commission and the rest is history. He'll tell you how he worked with all the greats at USO shows across Europe. All lies. Brooks was responsible for their luggage. He was nothing more than a glorified bell hop with officer's bars."

"He kept buying the drinks, blew what money he had, burning friends and bridges along the way." Stella took another drag on her cigarette. "When the V-2 rocket blew away his pretty-boy looks, he climbed into a bottle and would have drunk himself to any early grave if we'd allowed him to. He's not here because of his injuries, there's nothing more that can be done. He's tagged as a suicide waiting to happen. Brooks doesn't want help or hope, just the next drink."

"Elroy's new best friend." Henry opened the window wider to air out the smoke. "Brooks is not exactly an ideal roommate for Earl, on the other hand if Earl keeps pushing Brook's buttons, who knows?"

"How are you and Ivory Burch getting along?" She chain-lit a cigarette, then tapped the butt out in an ashtray.

Henry took note that Stella only smoked half a cigarette at a time; unfiltered. "Ivory is a piece of work. Hate and anger pour from the guy like sweat on a hot Louisiana day. I think it's his anger that keeps him alive. He's got enough medical issues to kill off half of the other guys in the ward. I have to keep looking over my shoulder to make sure a knife isn't coming my way. Any chance you could transfer him to another ward?"

Earl shuffled by in his blue hospital nightgown.

Stella and Henry stifled their laughter as they watched Earl pass, his backside mostly bare. "Evening, Earl. You couldn't sleep?" Stella asked.

"Sleep," Earl answered, "personally I think it's a waste of time." He miscounted his steps to the day room. He took two steps backwards, turned to his right, and tapped with his cane until he found the doorway. "I never cared much for meadow larks. Damn things never shut up. If the damned window would open, I'd open it and let Brooks fly away home." He found the piano, the piano stool, sat, touched the piano keys lightly, still too drowsy to pick a tune.

"Henry," Stella said, "Ivory Burch is on the wait-and-see list. The doctors are waiting to see if he's got enough fight left in him to want to go on living. His immune system is shot to hell. His spirit is on the edge of a bottomless pit. He's lost a leg and the infection is spreading into his hip. If he doesn't snap out of it soon, he will die. Smart money says that he won't make it more than a couple of weeks. The long shot is that your presence will help bring on enough anger and hatred to energize his spirit with the will to live, even if that energy is focused on nothing more than rage and revenge."

"That's all I need. Why don't they just paint a bulls-eye on my back and give the guy a bow and arrow," Henry said, feeling much the sacrificial lamb.

"Move him in with us," Earl said, overhearing their conversation.

"What?" Stella exclaimed, not sure they heard correctly, she and Henry moved towards the day room door.

"I'm serious." Earl played an intense boogie-woogie, lost the keys, then slowed to a breezy jazz number. "It just might be the ticket." His fingers hovered above the keys in still motion. "The bastard you appointed as my chief executioner and roommate is doing his best to make my every waking moment hell. Bastard! And that is the nicest thing I can say about him." His expression showed true annoyance. "The way I see it, Brooks and me, have one thing in common: the dark."

He gave a short bitter laugh, shaking his head in exasperation. "I know I've seen my last sunrise or sunset. It isn't easy. I'm trying to learn how to live with that." His fingers hit four keys he hadn't intended, then hovered in stillness again. "Look at me. I'm trapped in my own worst nightmare. It's not exactly rosy being a blind man who is scared to death of the dark. Why do you think I sing all night? I've feared the goddamned dark since I was a kid."

Earl's fingers hit the keys with a flourish of anger mixed

with some profound blues that he played for half a minute before his hands stilled again. "Brooks and I are on the same night train, only I want to learn how to drive the damn thing. Brooks would prefer to lie down on the tracks. If there is a God, which I sincerely doubt, and he's the conductor, then this is a train wreck waiting to happen. Am I right, or am I wrong?"

Neither Stella nor Henry answered.

"That's what I thought." He turned his face close to where he thought they might be. "From what Brooks has told me, I'm pretty goddamned certain that he would not like what he would see if he could see himself in a mirror. The guy was a rich Hollywood Dapper Dan with limited talent and an unrelenting thirst for booze. Which reminds me, is there any way you can put Elroy on a short leash? The rotgut he's selling Brooks will kill him."

Earl played the first verse of a song he seemed to know well, then changed abruptly to something else. "Brooks lives behind a mask of lies so thick that he doesn't know what the truth is anymore. He is not in there whistling like a goddamned meadow lark because I sing, that's horse crap. He's whistling because he's scared to go on living. If someone doesn't give him something to hang on to soon, the guy will find a way to jump off a cliff.

"The way I see it, Brooks and I need a lifeline. It sounds like this fellow Ivory what's-his-name has more problems than both of us together. Maybe by giving the guy a hand, we can drag our pitiful asses out of this black lagoon we're mired in."

Stella looked at Henry. "It just might work."

"I've seen crazier things," Henry answered. "What

about the doctors? Think they'll go for it?"

"I'll make the transfer first thing in the morning before rounds. The Doctor will be too busy to argue the point after the fact," Stella said, her smile as broad as the possibilities.

Damn, what have I gone and done now? Earl thought as he brushed the keys and whistled. "Send in that clown, I'm a crooner, not a god-damned bird."

"Earl, if we move Ivory in, you and Brooks are going to have to can the night music," he heard Stella say.

"On the contrary. If anything, we'll need to ratchet it up a notch. I've got a feeling Ivory can make his own night noises." Earl changed tunes and began to play the same tune that Brooks was whistling down the hall. "I'm in here, Tweety."

9
SOUL-SUCKING DREAMS

Earl sat on the edge of his bed tapping his cane repeatedly on the floor. For three days and nights he and Brooks had made no progress in connecting with Ivory Burch.

Ivory lay sullenly on his bed, his eyes wide open, rarely blinking, as he stared at the nothingness of the plain white institutional ceiling. The room was officers' country, he wasn't an officer and didn't want any part of it. It had been the officers who had ordered him to surrender. He had been trained to fight, then ordered to lie down like a whipped dog. And where he had been dogs were treated better. The shame would always be with him.

He didn't care, not any more. He had died months ago back in the jungle, but God had forgotten to take him. Ivory felt he had no right to go on living, but he lacked the courage to do anything about it. And so, he waited. In time he would fade away to oblivion, finally to answer the last roll call with his lost company.

Reporting for duty, Sergeant Ware. Sorry I'm late.

His new roommates, officers, were both blind, nosy and noisy. They never shut up, bickering like two old women. When they were not talking, one would whistle or the other sing, it didn't matter what time of day or night.

The only good thing was that he hadn't had the night-mare in three days. Everything would be just fine now, if those two blind fools would just leave him alone. One, a Captain Brooks something or other, was the worst of the two: a puffed-up Army washout whose head was wrapped up so tight it reminded him of an oversized egg.

The shorter of the two was either talking or singing. It was better when he sang, because when he talked he didn't have anything to say worth hearing. He didn't act like a high and mighty officer, but this was officers' country, and the first thing Ivory had learned in the Marines was never to volunteer and never to trust an officer. *I've got one good leg,* Ivory thought, *and if either of them gives me any more grief, I'll kick the hell out of him.*

The one who sang, tapped his way towards him. "It has been three days now without so much as a howdy-do. I consider that to be impolite, then I decided that you were just the shy type and didn't mean no disrespect."

He extended his hand towards where he thought Ivory should be. "Friends call me Earl." There was a long silence as his hand wavered in the air. "We were introduced by Stella. You remember her: a nice gal with a sensuous smoky kind of voice; head nurse around here." He pulled back his hand. "Hell's bells, you are a rude son-of-a-bitch, aren't you? Well, that's going to change right now." He pounded his cane forcibly on the floor. "Enough of this self-pity crap," he said accusingly. "You think you're the only poor son-of-a-bitch around here who came out of the war with a raw deal? Hell, and damnation, what do you think war is? Look at Brooks over there, talk about a raw deal. Son, you don't know the half of it."

"What?" Ivory rolled his tongue around his mouth to clear out the crud and cobwebs. "What the hell are you talking about?"

"Cut the crap, Marine. Who do you think you are, the lone survivor? Life is tough, then you die. Only thing is that you are still alive. What are you going to do about it?

You didn't crawl out of hell's cesspool to die of stupidity in a VA hospital, or did you?"

The next thing Ivory knew, the blind man whopped him on the top of his head with his cane. "What the hell was that for?"

"There, at least now I know you're still breathing," Earl said. "You've got to help me out here, son. I'm blind, not deaf or dumb, and I won't be taken for a fool."

"The hell you say," the other blind man said.

"Shut up, Brooks. If I think you got something worthwhile to say, I'll declare it a miracle, and go to church on Sunday. Don't hold your breath for long on that one."

Earl raised his cane as if to strike Ivory a second time. Ivory slid back, leaving the cane to threaten plain air. "Now you listen close, Ivory. I can call you by your first name because believe it or not I intend to be your friend. You listen really well, because if I have to tell you this twice, I'm going to be needing a new cane.

"Let us assume for the time being that I am the center of the universe. In doing this, we'll skip innumerable boring stories, which includes anything Brooks has to say; sagas of heroism, ballads of tragic love, the rise and fall of empires, whatever. Let's hurry forward to the only tale of any real importance." He stopped for a moment and brought the cane down to his side. Smiled, then cocked his head and pasted on a dead-serious face. "You and me kid, right here, right now." He stopped and listened to Ivory breathe. "There is no story, good or bad, that does not touch the truth, even if the truth is uglier than sin. I'll tell you what, I'll tell you mine if you'll tell me yours. If it helps,

I'll even go first."

"Go to hell!" Ivory spat. "I'm not interested."

"Dreams," Earl roared. "Soul-sucking dreams that draw you down like quicksand. No matter how hard you try to crawl out you're stuck in its foul muck knee-deep. The problem is, you're in head-first. I'll make you a deal. I'll trade your horror for the horror in my nightmare, then you try to do me one better. The loser gets to buy the drinks." He took off his dark glasses showing the angry red scars still healing.

Ivory shook his head. A single tear appeared in his right eye. "You don't want to know, so piss off, okay?"

Brooks abruptly stood. "Out of that rack, Marine, and stand to attention. I've had enough of your crap," he barked.

That-ah-boy, Brooks, Earl thought. *Show the kid what kind of asshole you really are.* "Feel free to ignore the man, Ivory. He's blind, dumb, and tone-deaf."

Henry was listening just outside the door. It sounded as if everything was going as Stella had planned. Earl and Brooks were going to push Ivory to the edge, to get him fighting mad. Henry was there to make sure things didn't get out of hand. When he heard Brooks order Ivory to stand at attention, Henry entered the room. Ivory swung his lethal glare from Brooks bandaged, faceless head to Henry's yellow-brown Japanese-American face. Henry could tell by Ivory's eyes that if given a gun Ivory would not hesitate to pull the trigger. He ignored it. "I bring gifts," Henry said as he placed a brown paper bag at the foot of Earl and Brook's beds. The third bag he placed on the center of the room's only table while deliberately keeping a safe distance from

Ivory, whose fists were clenched and visibly shaking.

The rattle of glass drew Brooks' attention. "What do we have here?"

"Something I know I'm going to regret; four pints of Old Charter whiskey," Henry said as he opened the bags. Then he passed a bottle to Brooks and Earl before uncapping his own. He wasn't comfortable giving booze to Brooks, but this wasn't just about Ivory. Brooks needed a major morale boost. Good booze rationed was far better than Elroy's cheap hooch in unlimited supply.

Henry placed the last bottle deliberately on a table across the room. "Ivory, if you want some, you are going to have to get up on your one good leg to get it." He turned back to Earl and Brooks. "Guys, you can thank Stella for this. The two of you are a hit in the day room; your music may be the best medicine we have around here. However, your mostly bare bottoms hanging out of your hospital blues don't make the grade. So here you are: new civvies. I hope Stella got the sizes right. You're going to have to dress yourselves, no help with the buttons and bows."

He looked at his watch. "Think you can get it together by evening chow? Why ask? Even if you put your clothes on inside out you'll still look a lot better than you do now." Careful not to give Ivory any clues of his Stella's plan, he left without further word or encouragement.

Ivory sat expressionless with lips tight as stone, which of course left no impression with Earl, who could only sense the man's attitude. "Knock it off, Marine!" Earl gave him a another rap on the head with his cane.

"OUCH!" How the hell does he do that? Ivory thought, the bastard can't see me, but he nails me every time.

"I don't have to see to know that given the chance you

would like to carve Henry Akita into dog chow. Henry is no 4-F draft dodger; he's earned his stripes and then some. Henry's got his story just like you and me. He was a medic with the 442nd, the all-Nisei Regiment, in Italy.

"The 'Purple Heart Battalion' went into the field in Italy with 1,432 men. Less than a year later they were down to 239 infantrymen and 21 officers. Not many medics made it out alive. Too many good men died in that war, all good Americans. Why? So, you can sit here and feel sorry for yourself because you came out alive. Life isn't fair, and there's not a man in this place that doesn't know the truth of that."

A funereal silence filled the room as Earl stood silent his cane wavering within striking distance.

"Thanks for the history lesson. I lost every man jack in my outfit," Ivory snapped. "Call him whatever you want. I know what I see. He's a goddamned Jap. He doesn't belong here. It just ain't right." The anger brought a flush to his parchment cheeks and enough adrenaline to make him antsy. He rose, slipped on his one slipper, grabbed a towel and slid into his wheelchair. "Come on, Sarge," he grumbled. He picked up the remaining pint and rolled out the door with thundering anger, "this place stinks of Japs and Jap lovers."

Earl almost had to bite his tongue when he heard Ivory talk to a man who wasn't there. "Brooks," he said in a low voice, "did you hear—?"

"What?" Brooks had a narrow attention span, his mind fixed on his pint of good whiskey.

10

ONE BOURBON, ONE SCOTCH

Ivory muttered bitter expletives, plotting murder with the ghost of Sergeant Ware, fueling his rage. When he saw Stella talking with Henry in the hallway he threw the towel back towards his door and rolled on by. He didn't want a shower, bathing took too much effort. If he smelled a little ripe that was OK, he didn't want to get close to people anyway.

Instead he rolled his way to the day room, which normally was off-limits until after supper. For the moment all he wanted was to be as far away from *King Earl the Bastard* and *Brooks the Pompous Ass* as possible. Stella saw him, smiled, otherwise ignored him. It was her meddling that had put him in the room with the two warbling troubadours and he didn't need one more meddling nose in his business, especially a female. He slammed the door to the day room open and rolled himself to the back of the room, opened the bottle and took a long pull of the whiskey. His empty stomach growled as he tried to put aside everything *King Earl* had laid on him. He was beginning to feel a little light-headed, but he continued to sip on the whiskey. It was the first booze he had tasted since being captured by the Japanese. He sat alone with his back to the door and sipped on the whiskey, fighting off the images he knew would come.

The stark black and institutional gray furniture blurred as he saw, smelled, and tasted the jungle, and in a moment, he was back there. Just outside the camp, the dead Jap soldier who had come so close to killing him lay crumpled on the trail, his skull split open like an overripe melon where Sarge had taken him out with a rock.

The sarge lay nearby, just as dead, his cold dead eyes staring at him accusingly. "Sarge, here, I brought you something to ease the pain." He held out the bottle with a trembling hand. "You should have let me go and saved your own miserable hide, Sarge... I..." He words fell silent as his ghost refused to answer.

Stella knocked on the door. "Earl... Brooks, are you gentlemen ready?" She didn't wait for an answer. She had seen it all before. Earl was mostly dressed. Brooks needed help. She took the bottle from him.

"Hey, I'm not done with that," he groused as he reached blindly for the bottle.

"You can have that back after you're dressed and on stage."

"On stage," Earl enthused with a broad smile. "Now you're cooking."

"I wasn't sure until this moment, but you gentlemen are about to become the best medicine there is around this place. Ivory," she said as she began to dress Brooks, "is teetering on the edge of a cliff, and all the words in the world aren't going to help him if he wants to jump.

"Earl," she said, her voice warm as a new summer's day, "in the short time you've been here you've taught me that music can reach a person's heart before they have a chance to think about it. If that's true, then we have a chance to find Ivory's soul, to touch his heart, to laugh or cry, to feel some emotion. He's drowning in guilt because he came back alive when others didn't. He needs to cry a tear from passion instead of pain. Do you think you can help me help him do that?"

Earl blew out a long-drawn-out whistle as he thought about it, then tipped an imaginary hat. "At your service, doll." He lowered his voice to a friendly whisper, knowing that Brooks could hear everything he said. "Say, what about Brooks? When he sings, grown men cry from the pain."

"I heard that." Brooks complained as Stella fitted his bow-tie.

"Earl..."

"I guess he can tag along." It was hard for Earl to say no to anything Stella asked. "Brooks, you're OK on the piano. Just OK. But you've got a mean whistle. So, pucker up whatever you have left behind that mask of yours and let's see if we can make Stella's day."

As they left the room Earl put his hand out for Stella. She took it. He gave it an affectionate squeeze. "On the other hand, let's make it Ivory's day."

Henry met Stella as she helped guide Earl and Brooks towards the day room. He kept the blind troubadours quiet while Stella, on cat paws, entered and placed a Gibson guitar she had hidden earlier quietly in the chair behind where Ivory sat.

The disturbance had been just enough to get Ivory to stop staring into Sarge's dead eyes. He took a sip of liquor, but otherwise gave no indication of recognition, when it sounded as if someone had sat in the chair behind him. He eyed the radio on a nearby table and inwardly shuttered at the thought that someone might turn it on. If some asshole wants to listen to a goddamned baseball game, he's got another think coming.

He hated baseball. The Japs were obsessed with the

game and had forced the prisoners to play against them. He remembered barely being able to hold up the bat, striking out earned one a beating, and hitting a home run often proved to be fatal.

Stella motioned for Henry to help Earl and Brooks to the piano. She sucked in her breath trying not to laugh as they entered. Earl wore a skewed dark blue beret, heavy-rimmed dark glasses, an Irish wool sweater with rainbow suspenders that brought out the gold in his smile.

Brooks, his entire head freshly wrapped in white gauze, except for the openings for his nose and mouth, wore a white tux, a clip-on bow tie worn at a curious angle, white button-down spats, with a frayed white top hat, the pawn shop's price tag still pinned to the brim. She should have taken it off, but what the hell: Brooks can't see it, and it's good for a laugh. He really needs to lighten up.

Henry waited a moment to make sure the guys were ready, then stepped back from to the piano, bringing his clarinet up. Time to wake the place up. "One... two... and..." he counted off, his first note clear, rich and haunting.

Ivory sat up and turned as Stella started to sing....
'There are blues you get from loneliness
There are blues you get from pain
There are blues when your lonely for your one and only
Blues you can never explain'

Henry's clarinet, Stella's voice, and Earl's piano echoed through the mostly empty room. Earl held his head up high, slightly cocked to the right side, for better hearing. Brooks stood motionless, listening, tapping the rhythm with his left foot, wanting to be part, not sure when. Henry's eyes were closed as he faded out with one long sensuous note. Stella sang to the man, the one who she really needed to reach.

"Ivory, damn your dream, come to me..."

The sarge's eyes showed a little light, his face still a mask of death. "OK, Sarge, if I answer the lady. You and me... We..." It was the first time he had heard the sergeant's voice since the day back at the camp when the sarge's last words were cut off as his body was ripped apart with bullets. It almost seemed as if he could hear the sarge urge him on. *"Move it, kid."*

The music emptied the wards as the patients jammed the doorway. Those who were ambulatory aided those who were not. This was the first sweet sound of live music most of them had heard in a long time.

"Where the hell do you think you are going?" Elroy spat the words into a patient's ears as he forcefully spun him around. "Get the hell back in bed before I break your scraggy neck." The frightened man pointed towards the sound of the music, then pushed away. Elroy tried to stop another, but the music was more powerful than his threat. "Damn it, everyone back to the dorms. If the doctors wanted you to have music, they would have written a prescription."

No one listened.

"Don't blame me if you all lose privileges. Damn fools!"

Waves of music filled the hallway and there was nothing Elroy could do about it. His face beet-red, he turned angrily and stormed towards the elevator, toppling a man on crutches in the process. "The hospital administrator will put a stop to this crap." He pounded the elevator button.

The crack of Ivory's whiskey bottle went unheard as he let it slip from his hand. The pungent odor rose around him as he turned to face the music. This sure ain't no baseball game, he thought as he turned.

Stella sang straight from her heart as she motioned, palm up towards the guitar, while her lips read, "Join me." A simple phone call to his doctor at Oak Knoll had told her that before the war Ivory played the guitar. She had hoped that here she might be able to touch his heart. Ivory didn't move, so she went to him, picked up that beautiful wooden instrument and held it out. "Ivory, this is for you. Will you play something for me? Please."

With tears in his eyes he slowly reached out as Stella sang, accompanied this time by Brooks' rich whistle. His hands shook as he slowly reached out for the guitar. Tears flowed freely as his finger touched, then pulled back, fearing that it might be as fragile as a glass blown quail's egg. Stella pushed it forward an inch until it touched his quivering fingers. "Please." He took it, cradled it in his arms, then lovingly turned it until he touched the strings. Brooks continued to whistle as every eye in the room turned towards him.

Henry held his clarinet up waiting...

King Earl the Bastard turned the ivories into magic.

The sweet shrill of Henry's clarinet touched a part of Ivory's soul he thought long dead. He softly plucked the first notes, his vision blurred, his eyes stinging with salty tears, as he looked at Henry's hated Asiatic face. How could he hate someone who made such beautiful music? Hate was something the war had given him, hard-earned and bittersweet.

He gave Henry a long, measured look and found himself unable to trade his hate for compassion. The ghost of Sergeant Ware now stood amongst the crowd, a reminder of the barbarity, the putrid hell he had somehow survived.

"You got one job, Marine, to hate and to go on hating Japs until there are no more of the parasites left to kill." Foul ooze dripped from the specter as it leered at him in final warning. *"You got that, Marine?"*

Right now, he could taste the man's music and hate with bitter rage where it came from. Nothing personal pal. You were born Japanese on American soil, and I have taken a solemn oath to despise the color of your skin, your very existence.

The last note spun from Henry's clarinet as Stella encouraged him to play. Ivory plucked a few strings, as dozens of slippered feet filled the room. "Earl... Brooks, hit it, boys." There was applause and laughter as Earl sang an old drinking song, allowing Brooks to back him on the keyboard.

Ivory struggled to find the right chords, finding himself unable to either sing or play as the dark clouds of long-buried emotions finally peeled away. For the first time he openly wept as the faces of the dead, brothers at arms, faces that screamed in his nightmares began to let him go.

* * * *

The sarge held on, loyal and true.

Ivory stared into the malevolent eyes of the Japanese soldier whose long narrow bayonet wavered menacingly an inch from his throat. The angle of the blade changed as the soldier suddenly shifted his aim towards Ivory's emaciated stomach.

"God no...!" He wailed in terror as he waited to be gutted like a fish. The hate in the eyes of his executioner blazed with stone-cold malice as he understood that the

Jap soldier wanted to prolong his death as punishment for his attempted escape. Overwhelmed with terror he watched helplessly as the sharp tip of the blade started to fall.

The cold sneer of his assailant changed suddenly to shock, pain, and bewilderment as a large rock crashed into his head, once, twice, his skull splitting open, spilling gore as he fell aside. The bayonet fell, stabbing into Ivory's calf, striking bone, the pain sharp, as the blade pulled free.

"Go," Sergeant Ware hissed, and he indicated with his eyes the trail leading towards the cliff and the river below. He brought the stone down a third time. "Go!"

Ivory scrambled backwards on all fours, his eyes never leaving the crushed in skull of the Jap soldier. "Jesus, how?"

"Go, dammit." The sergeant looked up the trail. More Japanese soldiers were coming.

Ivory stumbled to his feet, his hand coming away from his leg red with blood. He eyed his wound. There was a lot of blood, but at least it wasn't gushing. He wasn't going to get very far unless he stopped the bleeding, but for the moment there was nothing he could do but run for his life.

Fear, just short of blind panic, drove him through the moss-covered undergrowth towards the cliff's edge. He lost the trail, turned back towards the sergeant whose eyes suddenly went wide as a bullet exploded through his chest in a blossom of dark red. There were three more shots. The sergeant was dead before he hit the ground.

Ivory stumbled backward. "The trail... where?" His words those of a stranger, as his heart thundered through the ringing in his ears, pain stabbing through his straining chest as he gasped for air.

The Japanese screamed close by as bullets shredded

through jungle undergrowth that tore at his flesh and
blocked his way. He heard a bullet slice through a leaf near
his ear as his feet abruptly went out from beneath him and
he tumbled head over heels down a steep cliff. The river, a
spinning green whirlpool rose to meet him.

* * * *

Stella put her arms around Ivory as he wept, for the first time remembering every horrifying detail, his nightmare finally complete. "The Sergeant, he..." Ivory whispered dryly...

"Saved your life." She finished for him. "Is he here with you now?"

His tears slowed as he looked into her eyes and saw no fault or blame, only compassion. The room, the faces of his fellow patients, who a moment before had come alive with the joy of the music, had grown silent as he struggled to push his terror away. He closed his eyes and sucked in a deep breath. His fingers plucked a note from the guitar strings, and then another, as one last tear fell from his cheek as Stella released him.

"Don't stop now, boys, the party is just getting started." She winked at Henry as she brought back her own smile.

Stella and Henry passed out small paper pill cups filled with whiskey to each man in the room. Real whiskey, not the rot-gut hooch Elroy hawked for his personal profit. With one eye on Ivory, the other on the door, Henry and Stella felt the energy. It was working. The dark cloud of hopelessness was breaking for Ivory and for others.

Brooks whistled as Earl began to play again, his voice raw magic. Stella cried as she watched her patients, her poor pathetic men, raise their little white pill cups and sing in unison.

Elroy abruptly appeared in the doorway, with Herbert Mann, the Hospital Administrator, in tow. Elroy gave everyone a hard look, then whispered something to Mann, who nodded his head, saying to Elroy, "Choose your battles carefully. Don't let them choose you. Let them have their fun. They will find out soon how expensive it will turn out to be. When Stella and Mister Akita attempt to leave, kindly escort them to my office." The Administrator said as he turned to leave, "Make sure they understand that this is not an open-ended invitation."

Elroy stayed a minute longer until he caught Stella's eye, then drew and pointed his finger at her as if he held a gun.

They played another hour or so, leaving most of the patients to listen from their beds. Ivory played until he could play no more. Brooks whistled 'Shoo Fly Pie and Apple Pan Dowdy,' most everyone recognized from Billboard Magazine's best seller chart.

Stella and Henry left them to their music, as the next shift of orderlies and nurses came on duty, staring wide-eyed with disbelief as they passed the doors of the day room. Henry turned and took one last look at the trio he had brought together, and marveled at Ivory's lifted spirit.

Earl seemed to give Ivory room, as he played down, and sang down to Brook's range, where Ivory could jump on board. Unbelievable, he thought. Earl is like a caged bird begging to take flight, yet he's holding back for Brooks, a guy he doesn't even like.

Henry put his clarinet away, it was time for Earl, Brooks, and Ivory to stand on their own without any more outside help. If Ivory could willingly stand again on his one good leg, then perhaps tonight he had taken his first step.

Ivory missed a chord as he watched Henry and Stella leave. His fingers wavered, motionless, above the strings as he studied the smile on Henry's face. What was it that Henry had said the first time they had come eye to eye? *Oh yes: Take it easy fella, it's only a dream.*

11
GOODBYE, MR. AKITA

Stella let the door silently slide shut as she listened one last time to Ivory strum his guitar. She smiled. Earl generously took a back seat on the piano, letting Ivory take the lead. She sighed as she looked at Ivory in wonder. Neither she nor Henry had anticipated his response.

Too few men recovered when their war-shattered minds took them as low as Ivory had gone. The music... Earl, Brooks, she and Henry had all extended a hand, doubtful that Ivory would lift a finger back in their direction. He had. He had catapulted out of the depths of his own personal hell and landed on solid ground, with a tear to acknowledge where he had been and a song to rejoice in the light. Too much, too fast. She knew he would slip back, perhaps all the way. But for now, there was hope: Ivory was no longer a wait-and-see patient. He now knew that he didn't have to live burdened forever with guilt, tortured by the accusing faces of the dead. A little light had seeped through a crack in the wall, beckoning him to begin the journey into the light of day and life.

The smile in her eyes changed as Elroy stepped up behind Henry.

Henry saw Elroy's reflection and braced too late as Elroy put a vise-like grip on his elbow, twisting just hard enough to control his movement. "Mr. Mann requests" — his voice more than threatening — "he demands that" — he looked at Stella — "you come with me to his office. Now!"

"I'm sure that whatever—" She was cut off in mid-sentence. The look in Elroy's eyes was malevolent, giving her a cold shiver as if she was about to be violated. Her breath caught as Elroy gave Henry a sudden forceful shove, knocking him to the floor. "You have one minute to get your Jap ass out of my hospital," he said. He pulled an envelope out of his pocket, took the cash out of it for Henry to see, pocketed it, then wadded up and threw Henry's pink slip on the floor next to him. "You are fired, effective immediately, wages owed and paid"… he patted his pocket… "and deducted for damages."

There was a brief sullen silence. Elroy baited Henry for an argument, any sign of defiance, relishing the opportunity to pummel and throw Henry out onto the street like so much garbage.

Henry started to rise.

Elroy moved as fast as a predatory cat, kicking Henry back onto his knees.

"Henry don't!" Stella screamed.

Elroy swayed back and forth on boxer's feet, looking for an excuse to attack either of them. "Come on, give me a chance to send you back to your ancestors."

"Henry, please," Stella said, her voice just short of a whisper, "don't give him an excuse. I'll talk to Mann." We both know where that will go, she thought, knowing that Herbert Mann would not lift a finger to help either of them. He was as much a puppet of Elroy's as anyone. Her eyes were dark with a woman's scorn as she glared directly into Elroy's eyes. "Dr. Garitty will do something…"

Elroy snorted a single laugh. He looked away from Stella and gave Henry a second kick.

Henry crawled backwards, struggled to rise to his knees, then to his feet in a defensive position. Strong arms grabbed him from behind, Simon and Alex, two orderlies restraining him, twisting one arm painfully behind his back, another wrapped around his neck. Elroy twitched, ready to deliver a fist or a kick into Henry's gut.

Stella blocked his attack by placing herself between them, her back to Elroy. She knew the two orderlies were harmless cowards by themselves, afraid to refuse Elroy's bidding. Frequently drunk from the bad hooch Elroy provided, they were incompetent puppets who kept their jobs only on Elroy's whim. She hadn't seen them coming, but now that they were here, they might prove to be useful. Stella caught their eyes, drawing their attention away from Elroy as she addressed them in her most authoritative head-nurse voice. "Gentlemen, Mr. Akita was about to leave. Would you please escort him to the front door, then stay there to make sure he doesn't try to return?"

Henry's eyes went wide with indignation and a sense of betrayal. She couldn't help that. Elroy could and would do serious harm if given a chance, and his fuse was short and burning.

"Goodbye, Mr. Akita."

Simon and Alex looked beyond her at Elroy, then without further hesitation dragged Henry towards the stairwell door.

"Stella..." Henry gasped uselessly as his arm was twisted harder.

Losing his prize, Elroy needed to vent. Stella had interfered once too often. He wrapped his arm around Stella's waist and spun her around. She slipped from his grasp faster than he thought possible, then spun around twice as he reached for her again. And missed. Henry's cry as he wrestled with his escorts in the stairwell distracted Elroy just long enough for Stella to reach the open door to the elevator, which slid shut behind her before he could stop it.

Stella's mind raced faster than her labored breath. What the hell was happening? She knew that there was no love lost between management and Henry. The fact that he was a war hero with a bronze star was the only reason he had gotten the job. Japanese-Americans were still not welcome back in this shining city by the bay. Elroy had been more than self-confident and cocky with Henry. Whatever is happening must be sanctioned by Herbert Mann. That being true, what of my fate?

Her breath steadied as she tried to get a fix on... No sooner had the elevator door begun to open than a strong hand slipped through, followed by Elroy's menacing face. Before she could step back, his thick ham-hock sized hand seized her by her throat, lifting her from the floor as he forced her to the rear of the elevator. Her eyes bulged with panic as she struggled to find her footing as the door slid shut. With a free hand he punched the stop button, freeing the elevator in place, then drew it roughly down to her breasts, crudely cupping them as he tore off two of her blouse buttons. His breath smelled of cheap tobacco and rank with alcohol as he licked her left cheek.

"It's payback time, bitch," he swore as he tried to force his tongue into her mouth, only to have it bitten. This brought a strong backhanded slap which drew blood. "You've screwed with me one too many times. Now I'm going to screw you until you beg..." He ripped off another button, snapping her bra, as a fingernail dug into her breast as he leaned in to capture an exposed nipple.

Stella brought her knee forcefully into his groin.

"JESAHGOD!!!" he swore as he sucked in his breath, arching his back in agony. He dropped his grasp on her throat as he slumped forward, which allowed her to bring her other knee up in a driving force into his chin. That was all it took.

Stella had no time to gloat as she spun around, triple-tapped the open button and flew out of the elevator as fast as the opening doors would allow her.

Herbert Mann stood outside his office door as Stella burst out of the elevator. He had been waiting outside for Stella to be delivered. When Elroy had vaulted from the stairwell and forced himself into the elevator he had almost smiled. It brought on a slightly jealous rush, if not a sexual urge. He knew what Elroy wanted and could only imagine the pleasure he would receive at Stella's expense. She deserved everything coming to her.

He couldn't have been more surprised when it was Stella who came out of the elevator. Seeing Elroy slumped on the floor of the elevator as she came out seemingly unscathed, he sputtered something unintelligible beneath his breath, then turned to the sanctuary of his office.

Stella's first inclination was to flee to the stairs, down and out of the hospital, before Elroy could manage to get to his feet. She wasn't about to underestimate him. He was dangerous, and now that she had put him on his knees, he would be after blood. That was, until she saw Mann. "You asked for me?" she demanded with a voice demanding his attention.

Mann turned to face her, annoyed with her attitude. He had intended to reprimand her for her insolence, but froze as she approached, fast and far more determined than he was prepared for. A second later she stood eye to eye with him.

Stella was disgusted with the man, but she would not

let him look away. "I've seen my share of ugliness, horror, stupidity, and inhumanity in the last few years! This..." she sputtered, never leaving eye contact, "this takes the cake. You wanted to see me. Here I am, you miserable..."

That was all Herbert Mann heard. Her unexpected and painful slap to his face sent him reeling and he fell backwards through his open office door. His secretary, who had been watching intently from her desk chair, shrieked at the sudden violence, only adding to his humiliation.

Stella shook out the pain in her wrist as she smiled meekly at Mann's secretary. Her smile broadened into a mask of contempt as she returned her glare to Mann. "And since you won't be needing me any further, sir, I've got rounds to do."

She shut the office door behind her as she turned towards the stairs. Not so fast, she thought, as she eyed the elevator where Elroy lay in a fetal position gripping his injured manhood. Some unfinished business. She walked over to the elevator, reached in, tapped the Alarm button, and then the Close button. She knew that more than one door had just been closed. Her career was down the drain. Her only thought was to find Henry.

12

WHERE DOES ONE BEGIN?

Exhausted, Earl slept briefly.

He dreamed of pleasant days, back in Kentucky before the war. In dreamlike reality he saw endless rolling hills of green under an intense blue sky. The hills rolled by until finally his vision settled on the country club where he had worked when he was a younger man and all the world lay before him.

In his mind's eye he was there just as if it had been only yesterday, serving drinks to the beautiful young women who sunned themselves by the club's poolside. They were rich and sensuous, and off-limits to the staff, except for a daring vixen who chanced an adventure with a man below her social class.

His dreams were not usually filled with dark, haunting memories of war and death. His were often enough filled with pleasant thoughts of what life had been like when he had his sight. And always there was music. The music in his head came in waves of color and light. And then a black curtain would drop, he would wake, the music would stop, and he was back. That was when the fear came, when the black serpent drew near, bringing with it the unforgiving dark.

He woke.

The hospital was quiet, with fewer screams to shatter the night. He remembered the party and chuckled. *Yes, sir, that was all right.* Careful not to disturb Ivory or Brooks, unable to find his slippers, he padded barefoot back to the day room anticipating a replay of some of the tunes from the night before. On his terms this time, of course.

Ivory lay on his bunk unable to sleep, confused by a whirlwind of emotions he desperately wanted to sort out. He just couldn't get hold of one. It was kind of like trying to read a book upside down and backwards. Nothing made any sense. Yet, he hadn't felt this alive since his first days in China.

He had grown up in a small dusty town in rural Texas where the

Depression had been deep, the work hard, the view tumbleweed desolate. He had sought adventure and found it in the Marines, where he had been sent to mystical, crowded China, far on the other side of the world. He had wanted adventure and had gotten it. Then came the war. He felt his heart race but couldn't run from his thoughts. King Earl the Bastard had been right. It was time to stop feeling sorry for himself and get on with living. He owed that much to Sergeant Ware.

He heard Earl rise and thought about saying something. What? Where does one begin? He started to say something, but Earl was out the door before he had a chance.

On his way to the day room Earl couldn't help but think about Brooks. Maybe, just maybe, he might have the guy wrong. Forget it, that he can whistle up a storm doesn't change the fact that he is an insufferable prick. Earl reached the day room door and found the knob. It was locked. His hands found the cold metal as he rattled the chain, the padlock, cold, heavy and unyielding. "What the hell is this?" He rattled the chain again as he wondered if he had taken a wrong turn somewhere and was at the wrong door. He mentally recounted his steps. No, this here is the door to the day room, and it's locked tighter than Dad's gun closet.

"Hey, Henry, Stella, someone, what the hell is this?" He rattled the chain vigorously and kicked at the door. "Damn, that hurt." He hopped on one foot while reaching for his stubbed toe, then fell flat on his ass. "Damn it!" he cursed. Someone's going to pay for this. He felt the cold on his bare ass and had to laugh at the mental image of himself sprawled out in his hospital blues.

Sleepy voices rose from the ward across the hall. Earl's laughter, followed by explicit expletives, could be heard across the hospital. Small groups of men began to appear in the hallway. Few spoke, none offered to help; they knew trouble when they saw it.

"Mr. Crier, I'll see you in my office." The voice belonged to Herbert Mann, the hospital administrator. Elroy took Earl by the elbow and pulled him none too gently to his feet. Elroy had a smell Earl knew well: the stench of bad booze oozing from his pores. "Get your hands off me, you goddamned storm trooper!" Earl demanded as he tried to pull away from Elroy's almost painful grip.

"I said that we will speak in my office. Elroy, bring him along."

One man booed and then another as Elroy manhandled Earl towards the elevator. Mann stood facing the elevator door, ignoring the protests as he waited for the door to open. Next to Elroy, the administrator looked somewhat like Charlie Chaplin, with a pot belly, thinning gray hair, and a mustache too full and dark for his facial features. A comical character, feared by most, who stood back unwilling to lend a hand.

"Someone get Stella," a voice called out.

"Too late," another answered, "the bastard fired her as

she left the party. Henry Akita, too."

The elevator door closed as Earl weighed those words.

Fired?

13
WHERE AM I TO GO?

Earl's toe throbbed like a son-of-a-bitch, and he did not need the distraction as he tried to get a sense of the administrator's angst. He knew he was in an awkward position, and it wasn't just his bare bottom in his hospital blues that sent a chill through him. He was vulnerable, and he knew it. No chair offered, he leaned forward on his cane and mustered the best bravado he could find. "Did I hear right?" he asked incredulously. "You fired Stella? Why? Henry, let me guess."

Mann motioned to Elroy with a flick of his hand. "Elroy, you know what to do, be quick about it." He then spoke to Earl without looking at him. He had dealt with Earl Crier before and found being stared down by a blind man quite unsettling. "Mr. Akita has been dismissed. Miss Tate — Stella — has been reprimanded and been given two weeks off without pay. I can assure you that if there was not an acute shortage of nurses, she would have joined Mr. Akita in the unemployment line."

"You had no right—"

"That is where you are wrong." His voice was condescending. "I have every right. I understand that this so-called celebration was your idea. Patients in this facility don't have ideas. We have rules. Your opinion amounts to nothing. Elroy informs me that you have been a consistent troublemaker from the first moment you arrived here. That is going to change," Mann said with a vindictive tone to his voice. "As of this moment you are dismissed from this facility."

"You can't—" Earl started to say, his anger rising, before he was cut off.

"I can, and I have. This is a veteran's hospital, and you sir, are not a veteran. You served with the Merchant Marine and are not entitled to veteran's benefits. At the request of the United States Navy you were given temporary shelter and medical care in exchange for your silence regarding the incident and cause of your injuries, just if you obey the rules. The rules, as I see it, are what I determine them to be. On my recommendation the Navy has agreed to immediately terminate any agreement you might have thought you had."

"I..." Earl stammered. He hadn't anticipated this.

"Enough!" Mann ordered. "One more word from you and you will be charged for your stay and required to pay back every penny for expenses incurred by the United States government. Do I make myself clear?" He plucked an envelope from an open drawer to his desk and forced it into Earl's hands. "This contains your discharge papers and sixteen hundred dollars in cash, back pay owed you by the Merchant Marine." He looked at Earl's dark glasses. "Do you want me to count it out for you?"

There was a rapid knock on the door as it opened.

"Ah, there you are Elroy," Mann said. "Elroy has been kind enough to collect your things. Everything is in the paper bag. After you have changed into your civilian clothes, you will be escorted to the rear parking lot, where a cab is waiting."

Earl dropped his cane and the envelope as his clothes

were forced into his hands.

"Where am I to go?"

The administrator turned his back and left without an answer.

"Get on with it, the meter is running on your cab," Elroy said as he picked up the envelope, opened it and quietly pocketed most of the cash. "It's your dime, pal."

14

TIME TO MAKE A STAND

Ivory pushed open the bathroom door just in time to catch a glance of Elroy, a bag in hand, as he bullied his way through the hallway. There was a palatable tension in the air. Small groups of patients huddled here and there in whispered conversations. Something had them spooked; they grew quiet, eyes downcast as Elroy passed. The expression on Elroy's face read trouble, and a glance of Earl's new tux poking out of the bag Elroy carried raised the hair on the back of Ivory's neck. He pushed his way through the crowd in his squeaky wheelchair. "Come on, guys, get out of the way." Voices rose, angry and confused, their focus on the day room doors. He grasped the padlock, gave it a firm tug, then let it drop back with a solid thump against the door. "My guitar is in there," he said, surprised at how much its sudden loss meant to him. He kicked the door with his one good leg but lacked the strength to do any damage.

"Stella?" He searched the hallway. Stella was nowhere to be found. "Henry..." He stopped mid-breath as he realized who he was calling. "Henry Akita..." He called again, kicked at the day room door from his wheelchair, then turned and rolled towards the elevator, punching the Up button angrily multiple times. The tracking light remained on Five as he continued to punish the button.

"Hey, what gives?" demanded a bear of a man, his voice sounding like rolling gravel on a dry creek bed. He stood well above everyone else, his hospital blues two sizes too small, which made him appear even more gargantuan.

"Bastard," Ivory swore as he turned back towards the locked day room door. He was steamed. It felt good. The raw emotion, a valve to let off the weight of anger and frustration that had been holding him down too long.

"These bastards don't give a rip whether any of us live or die." A guy named Sully, whom Ivory had met at chow, edged his way through the crowd. He was a nervous little man, all of five foot two, with an annoying facial twitch and wild, darting eyes.

"I've had enough of this crap," the big guy said.

It was then that Ivory noticed that the giant lacked a left arm from the shoulder down. His right hand was missing the thumb and the top third of the first finger. Ivory just stared for a moment. The man was a mountain, a living pack mule, a man who could carry his weight and yours when things got tough and not break a sweat. Now, he couldn't light his own cigarette.

Ivory looked down where his own leg should have been and for the moment realized that he might just have gotten off lucky. He looked at the maimed giant, nervous little Sully, then back at his own amputation, and sighed.

"We're not exactly going to storm the citadel, are we?"

The giant looked down at Sully and back again at Ivory in his wheelchair. "I reckon not," he rumbled. He grew silent again, as if searching for words that were not his to begin with. "It ain't right, letting them get away with crap like this without us lifting a finger." He held out his mangled hand, pondered it for a moment, as he stared at the chain and padlock securing the day room doors. "No, sir, it ain't right. We're going to take back what's ours."

He pushed with his shoulder against one of the doors,

then pointed the best he could at one of the door's hinges. "We'll need something to pry these loose. Who's with me? We'll take the doors down, chain or no chain."

The crowd shrank quietly back into their wards.

"That might work," Ivory said. "Then what?" *At least I can get my guitar,* he thought. *That doesn't do anything for Stella and Henry... or Earl.*

"Earl?" someone asked.

"Earl should be in the day room, only he isn't here, is he?" Sully said, "I've got a bad feeling about this. I just saw Elroy go by with Earl's tux. Any bets that Earl is up on the fifth floor?"

Ivory eyed the frozen elevator light button. Everyone spoke at once, low voices, no one willing to say what they all knew to be the truth, that Earl was as good as gone. Ivory clenched his fist. "It ain't right."

"That's God's truth," Sully said, "and being that Mann is God and Elroy is J.C., there is not one damn thing we can do." Suddenly, Sully jumped as if he had been hit by an electrical charge. "We'll hold ourselves a little protest and take back what's ours." He spun around and ran like a baying coon dog down the hallway and into the chow hall, returning a moment later with two dull table knives. "This ought to do it."

The giant rolled one in his palm until he had a grip on it and began to chisel away the dry paint that held the bolts in place. Sully worked on the lower bolt while Ivory kept an eye on the elevator.

"Burrell Smith," the giant said to his new friend as he pulled the first bolt. "Pleased to meet you."

"Ivory," he answered. What little energy he had was sputtering. Things were happening so fast. Part of him wanted to retreat into the old fog where he didn't give a damn. His hands began to tighten on the wheels to his chair as he started to push himself back.

"Lewis," said one of the other men who had stayed, "and this here is Tony. We're going to need more help with these. Those doors look plenty heavy. Tony lets you and me round up a few of the guys." Tony looked uncertainly back. "And don't take no for an answer. Burrell is right; it's time we took a stand."

The doors were opened.

Ivory, Burrell, Sully, and sixteen others who were dragged from the wards filled the day room. Lewis and Tony set the doors back in place, minus the bolts, then sat back and waited with a few other curious souls. "We've got the best seats in the house," Lewis told Tony. "Nothing is going to happen in there until shit happens out here."

15
LIFT EVERY VOICE

"Get back to your rooms," Mann demanded as he stepped off the elevator. "The day room is closed until further notice. If you give me any trouble, I'll have it converted to a staff lounge." He grabbed hold of the chain giving it a solid tug to emphasis his point. The cowed patients remained expectantly silent. Mann's wrist had caught in the chain, pulling him off his feet. The heavy doors fell back with a thunderous crash.

Ivory was sitting in the middle of the room. As the doors collapsed, he began to strum his guitar and sing an old protest song by James Wilden Johnson:

'Lift every voice and sing
till earth and heaven ring,
ring with the harmonies of liberty.
Let our rejoicing rise...'

Mann, pride and flesh bruised, sat up, holding his wrist and raged, "Elroy!"

The song was contagious. Patients gathered in the hall joined those inside:

'We have come over a way
that with tears have been watered;
We have come, treading our path
through the blood of the slaughtered,
Out from the gloomy past,
till now we stand at last,
Where the white gleam of our bright star is cast.'

The sarge rose menacingly above Mann as Ivory

struggled from his wheelchair to stand on his one good leg. "I'm no wait-and-see patient, you sorry bastard. Ship me back to Oak Knoll where I can get this leg fixed and get on with life." For a moment it seemed to Ivory that the sarge's apparition had just given him a conspiratorial wink as Mann stumbled and fell once more.

16

THE BLUES HAVE NEVER SEEMED SO DEEP

The cabbie grew impatient as he drove slowly up one street and down another waiting for directions.

Desperation seeped into Earl's soul as he felt the cold foreboding wind blow against his face. He had to have the window open lest he suffocate; the world as he had known it was shrinking with each breath.

"It's your dime, buddy. We've been by this way three times with no luck. If you can't give me an address, name of the place, or tell me what the place looks like, we can be at this all night. Do you know how many bars there are in this city?"

Earl sat facing the open window, the cold, and smell of salt air, a dark memory of his days at sea. "It's within walking distance of the hospital," Earl said. "Just keep trying, I'll make it worth your while."

Two blocks farther on, the cabbie pulled to a stop. "Okay, pal, this one here is the last one in the neighborhood. It's a local dive, if I ever saw one. The place looks empty."

"Describe the building to me," Earl asked. "How many stories?"

"It's a two-story, white stucco dump with peeling paint. It doesn't look like much. There are two front windows with blackout curtains still in place. It's dark except for an 'Open' sign buzzing in the window. The name of the place is painted on a small window in the door, but I can't read it from here. That's it, Mac. Take it or leave it. It's your dime."

"Help me to the door. I've got a hunch this is the place."

Earl hesitated at the door. God, he hoped he had the right place. He had nowhere else to go. He took a deep breath and sang low to himself to steady his nerves.

The bar was quiet. A baseball game was playing on a radio, not in the bar, somewhere outside. The San Francisco Seals were two up, in the third inning. The place didn't sound like any bar he'd been to. There was no clicking of ice, drunken banter, or laughter, no music. He smelled stale beer and tobacco and something else he couldn't quite make out. As he stepped forward with the help of the cabbie, his foot crunched something on the floor. He sniffed and found the aroma of roasted peanut shells. Must be a pigsty, he thought and called out, "I'm looking for Henry Akita."

The crunch of the peanut shell alerted Gibby that some-one had come in. "Who's asking?" Gibby said as he turned towards the door. New customers were rare; blind ones, well that was a whole different story. He peered through the top of his glasses. "You must be the one and only Earl Crier. Henry has said nothing but good about you." Gibby stepped forward, shells crunching underfoot, and took Earl's arm. "Come on in. How much is the fare, cabbie?"

"First thing I learned about Henry," Earl said, "is that he's a lousy liar. If you want to know the truth, I'm a con-descending pain in the butt. Being that I owe Henry a favor or two, I'll behave myself, for the price of a cold beer." He settled into a seat, his bag on the bar in front of him, then searched the inside of his bag for the envelope which contained his discharge papers and back pay.

"Three-fifty," the cabbie said.

Gibby pulled out four bucks and sent him on his way. "My friends call me Gibby. I'd be pleased if you'd do the same," he said as he came around the bar. "Henry will be back in about twenty minutes. He went out to pick up some Chinese. Henry always buys more than we can eat, so you're welcome. What can I get you?"

Earl sat back and blew out a dry whistle. An hour or so ago, he had been booted out of the hospital, with no direction, nor a chance to say goodbye to his pals. He did not kid himself. The Veteran's hospital was a lousy place to be, a dead end for many; however, its dreary sameness was something he already missed.

The party Stella and Henry had thrown the night before had let in a little cheer, which everyone needed by the bushel. He couldn't recall hearing as much joy in the old veterans' tomb as had rocked the place last night. But, hell's bells, it had also opened a hornet's nest and God knows what else.

Ivory Burch, a guy wanting to jump headfirst into his own grave, had somehow been resurrected. Earl had known that the hospital brass was likely to get on his case for his part in the insurrection, but he had not thought that they would cut him loose and throw him out like so much dirty bathwater.

The hospital's bland routine had sheltered him from the terrors that lurked in the dark. He knew how many steps there were from one place to the next. He felt less handicapped when he was able to help someone more mangled than he. Less time to worry about where that damned dragon might be.

Earl felt his nerves begin to slip. The dragon was near. The cab ride had unnerved him, riding around in search of a place he did not know. The dragon was not far behind, or perhaps just ahead. Now, here he was, a blind fool on a fool's journey. He knew that he was close to the edge, with no idea how far the bottom lay.

He wet his lips. "A tall cold beer - leave the foam, if you please. Make it two, the first will be gone by the time you've poured the second."

Gibby laughed as he poured the first and brought the cool glass to Earl's fingertips. "Done with the hospital and got your walking papers. Bet you thought you'd never see the day. Pardon me, sometimes I'm too nosy for my own good. You have family waiting?"

Earl finished the beer with a smile and a frothy mustache as the second was placed before him. "No," he said. "I had a kid brother. He died on Wake Island. I had me a girl before the war," he said with a slight sigh, "but that was a lifetime ago. Home? No, sir, no place I can call home. The one I had blew away in the Depression.

"When I joined the Merchant Marine, my forwarding address became the next place I'd be." He laughed out loud. "Damn, I haven't cried in my beer, telling a good old-fashioned sob story to a bartender, in a month of Sundays."

He took a sip of beer. *I'd better shut up before he finds out that I'm about as vulnerable as an old coon dog sitting in the middle of two lanes of oncoming traffic.* A tear rolled down from behind his dark glasses. I should have had the cabbie stay. *I ain't got no right adding my burdens to anything Henry's already carrying.* He reached for his bag, found the envelope, and opened it. "How much do I owe you for the beers?"

"Your money is no good here," said Gibby. "You'll stay and have Chinese with us, and I won't take no for an answer. It ain't great, but I'll bet it's better than the hospital crap you've been eating."

Earl suddenly felt lightheaded as he counted the bills in the envelope. There were three left of what had been a couple of dozen. He pulled them out. "Help me out here," he asked with a slight tremor to his voice. "How much do I have here?"

"Three tens, thirty bucks," Gibby said, "but I won't take your money."

Earl folded the bills and slipped them into his pocket. *Thanks,* he thought, *someone else already did. I had sixteen hundred bucks. What the hell can I do with thirty bucks? I'm blind, homeless, and broke. Three strikes and you're out, and I guess this here is strike three. Time to take a flying lesson off the old Golden Gate Bridge.* His breath caught short; he felt the dragon draw near enough that he could almost smell it.

* * * *

The ship's klaxon wailed Abandon Ship. Earl's lifeboat station had taken a direct hit; not that it mattered, the Murmansk Sea was freezing, the waves fifteen feet, and the Nazi U-boat crews were machine-gunning any survivors.

The Master Chief grabbed him and Billy Bread, a skinny kid from

Wilton, North Dakota, and ordered them to go down into an ammunition hold and secure a rack of artillery shells that had broken loose. The Master Chief was the first in. Neither he or Billy were eager to follow. There was a good chance that the ship's boilers would blow before any lifeboats could be lowered.

Earl braced himself against the ice-covered rail as the ship rolled heavily. A nearby ship exploded in one massive fireball. A shrill whine sliced through the deafening rumble as a red-hot piece of shrapnel the size of a handsaw embedded itself in the exterior bulkhead just above the hatch the Master Chief had just passed through.

Earl was more terrified of going down into the hold than he was of the horror of war that surrounded him. He turned to tell Billy to go next, screamed in horror, then puked over the side. The shrapnel had sliced right through Billy; his intestines were snaking out of his body as Billy reached out, not knowing that he was already dead. Everything from his navel down slid into the ocean, and his upper torso slipped and slid in a steaming pool of blood.

Earl, caught between two horrors, dropped down into the service alley, which was lit only with red emergency lighting. The chief had already disappeared through a hatch leading into the hold. Earl followed, dogged the hatch behind him, then looked down into the dimly lit cavernous space.

The chief was halfway down the ladder. The hold was filled with explosive shells, hand grenades, mines, flame throwers and God knows what else. "Hell, I'm not going down there." Earl gripped the rail, his hands slippery with Billy's blood. One look told him that the situation was beyond critical. A Jeep was rolling freely about the hold. A rack of artillery shells had collapsed, the explosive shells spinning around like so many demented bowling balls.

Three more racks sagged as the Jeep battered against them.

"Crier," the chief bellowed, "quit your bellyaching and get your ass down here. I can't do this by myself."

Earl descended the ladder one precarious step at a time. The ship lurched, rolled heavily, the hull booming protest. He froze. The pounding intensified. The chief let out a blood-curdling scream. Earl looked down and caught the terrified death-look in the chief's eyes. The Jeep had caught the chief before his foot had hit the deck, spinning him around, then crushing him against a bulkhead. Blood ran from his open mouth. The ship rolled an impossible sixty degrees. The Jeep slid sideways, shearing off a rack of 75mm fragmentation shells, which thundered over the stricken man as he slumped lifeless to the deck.

The ship rolled out of a deep trough and listed sharply to port. Earl screamed, his feet kicking frantically for support as he tried to hold on. Everything loose rolled with the ship, a thundering herd stampeding, first one direction than another. He dropped to the deck, his left ankle taking the worst of the fall. The eerie red lights flickered.

There was nothing he could do for the chief, who lay limp and folded-up like a rag doll. The crush of projectiles shifted towards the bow as the stern of the ship rose violently. A searing flash followed by a thunderous explosion ripped through the bulkhead. Earl covered his face as he was hurled across the hold.

An explosion ripped through the hull. A horrendous fireball roared towards him, its searing heat burning his hair and blistering his skin. Then, within an inch of his life, the flames hissed in protest as they were extinguished by the in-rushing sea. An absolute darkness enveloped him, and he heard the ship begin to break apart.

His head spun from the impact, his back was one large aching bruise. He was dizzy and nauseous. He felt on fire as every inch of exposed flesh still reacted to the burns left by the vanished fire. The groans of the mortally wounded ship filled the pitch-black void, the sound of rushing water the most foreboding.

The eerie sounds suddenly seemed distant and everything blended into one shrill tone within his own head, the pain in his ears almost paralyzing. Surprised to be alive, he screamed for help, but could not hear his own voice. He was trapped alive in his worst nightmare: the dark. It was alive, and it was devouring him.

* * * *

Earl sat silent and morose for several minutes.

In the artificial yellowish hue of the bar, Gibby could see that Earl's skin tone had grown ashen, with a clear bead of sweat on his brow. His hands were shaking, his breathing shallow and rushed. Gibby reached out and caught the beer glass as it slipped from Earl's hand. "Earl are you, all right?" Gibby asked. "God in heaven, son, are you having some kind of seizure?"

Earl's face remained skewed in painful concentration. His dark glasses gave Gibby no clue as to what was going on in Earl's head.

Henry, where the hell are you? Gibby thought. What the hell am I supposed to do?

* * * *

The ship rolled, racks of explosives collapsed. It was dark, pitch black. Earl could not see his hand in front of his face. He panicked as a heavy canister brushed his foot. His left ankle seized with pain when he rose and tried to put weight on it. The shrillness in his ears lessened. A runaway oil drum slammed into him, knocking him back off his feet again. There were more. How many? Nearly paralyzed with fear he searched the dark, wide-eyed, each crash and thud his mortal enemy. A large metal drum thundered towards him. He tried to roll out of the way, only to roll in front of the Jeep. He screamed in anguish as it rolled over his foot, his ankle breaking. Fear outweighed his pain. He found a hold on the Jeep and pulled himself up and into the driver's seat. His leg was still outside when a half dozen oil drums slammed into the runaway vehicle. White, searing pain sucked his breath and every ounce of courage from him as he felt his leg fracture. He struggled not to pass out and painfully pulled his leg inside. Unable to move another inch, he sat alone in the dark. The pain, fear, and anguish of impending death were insurmountable.

A brilliant flash of light turned intense black into a storm of blinding white, yellow, orange, red, then gray, light as an explosion tore through the ship. The sea rushed in. Despite the glare of flame and explosions around him, Earl could see through the ruptured bulkhead the sea and a deep blue sky laden with stars in the Arctic day.

He felt a strange relief as his eyes locked on one brilliant but distant star. He knew that he was going to die and wondered if perhaps that star was his little bit of heaven. Music flooded his mind as tears blurred the heavens, and he began to sing. The deafening noise of the dyeing ship stole his words.

* * * *

"Earl?"

The brilliance of that starry night sped away in a whirlwind leaving nothing more than the dark of empty space. He heard a radio, distant, then a voice, followed by the warmth of a human hand as it touched him.

"Earl?"

"What? No! I can't swim!" Startled, he clawed at the bar and spilled his drink before slamming his hand down on a plate containing something slick and sticky.

A hand grabbed him before he could topple from the bar stool. "Easy there, pal, you had a bad dream. It's me: Gibby. You're waiting for your pal Henry. Henry Akita remember?"

Earl calmed. It had been the same nightmare that crept up on him when he let his guard down. He knew that he was back in the real world, for in the dream, as terrifying as it was, there was the remembrance of light and color. The stars, how he anguished to see those stars again. In the real world, it was now always dark. "I'm OK," he said as he lifted his hand from the sticky substance.

Tat... tat... tat-tat.

Earl heard the steady drip of the spilt beer as it dripped from the bar to the floor. His shirt sleeve grew wet, cold, as it sopped up some of the chilled brew. "I'm sorry." He brought his hands together spreading the stickiness. "What is this?" He brought a finger to his nose, then tasted it.

"Honeycomb," Gibby said, and he padded a large bar towel onto the spilled beer. "Clover honeycomb. I'm partial to it with some sourdough toast. Here." He jammed the wet bar towel between Earl's hands before he spread the honey any further. "No harm done, but let's get you cleaned up before it gets any worse."

With some trepidation he helped Earl behind the bar. A neurotic blind man among all the liquor bottles was an invitation to disaster. Gibby turned on the water, not too hot, eyed the honeycomb slathered throughout both of Earl's hands, and chuckled.

"EUREKA! Today I'm going to kill me a Jap!"

Gibby's caught short his laugh as the front door burst open with a loud crash. He turned just in time to see Henry Akita fly through the doorway as if he'd been hit by a run-away cable car. Four tough-looking street thugs followed, whooping and howling as they kicked and punched Henry with savage delight. They were the same four who had come after Henry the first time he had come into the bar.

"What the hell!" Gibby screamed. "Henry, get to your feet!" One look told Gibby that Henry had already taken a beating and couldn't take much more. "Earl, you stay put," he said, and he pushed Earl down by the shoulders. "I've got enough problems without worrying about you."

He left Earl kneeling by the sink, water running, grabbed the baseball bat, and stormed out from behind the bar. "Get the hell out of here, you scum bastards." The bat swung through the air as he ran at the largest of the thugs. "Henry, roll away!"

Earl was not one to run from a fight, especially if a friend was in trouble. "Henry? Gibby?" What the hell is going on? He heard a thump and a crash as a table clattered to the floor. Gibby let out an awkward wheeze as something struck him. The noise, chaos, screams, and cries of pain told him that both Henry and Gibby were in serious trouble. His hands were still wet with a little sticky honey, and he felt anxiously around the bar for a weapon. Finding nothing, he reached lower, found a drawer and pulled it open.

Henry struggled to get to his feet, but the assault was too overwhelming. All he could do was roll in to a ball and cover his head and face and hope for the best. Through the corner of his eye he saw one of the thugs whip a bike chain low, cracking Gibby in the knee. "GEEYIKES!" The bat slipped from Gibby's grasp as the old man cried out in pain. He was yanked off his feet and thrown against a table. Gibby, the table, and two chairs, tumbled across the room as the baseball bat clattered to the floor, the bat scooped up by one of the thugs.

"This will do just fine," the thug grinned, showing rotten teeth, and he weighed the bat for measure, then slapped it against the palm of his other hand. "First we bash this Jap's head in, then we'll teach the old man a lesson for being a Jap lover." He raised the bat above Henry ready to strike.

"God... No..." Gibby cried from nearby. "Don't... for Christ's sake it's murder!"

The gun thundered as a bullet struck the ceiling just over the thug's head just as he prepared to strike. He froze. The thug crouched, the bat still raised, and he turned to see a man with dark glasses standing behind the bar with a nasty-looking handgun, still smoking, pointed in his direction.

Henry managed to roll a little farther out of reach.

"What the hell is this?" The thug stepped back, not sure what to do. He could see the man's hands tremble as he moved the gun first to the left, then to the right, aiming at no one.

"Get the hell out before I blow your balls off!" The

man with the dark glasses roared, and he cocked the gun. "Now!"

A chair clattered as the old bartender, breathing heavily, tried to get to his feet. The barrel of the gun moved quickly towards the sound, then back again, as the thug took a step forward, a nut shell crunching beneath his foot.

"The bastard's blind," the thug with the bike chain said in a loud, useless whisper as he slowly worked his way quietly to the right.

"Earl don't point that damn thing at me," Gibby urged.

The gun moved back towards the one with the bat.

The thug lowered the bat and took a cautious step forward. "Well, well, ain't this something." The barrel of the gun was pointed straight at him. He gave a nod to his cohort with the chain, who moved quietly towards the bar, readying the chain to strike the gun from the blind man's grasp.

Henry looked up from the floor in horror. "Earl..." he started to shout a warning but shut up when he realized Earl did not need any distractions.

The gun grew heavier, the longer Earl held it straight out in front of him with his finger on the trigger. There were four men that he knew of. One was straight ahead. He was certain that one had Henry and another, Gibby. Where was the third, or fourth? Had he miscounted? How many bullets were in the gun? "Gibby, Henry, stay down," he said. "Stay quiet".

A chair tipped over to his left and he quickly moved the gun in that direction. That would be Gibby. He could hear him wheeze as he fought to get his breath back. He moved the gun back towards where the thug with the bat had been.

"A blind bastard with a gun, ain't that a crock?" He

heard someone whisper. At least now he knew where the third one was - near Henry, a few steps behind the bat man. Where was the fourth?

"Well... well... what do we have here?" He heard the bat man say. Earl kept the gun pointed at the most threatening and promising target. The man took a step forward. Earl tightened his finger on the trigger. The thug stopped. He could hear the wood of the bat slap against the sweat of the man's hand. This was the leader, the most dangerous, the one he needed to take out. The room grew quiet. He could hear their breathing. There were two to his right: one was with Gibby, one was by Henry — not a threat, at least not yet. One man was missing. The hair stood up on the back of Earl's neck. One of them was about to make his move. He could feel it. The wall clock behind him ticked hard.

"Earl..."

That was Henry. *What is he trying to tell me?*
CRUNCH!

He heard the crunch of a peanut shell just a few feet from his left. He turned and fired. The gun thundered, kicking back in his hand. There was a scream followed by the sharp clang of metal on wood as something slammed into the bar dangerously close to where he stood. Whoever he had shot stumbled back, then fell hard.

The bat man had been watching eagerly as his crony crept up to the bar undetected, the chain held ready to strike the gun from the blind bastard's hand. He bounced lightly on the balls of his feet, ready to move in with the bat. He did not care about useless peanut shells by his feet.

The blind man turned — no warning — and fired.
BLAM.

The bike chain slammed into the bar inches from where

the blind man stood. Helpless, my ass, the bastard just blew away... As soon as the bat man saw the bright splotch of red spread across his partner's chest, he charged forward with every intention of bashing the blind man into a bloody pulp. His scream of rage caught in his throat as he saw the gun swivel back in his direction, the blind man's finger closing tight and fast on the trigger. He died as the bat flew harmlessly over the blind man's head.

17
OH, HOW HE SANG

Later the next day. Earl sat silent and listened to the rhythmic tick of the wall clock and the radio's endless chatter. Ferris "Burrhead" Fein, with the San Francisco Seals, slammed one out of the park with two men on base. Earl smiled faintly. He crunched a peanut shell between his fingers and popped the nut into his mouth. He remembered a game with the Kansas City Blues back in 1938. That was the glory year, when the Blues won the Little World Series. Ahhh, those were the days. The sky never bluer, the ladies radiant and young. The beer never tasted any better, the peanuts straight out of the roaster. I'll never see a day like that again. His smile faded.

A key rattled in the lock to the front door. "Sam, we've got company," he said.

"I got it," Sam cautioned. "Unless you gave the perps keys to the front door, that should be your two pals back from the hospital." He unsnapped his sidearm just in case, stood, and stepped back into a shadow.

Officer Sam Newman had been assigned to keep an eye on Earl while Henry and Gibby were in the hospital. Sam had been one of the first cops on the scene, arriving in time to hear the two point-blank shots that had killed Louis Stark, a known and violent criminal. He had been the thug with the bat.

Earl had killed both of his assailants — the other, a John Doe — in self-defense, which was no small undertaking. The other two thugs had fled the scene. While not known to be armed, both had extensive records, including assault and battery. The press had made quite a hero out of Earl Crier, and the Chief of Police wouldn't take it too kindly if anything happened to him.

Gibby pushed open the door. "Damnations, it's hard to get good help these days," he growled as he took in the room. "Earl, I thought you would have the place cleaned up by now."

"The cops wouldn't let me touch a thing." Earl shrugged without turning towards the sound of Gibby's voice. "While you two have been schmoozing with the nurses, I've had my hands full with all the friggin' reporters," he added glibly.

Sam relaxed and stepped out into the light.

"Are you expecting more trouble?" Gibby asked.

Sam was about Gibby's height and build and close to retirement. Take him out of uniform and he might pass for Gibby's twin brother. "Just playing it smart. It wouldn't look too good if something happened to Earl here."

Gibby shook his head as he eyed the crime scene with its chalk markings around two large red stains that marred the floor. Furniture that had been overturned remained exactly as it had been when he and Henry and been taken to the hospital. He righted a table and a couple of chairs and swore as he calculated the damage to the bar.

It had taken two shots for Earl to down the last assailant but not before the bat had sailed just over his head into a shelf of liquor bottles, which had crashed down onto a second line of bottles shattering most. "Keerist! This is gonna cost a fortune."

"I've got thirty bucks you can have, if it will help," Earl

said.

Gibby, stopped, looked at Earl, then muttered under his breath, "What are you, some kind of gunslinging saint?"

"You might be right," Henry said as he limped through the door. "Ouch, they did a number on the place didn't they?" His arm in a sling, Henry tried to right a table with his left hand. "I guess things could have been worse."

Gibby looked behind the bar at the lake of booze and shattered glass. "That's a waste of fine liquor and a hell of a lot of dough," he said as he tried to add up the cost. *The mirror has a crack, otherwise it's whole. at least that's something,* Gibby thought. "I can't raise the prices. If I can't find a way to bring in new customers, I might just have to close the place down." He righted a chair, then sat down, feeling a little lightheaded. His right arm seemed a little numb, but he put that off to the beating he had taken the day before.

"Henry," Earl sounded off, "by God, it's good to see you back." He raised a hand, questioning his own words. "Well, you know what I mean. Are you all right, nothing busted?"

"Earl, would it have been too much to ask, 'Gibby, are you all right, anything busted?' Jesus, Paul, and Mary, that's the thanks I get," Gibby fumed.

"Sorry," Earl said, "didn't mean no offense. Gibby, are you—"

"Don't ask," grumbled Gibby. "Don't ask." He wiped his brow. The numbness in his arm still hadn't gone away.

Henry got Sam to help him move a couple of tables from the right side of the bar, then stepped to the door, and waved with his good hand. "In here, guys." A moment later, two workmen carefully jostled a Steinway Parlor Grand Piano through the door and rolled it over to the spot

Henry had picked out.

Gibby felt pressure in his chest as he watched the piano being wheeled in. Jesus Christ, how much is that thing going to cost me? He started to speak but couldn't quite catch his breath.

Earl turned in his seat, puzzled at the sounds.

"Gibby," Henry said, "I know what you're thinking. The piano is not going to cost you a dime. While in the hospital I had a visit from an old friend, Professor Munemori. Before the war he taught at the Nisei school in the Kinmon Gekuen building on Clay Street. Since 1942 the building has been used as the Booker T. Washington Community Center. Now it's a men's hostel for Nisei who've been left homeless by their internment." The sadness and anger were both detectable in Henry's voice. "They were going to sell it. I got a good deal."

Henry looked long and hard at the old man whose pallor was beginning to give him some concern. "I know we haven't talked about this. You're the boss but hear me out. I told you I made a good deal. The piano is on loan for as long as we need it. The price? Nothing. In exchange you open the bar one night a month exclusively for Nisei customers, no discount, no credit, they'll pay cash. My

Japanese-American brothers are fond of jazz and, man-oh-man, once they hear Earl play, they will fill the place up."

Close the place up for a night to entertain a bunch of Japs. Gibby thought about what some of his regular customers would say and shook his head. *There ain't no way.* Then he thought about his son, studied Henry, who had become like a son to him, sighed without knowing it, and rose to his feet. As far as he was concerned, Jap money was as good as the next guys.

Henry guided Earl to the piano where he adjusted the stool, felt the keys, got a measure of the ivories, then began to play a sentimental Duke Ellington number to set the mood. Moving quickly to a stepped-up version of *G.I Jive.* (4) The piano needed tuning; nevertheless, it showed Earl's gift on the keyboard. "Johnny Mercer can play and sing circles around me on his tune – but ain't she sweet."

After righting a table, a few chairs, and wiping them down, Gibby sat down again and listened to Earl play. He was everything Henry had said he was and then some. "Earl," he finally said, breaking his pondering silence, "you've got yourself a job." His old-man scowl shifted to a grin as he looked Henry straight in the eye. "And you can thank your Nisei pal here. I'm only going to say this once, cause if I must think about it, I'm apt to change my mind. I want you to move in. If you say no, you're a fool, and I don't take you for a fool. There's some space back behind the storage room that I used as an office. It ain't much, but it will hold a bed and a small wardrobe. You won't have to mess with the stairs that way. The bath is upstairs, and there is a can down here, so you'll make out just fine."

"I can't pay much," Earl said, his pride caught in his throat. Shut up, fool, he thought. You got any other offers? "I appreciate the offer, but I don't want to be a burden, nor do I want charity."

"Charity? You'll earn your keep same as Henry here. Henry, help Earl over here, and we'll seal the deal with a bottle of champagne."

"Now wait a moment," Earl protested. "Nobody has agreed to anything, at least not yet." He started to rise.

"Sit," Henry ordered as he rapped his knuckles on the

piano bench and pushed him back onto it.

"Earl," Gibby said matter-of-factly, "I'm going to charge you the same rent I charge Henry, and you can start earning your keep right now. Henry says you're a genius on the piano. So, Saint Crier, why don't you make like an angel and turn this musty old place into a little bit of Heaven with the type of music that will fill the place with paying customers." He glanced at Henry through smudged spectacles that rode haphazardly on his nose. "And that includes an all-Nisei night."

The words caught in Earl's throat struggled for air. His head swam as he counted the money he did not have and the options that did not exist. After what seemed an unbearable pause, he found the word he was looking for and blurted it out. "Deal!" He turned on the bench and felt for the keyboard, tested the keys, caressed the mahogany and ran his fingers across the word embossed just above the middle. "Steinway?" Ignoring his tears, he began to play, his finders moving from a well-known tune to an original, six tunes blending together as if they were written that way.

The champagne cork popped. Gibby poured beer for the workmen and Officer Sam Newman.Gibby was mesmerized by Earl's dexterity and speed on the keyboard. He didn't miss a note. Gibby had heard a blind man playing the piano once - that had been on the radio but seeing was believing. All he could say was, "Well, I'll be damned."

The men sang and raised their glasses as they watched him work his magic as his fingers danced as one with the ivory keys.

As Earl finished, Henry brought out his clarinet from behind the bar and tried to play, his injuries silencing him. Earl gave him a wink, his fingers danced and oh, how he sang.

18
I'M NOT NUTS

Brooks sat alone in his hospital room, waiting for his poker pals to show up. Playing five-card stud with Self-Pity and Desperation is not for the faint of heart. The last time he had played and called their bluff, he had drawn two deuces wild and lived to tell about it. Perhaps today he would have better luck.

He shook his head in bemusement, then spoke aloud, needing to hear his own voice. "I'm not nuts, at least not yet. Yes..." The word was long and drawn out. "I talk to myself, and from time to time I even answer. Sometimes my mouth just starts talking and it takes my mind a while to catch up. A little talk never hurt anyone, and it's a hell of a lot better than raging at Mr. Dark. I do try to carry on the other end of the conversation - no sense being rude.

"Now if I were to start singing in three-part harmony, that would be a whole different kettle of fish. You see, I've got this permanent reservation at the No See Motel, and from time to time I'd like to get a fix on whether I'm awake or only dreaming. It's not easy, and that is the damned truth. But at least for the moment I'm keeping my head above water."

He ran his hand over his cheek, then up to his forehead, the coarse bandage never ending. He gave a short bitter laugh and shook his head in exasperation. He then shifted his weight as he let out a sudden bark: "Earl, you pompous bastard, where in this big black universe did you get off to?" He heaved a dramatic sigh. "You were always trying to do me one better. You dreamt in all the colors of the rainbow — or was that another crock? Me, I was never a big dreamer, at least not since I was a kid. I always dreamt in black and white. Now I don't get the white." He sat silent for a moment in the deep velvet of night with neither the stars nor the moon for company.

Brooks had begun talking to himself shortly after being left alone in his small, forbidding hospital room. He never thought he would miss Earl. They hadn't liked each other from the first moment Stella had made them roomies. Now they shared uncommon bonds: the black that was all-consuming, music, and their loathing for each other's company.

"Earl," he continued to speak aloud, "one thing I do know is that you are not out there selling pencils on some damned street corner. No, sir, you're playing the piano, right as rain. What galls me is that you're out there singing up a storm and I'm stuck here in this pit." And then he added, with an odd catch to his voice: "God bless you anyway, you annoying egotistical prick."

The grumble in Brooks' belly interrupted his thought. He was having a hard time adjusting to the tedium. Somehow 'tedium' fell short of any relevancy once he had lost his sight. "I know Tedium, he's a fair-weather pal of mine. Hah! You've got to watch out for the guy. He's a crooked son-of-a-bitch who will turn on you soon as you're not looking. He's a chameleon.

"One moment you think you're in the doldrums or caught in a ho-hum moment, you're bored and can't quite stifle a yawn, and then to your chagrin you find out that it's just good old Tedium paying his respects.

"You just never know when or where the bastard will show up. I've known him to lurk in the bottom of a cold cup of coffee or come wrapped in a pack of Camel cigarettes. Hell" — Brooks gave an incredulous laugh — "you meet up with Tedium often enough you learn that he's not the enemy. He's a pal. Old Tedium is one hell of a drinking buddy."

Brooks had been lucky. He and Tedium had met mostly on safe ground. Brooks had not spent long weeks at sea sweating in the stinking hulls of ships, playing cards, and telling lies about the girls back home, while waiting for orders to storm a worthless beach in sheer terror. "It's a sad commentary," he remembered saying to Tedium, "when a human being prays for instant obliteration versus the agony of lying on the sandy beach with a limb blown off or your guts ripped out as you scream for a mother who carried her own pain when she brought you into the world." Brooks never had to look out from behind a thin plexiglass wind-shield at forty-five hundred feet as thousands of rounds of ack-ack exploded around him while the bombardier dropped a payload of fire bombs on Dresden, burning the civilian population. Many a soldier knew Tedium, and they knew that as soon as the shooting started Tedium would abandon ship to wait for his pals at the nearest pub back in merry old England.

"Yes, sir, old Tedium is a real squared-away guy." Brook's sigh was antagonistic. "Like I said, Old Tedium is a fair weather... fraud." He paused, taking the opportunity to contradict himself while he reflected on where he had spent most of his war. He had been a Special Services Officer shepherding Hollywood's elite to entertain the troops in the rest and recover staging areas, to relieve them of Tedium's odd sense of humor before sending them back to the thrill of war. The truth was that Brooks hadn't really been needed. He had been nothing more than a glorified bellhop with officer bars. Hello and welcome to London, Mr. Hope. I'll see that your luggage catches up with you. General Ulysses Fatass would like you to join him for drinks at five. He had never had enough rank or pull to be able to socialize with the high and mighty, and boy did that burn him.

Most of the war, he and his pal Tedium were regular fixtures at the Crooked Billet, a pub off Southborough Lane in Brambly, where Brooks played a little piano, with Tedium lifting one more pint for those about to go out and do great deeds and die trying. He had been the life of the party until 9:15 Sunday evening, November 19th, 1944, when the bar took a direct hit from a Nazi V-II rocket. His face, his sight, and his future were blown away. After that, it hadn't taken long for Brooks to take a personal dislike for his old pal Tedium. Tedium moved in like an unwanted in-law who yammered at him, saying nothing, just yammering on and on. "What could you possibly offer me that is worth the price of remembering? Get the hell out of here, yah good-for-nothing bum," Brooks swore as Tedium offered him a cigarette, which Books couldn't smoke with his face blown away. Slowly Brooks began to develop new friends and listen to the wise council of Mr. Dark, Self-Pity, and Desperation. If you played your cards right and ignored their slight- of- hand, you just might buy that losing hand. "Say goodnight, Gracie. Goodbye, Tedium. I won't say it's been nice knowing you."

Brooks sat alone, his sole companion Mr. Dark. He wet his lips as the craving for a strong drink answered the growl in his stomach. "We have a visitor," he said with a dry chuckle. "Our old pal Tedium has come to pay his respects. We were just talking about you. Let's have a

drink for old times' sake. Dammit," he swore as his belly
growled in agreement, "I want a Tennessee bourbon,
make it a double." There was a slight hiss as he pushed his
breath through his teeth and the hole in his mask. "Ssssss...
NOW!" He slammed his fist down on his knee. *Where the
hell are we going to find one?* He thought in frustration. He
brought his hand up to the woefully small mouth hole in
his bandaged head. How can I drink without looking like a
pitiful fool? This thought was followed by a dry chuckle.
"Without ruining my mascara." He laughed aloud.

His old pal Self-Pity came in with a freshly shuffled
deck and whispered sweet nothings in his ear. Since Earl
had been kicked out, and Ivory had disappeared, and
Henry and Stella had been fired, Brooks' narrow world had
spiraled into a dark bleakness that was beginning to suggest
that there was nothing left worth living for.

"I will not go quietly into the night," he exclaimed
with a poor imitation of a British accent. "If I have but one
life to give, then I choose to drown in a vat of bourbon.
Tedium, old pal; Self-Pity; Mr. Black, you guys game? Say,
where's

Desperation? Never mind, he'll show up in his own
good time."

"Where the hell are my clothes?" Stella had bought
him a tux. It wasn't hung up where he could find it
because there was no one to do it for him. Instead he had
to search in the dark for his pants, shoes, a shirt with too
many buttons, and figure out how they all came together.
Desperation chided him, but he didn't rage. There was no
one to hear him except for his three drinking buddies, and
they had all heard it before. He could not cry, for he had no
tear ducts. "Tedium, I'll bet you a dime to your doughnut

that Self-Pity can drink you under the table any day of the week."

He found his tux, and after exasperated fumbling and muttered cursing he had most of the buttons buttoned, though not all where they should be. At least his pants were right side out, or so he thought. Whatever he looked like, it was better than the hospital gown with the drafty rear-room view he was forced to wear.

He had a stash of dollar bills in a sock, which he shoved into his coat pocket. He stood up, gripped his cane, and wondered if he had the guts to do this. "Hell, I'm already talking to myself. If I stay here much longer, I will go nuts."

He stood tall and tossed his bandage-wrapped head back as best he could and proclaimed, "Come on boys, the fleet's in."

At the door he went pin-drop silent. He slowly pulled open the door and listened within the dark to the hospital sounds one last time. He knew where the elevator was by sound, but he hadn't a clue as to which floor he was on, how many floors there were, or where he needed to go.

When the elevator door closed, he punched all the buttons. The motion told him that he was going down. That was good, perhaps. He self-consciously checked the buttons on his pants as he felt the need to take a pee coming on. Damn, why didn't I think of that before I got the damn buttons done?

The elevator door opened to a damp, musty-smelling place that gave him the willies. After an eternal twenty minutes of wrong turns into pitch-black dead-end places, he lost any sense of direction or hope for recovery and stood with his back to the door inside a locked storage closet and called out with what little dignity he could muster. "Help, someone. I'm a poor blind sheep who's lost his way... And damn but I need to pee. Help? Anyone?"

He knew that he was in some sort of small room. Tedium and Self-Pity were hogging the space. "Get out of here, you bum. You're beginning to stink up the place. What's that? Mr. Black? No, no need to apologize. Believe me, I wish you could leave. If I could grab you by the throat and squeeze the life out of you, I would without a moment's hesitation. But I can't. You, pal, are my doppel-ganger, my faithful second self, and we're stuck together until death renders us apart. Hmmm, now there is something to ponder."

A janitor found him and got him to a bathroom in time. He would have cried if he could, because he urgently needed the janitor's help with the buttons to keep from peeing all over himself. That done, the janitor escorted Brooks back to his room. Brooks' protests fell on empty ears while his drinking pals laughed at his expense.

Again, the bourbon beckoned, and Brooks found himself alone with Mr. Black, while Self-Pity copped an attitude. Tedium had gone ahead to reserve a table. It didn't take long for Tenacity, who had invited himself to the party, to give Brooks a sharp kick in the ass. And they were off again. Brooks was halfway to the elevator when a nurse found him and kindly helped him back to his room, back into his hospital gown and into his bed. She had heard about his misadventure in the basement and gave him a pill to help him sleep and to keep him from wandering off again.

Self-Pity had gone on to join Tedium while Desperation shuffled the cards and dealt the first hand. Brooks pushed the cards away. As soon as the nurse left, he counted to twenty then spit the pill out, which was not easy to do through the damned mouth hole. The nurse, bless her heartless soul, at least had hung up his clothes, which had to count for something. He dressed and this time he only buttoned every other button on his fly. No sense taking chances.

Back on the elevator he found the second button from the bottom, pushed it, and held his breath. The door opened to the first floor, where he felt a slight breeze that carried with it the salty taste and smell of ocean air. Forty-two steps straight forward and the street sounds told him that the front door was just ahead. He felt the tempo of his heart increase with the excitement.

"Excuse me, sir?" Brooks stopped dead in his tracks. It was a woman's voice, a nosy one at that. "You shouldn't be here. If you are checking out..." She looked at a clip board then back at the blind man who had suddenly appeared before her. "If you are being released, I would have been notified right here." She tapped the clipboard purposely to show him where his name should have been written. Her authoritarian bag of hot air suddenly deflated when she remembered that he couldn't see. "Oh... I'm... I didn't mean..."

"Oh, that's all right, miss, I was just visiting a friend I hadn't seen for some time." Desperate times call for prime-grade bullshit, he thought, and he tried to put on his best smile, which of course she couldn't see beneath his Humpty Dumpty mask. "Would you mind calling me a cab?"

She peered over the top of her glasses. The man was dressed in civilian clothes. A tuxedo. No patient here would dress like that. A blind man couldn't find his way around this place without help. Well, he certainly had. Hmmm, a most unusual man. "Why certainly, let me help you find a seat, and I'll call one for you."

"Much obliged," Brooks responded. "I'll just wait outside. I'm partial to the sea air." Brooks tried to appear self-confident as he used his cane and followed the sound of the woman as she scurried to open the front door for him.

The cabby had gotten a call to pick up a handicapped ride at the veteran's hospital. The hospital parking lot was not well lit, neither was the entryway. In the pale-yellow light near the hospital door stood an apparition dressed to the nines in black; only he had no face.

"You gotta be kidding me," the cabby said and swore. The chewed butt of an unlit cigar clenched between his teeth remained motionless while the rest of his face skewed. "What's this, a mummy going to the opera? Somebody must be making one of those horror films with what's-his-face... Karloff." The tall, coal-black praying mantis character gave him the creeps and he thought about driving on. But he had not had many fares so far, and if he didn't come up with enough dough for the rent, his old lady would be busting his chops. He leaned over and rolled down the passenger side window. "Hey, buddy, you call for a cab?"

A white cane came out of nowhere and wavered in his direction. "You got it, Mac."

The cabby got out and escorted him none too gently to the cab. "Say, wait a minute, you got any dough?" the cabby demanded, and he gave the blind freak's elbow a slightly painful twist.

"How far will this get me?" Brooks held out two bills.

The cabby counted two fives. "You've got two bucks, which will get you to a couple of swell joints I know."

"Name them," Brooks demanded.

Caught off-guard, the cabby responded, "I'd recommend either the Stardust Lounge or Roland's.

"The Stardust," Brooks answered as if he knew the place. "Take the shortcut, you know the one I mean, and you can keep the difference as a tip."

"You got it, Mac." Five minutes later, the cab pulled up in front of a seedy neighborhood bar. The cabby helped his fare to the front door and took the two crumpled bills from the blind man's hands. He could see the beginning of what might be a grin, peeking from inside the mouth hole, in the tightly wrapped bandaged head, and it gave him the willies. "Need any help from here?" His tone implied a less than genuine offer.

The cabby hopped into his car, slammed the door, inserted the key, then looked at his loot. Ten buck's easy money. "What's this? Well, don't that beat all." The dough the blind man had given him was two one-dollar bills. He hee-hawed at the jackass he had been.

Brooks stood for a moment outside the door collecting his wits. He could only guess at how he would be received. Self-Pity was throwing a party inside in his honor, and he shouldn't keep them waiting. He sucked in a deep breath, squared his shoulders, felt for the door and then opened it. Come on, Self-Pity, you've got a few pals in there. Call in a few favors. How about giving me a break?

The bar smelled and sounded just like the type of place where he could drink until he was seduced by the siren

Oblivion. He stood inside the bar and waited. If people were going to gawk at him, they could get it over with now. He intended on standing there until hell froze over before he would give them the satisfaction. *Oh, please help the poor defenseless freak, h*e thought. *No, dammit, I demand the same courtesy as the next guy. They can see — that I cannot. I will not flounder around like a fish out of water looking for a seat.* It took only half a minute before Desperation tapped on his shoulder. "Come on, pal, the hell with your pride. I'm thirsty."

The bartender, a short muscular man with a marine buzz cut, glanced up from his whispered conversation with one of his regular customers. "The circus must be in town. Nate fix an eyeball on this."

Nate had been telling the bartender about a hot bimbo he had picked up in Reno. He stopped in mid-sentence and turned on the bar stool as he followed the bartender's gaze. He blew out a long low whistle as he set sight on an unusually tall man in a black tux. His entire head was wrapped in gauze. He had no face. The din of drunken laughter lowered to a murmur as all eyes settled on the freak.

Brooks reined in his rage as he checked with Self-Pity and Despair to see if either had found a table.

Nate took in the room and spoke to the bartender without taking his eyes off the floor show. "Claude, why don't you give the guy a break?"

"What?" It was less a question than it was ignorance.

"Claude, a hundred bucks to your one the guy is a veteran."

Claude shrugged his shoulders. "So? A lot of guys came back from the war with a few parts missing and their ass dragging. Does that make me their keeper? No, I don't think so. OK, the guy got a lousy deal, but that don't make it right for him to come in here and give my customers the creeps. Folks want to forget about the war and get on with life. You think they can do that with this freak coming in here dressed like a Christmas package. 'I'll be home for Christmas...' He sang the beginnings of the song poorly. "They should have given the poor bastard a ribbon."

They most likely did, Nate thought as he caught a glimpse of the tattoo on Claude's bicep. "You're all heart, Marine, a real peach of a guy." He turned his back to the faceless man and stared into a flyspecked, smoky bar mirror where he could not take his eyes off the tall dark stranger who could not return his gaze. His head slowly nodded as he watched the reflection of a courageous man who somehow managed to retain some dignity when he was surrounded by jerks like Claude. He pushed his empty glass forward and threw a buck on the counter. "One more, a fresh glass, and watch the head."

Claude poured a draft beer and swept the foam from the top of the mug with a knife then slid it across the counter. "So, what happened between you and the hot number you were telling me about?"

"Use your imagination," Nate groused as he got up, pulled a straw from a box at the end of the counter and left the bartender to finish the story with imagination he didn't have.

"Take no mind of these bums," he said as he reached the tall faceless man. "They're just jealous of that swell tux you're wearing. There're an empty table three steps straight on the clock and one to the left. Watch out for the extra chair." It didn't take imagination to see the beginnings of a horribly scarred face hidden beneath the layers of cloth that covered the stranger's head.

"Thank you," Brooks said. "You are most kind. How many seats are there? There will be three other gentlemen joining me." He found a chair and sat.

Nate set the beer down and slowly edged it into the faceless man's hands. He stripped the straw from its paper wrapper and plunked it into the beer. "I thought this might help. The bartender's name is Claude. He's a real dirt-ball. If he gives you any trouble, just tell him that old Nate will be back to settle accounts later." He pulled two more chairs up to the table and turned to leave, but not before giving Claude a hard look and a silent warning.

"Thank you," Brooks said as he tried to follow the voice. Citizen Nate had already departed. The cold sweat on the beer mug felt good in his hand. He felt for and found the straw and took a long slow sip. It wasn't bourbon, but it sure took the dry ache from his throat. He let out a grim chuckle. "Mr. Black, the first round is on you." His head turned towards the empty chairs one by one. "Gentlemen, shall we play a few hands? Five-card stud, nothing wild. I'm feeling lucky."

19
STELLA'S GUILT

Stella looked up from her book, Miracle of the Bells, unable to concentrate. The last time she had finished a book was in 1941. The war had interrupted so many pleasures in life. For years she had no time to read; now that she had did, she couldn't seem to get beyond the first sentence.

She was on disciplinary leave for insubordination to a hospital administrator with a Hitler complex. She was lucky to have only lost a few days' pay. Henry had lost his job, for which she felt very much responsible; that he was Nisei made it even more difficult. It had been her idea to allow the patients, who were able, to have a small taste of booze to brighten up the bleakness of their incarceration. Incarceration? It was supposed to be a hospital, where hope was promised, not taken away.

Mann, who rarely needed an excuse to fire someone, had used the alcohol as an excuse to fire Henry and to bully everyone else involved: staff and patients alike. The truth was that drinking was rampant throughout the hospital, especially amongst the staff. Elroy sold his cheap moonshine openly, and Mann never batted an eye, which gave her cause to question their relationship.

Having read the first line two, three, four times, she tossed the book onto a table. A dark cloud loomed over the hospital, and she sensed its's cold specter. If she had any savings she would willingly turn and run, with no looking back, until she could run no further. She couldn't, not if it meant abandoning her boys to the graft and insensitivity of men like Mann and Elroy, both the Devil's spawn, and there was little she could do to stop them.

If only she had the courage. Courage seemed natural for guys like Earl Crier, Ivory Burch, and Henry Akita. She remembered the look on Ivory's face when he had first opened his eyes and seen Henry, who, with great compassion, had reached out to a man who hated his very existence. "Take it easy fella, it's only a dream," he had said. Dreams? Few of the men in her care had dreams, thoughts and memories that refreshed the soul; most had nightmares. Maybe it was their combined weight that made the very air in the hospital foul and foreboding. The thought chilled her as she tried to push it aside.

She got up, put a log on the fire, warmed herself as she looked out from her small cold-water flat into the chill of the evening. She was forty-four; her entire career had been spent as a nurse. Had she a choice? She was not a secretary, a teacher, or a retail clerk.

She had never married, and for that matter had given up on the idea of ever doing so. She had seen too much suffering, anger and violence to allow herself to open her heart and be loved by and to love one man. She had a calling and a vocation in caring for the broken and battered souls who had paid a horrendous price for their service to their country in a time of war.

She had been one of the first nurses when the new Veterans' Hospital had opened in 1935. Her first patients had been Veterans' of the First World War and the Spanish-American War. After Pearl Harbor, the facility had been closed because it was too close to Fort Miley, and possible shelling from a Japanese invasion force.

She had transferred across the bay to Oak Knoll Navy Hospital where she worked twelve- to sixteen-hour days.

Oak Knoll was a major receiving hospital for the casualties in the distant war against Japan. She saw the worst of the worst and kept her emotions locked tight beneath her nurse's cap. Oak Knoll was a place she wanted to forget, and she jumped at the chance when the Veterans' Hospital reopened after the Japanese Empire crumbled under the intense plumes of two atomic bombs. San Francisco was home, and she often stared across the Bay at the city's welcoming lights. As the war raged, and the casualties mounted, she ached for her city by the Bay and her cable car bells. When the war came to a fitful end, she found a small apartment near the Veterans' Hospital and had been hired back as senior nurse.

Now that she was home, San Francisco was more beautiful than ever. It was the Veterans' Hospital that had changed. At Oak Knoll the casualties of war, no matter how difficult and ugly their traumas, were cared for. She soon discovered that at the Veterans' Hospital good medical care and kindness were not on the menu of everyday fare. It had become nothing more than a storage facility for those who were too scarred and maimed to return to the outside world.

The Administrator, a perpetual bean-counter, cared little for the value of a single human being. A penny saved was more important than a man's dignity or life. She shook her head. It was out of her hands now, everything but her sense of guilt for leaving those poor men behind. She reached for her coat and a scarf, needing some fresh air and a chance to think.

20

A BLIND MAN AND A JAP

Doctor Cornelius Fryback had little time or patience to spare. Of all the patients he had treated, few had suffered as much as the survivors of the China Marines, First Marine Battalion, Fourth Regiment. Most had not survived. Those who had would suffer life-long disabilities. War was hell, and Ivory Burch had served in the black heart of it.

A North China Marine, he was one of more than two hundred men who sank into POW hell before war was declared on December 8, 1941 and did not surface until the Japanese Empire surrendered unconditionally on September 2, 1945. Having suffered every single minute of the war under the most cruel and harsh conditions, Ivory crawled out of the Philippine jungle on September 3,1945. That he was alive was a miracle; that he would live doubtful. There was no space at Oak Knoll for patients considered to be beyond hope. Ivory was transferred to the Veterans' Hospital in San Francisco.

Dr. Fryback stopped in his tracks and put on his reading glasses when he saw Ivory Burch's name on the file. Until this moment, none of the wait-and-see patients he had consigned to the Veterans' Hospital had returned. That it was Ivory made it even more surprising. He read the file, bemused. He smiled as he knocked then pushed open the door.

"Well, Mr. Burch," Doctor Fryback said as he opened Ivory's medical file, "I didn't expect to see you back here so soon." He looked at Ivory over the top of his spectacles. Ivory had gained little weight since he had left Oak Knoll.

He appeared as frail as he had the day he had been carried off the U.S.S. Carton, and delivered to Oak Knoll, with a host of diseases and a poorly amputated leg.

Doctor Fryback cocked a bushy eyebrow and looked up curiously. "It says here that you were booted out of the Veterans' Hospital for insubordination to a superior officer. Is this true?"

Ivory smiled. His entire body shook, a gentle death rattle, a reminder that he still had more than one foot in a grave. Yet, there was a slight twinkle in his eyes that told the doctor that Ivory wasn't done yet, that his soul had somehow found the light of day.

Ivory looked at him intently before finally speaking, his voice a dry feeble quiver indicating that whatever had happened in the last twenty-four or, so hours had depleted much of his strength, leaving him pale and exhausted. "Superior officer?" Ivory said barely loud enough to be heard. "That's a laugh. Mann, the administrator, is a civilian 4-F prick. If I could have, I would have kicked his civilian ass into San Francisco Bay and fed him to the sharks. Only" — he paused with a mischievous smile — "I didn't want to give the sharks indigestion."

The doctor laughed, astonished at Ivory's hidden vigor. "I would have liked to see that." He laid the file down on his desk. "We've had more than one report on the administrator's callous behavior towards the patients. Perhaps in time you can enlighten us as to the true conditions over there?"

"Any time, doc, any time." His voice sounded a little thinner.

Doctor Fryback eyed Ivory a little more seriously. "Ivory," he said, "you were sent to the Veterans' Hospital because there was little more we could do for you here. The physical abuse you suffered along with the myriad diseases that have wracked your body should have killed you. You never should have come out of that jungle alive, but against all odds you did."

As if on cue the sarge appeared behind the doctor, giving Ivory a conspiratorial grin. His yellowish teeth, what there were of them, highlighting the dark abyss of his decaying face. Oh yeah, Ivory agreed with the sarge: Who said any of us survived?

"Unfortunately, your mental state was as worn down as your physical condition. Unless you wanted to live, there was little we could do to keep you alive." Doctor Fryback tapped the file with a long narrow finger. "I wrote here that you most likely would not last more than two or three weeks. Yet here you are, a dead man who is very much alive. Not in great shape, but alive. What magic bullet saved your life?"

Ivory's stomach grumbled, as he had not eaten much since the night before. "A blind man and a Jap," he answered as his stomach grumbled again.

"A blind man and a jap," Fryback repeated thoughtfully.

"Yep, and a nightingale named Stella."

"Stella Tate?" Fryback asked.

"All I know is that her name is Stella, a woman in her forties, with a heart of gold."

"It sounds like the Stella I know, and you're right, she is a nightingale if there ever was one." I'll give Stella a call, he thought. First this man needs to eat. "Are you able to keep down any solid food?"

"Yesterday I had Spam and eggs." He wet his lips. "And toast with... a dab of butter. I couldn't eat the Spam. It made my stomach ache," Ivory said, his mouth watering. "Real butter. It wasn't much bigger than a tiny old postage stamp, but damn, I haven't tasted anything that sweet since China."

"You remember China?" Doctor Fryback stood, turned Ivory's wheel chair around and guided him out the door. Most of the enlisted-rank patients were in dorms, twenty-four to thirty to a room. Ivory was to receive special treatment. Now that Ivory was no longer a wait-and-see patient, Doctor Fryback would do everything possible to make sure Ivory survived. His proudest day would be the day Ivory Burch walked out of Oak Knoll on his own.

"Do we remember China?" He turned slightly to see if the sarge was still there. He was. "Yes, I remember China. It's not easy, because back then everyone was alive, life was a grand adventure, we thought we were invincible. It's hard to go back: the faces, so many... so many.

"Doc, China was long ago, most of what I remember happened before the war. Everything else is a blank. I remember waking up on December 8th at Camp Holcomb, in Chinwangtao. My unit was to ship out on the 10th. We were surrounded by thousands of Japs. There were not enough of us to stand and fight. I... I..." His voice faltered. The sarge limped along behind followed by more shadows of the dead. Ivory's pallor paled as he grew silent.

Whether it was from exhaustion or the repressed memories, Doctor Fryback couldn't tell. "Go on."

Ivory didn't answer. He just stared ahead in silence. After a moment he licked his lips, then whispered two words: "Real butter."

A blind man and a Jap... huh, Doctor Fryback thought. He patted Ivory on his shoulder and steered him down a long white hospital corridor. *A blind man and a Jap? Just when you think you've heard it all, something new always seems to manifest itself.*

21
LIGHTS' LAST GLEAMING

The night air felt good. The foghorns seemed to bid Stella a personal greeting. She walked out the door with no decision as to where she might go. At the intersection she needed to decide: to go straight ahead, down the hill and around the park, then home; or turn left, walk two blocks to Shapiro's, a rowdy Union hangout. She could go to the right three and a half a block to Adam's Place. *Hello, Henry, you want to kick a girl when she's down? Here's your chance.* She knew what she needed to do.

The soft notes of a sonata softened the harsher night sounds of the city as she rounded the corner. She smiled; at least someone was sitting at home, warm and wrapped with pleasant thoughts and soft sounds. She looked up to see whose window might be open. The one she found was tuned to a Seals baseball game. No piano. The sonata faded, replaced by a cheerful Duke Ellington number, played on the piano. She stopped and listened. The music came from across the street where a warm yellow light bid welcome as she approached the door to Adam's Place.

"What on earth?" She gasped in surprise. The bar was alive, and Gibby was floating between tables, serving drinks and chatting it up with the customers. Henry looked up with a smile; he was filling orders from behind a crowded bar.

"Earl? How...?" Her breath caught in disbelief. She saw Earl sitting at a piano, smiling broadly, his fingers caressing the keys. He moved from the Ellington number to

White Cliffs of Dover. He was wearing the same Irish wool sweater and rainbow suspenders he had been given at the hospital. She giggled at his dark blue beret, which he had put on backwards at a rakish angle.

Gibby came over with a tray of dirty glasses in hand. "Stella don't stand there with your mouth open. Come on in." He looked around the room. "I don't have a table open, but I can make room for one more at the piano. Henry," he called out, "make room for one more there by Earl." He nodded curtly at a table where a customer looked impatient. "Yeah, yeah, don't bust your britches. I'll be there soon as I can."

"Earl? How?"

"It's a long story, sweetheart," Gibby said. "You go grab your seat before someone else does. All I can tell you is that when they fired Henry, they kicked Earl out with nowhere to go, nor barely a dime in his pocket. Some jackass at the hospital ripped him off. Can you believe that? Anyway, he found his way here, and heaven help me, I've adopted a blind man. I couldn't get rid of him if I wanted to. Look at this place."

"I am," she said as she unwound her scarf. "I am." She had known Gibby since before the war, and if there was ever a bartender with a good heart, a willing ear, loaded with sage advice, it was him.

Earl cocked his head as he heard a chair pull up by the piano. He sniffed, smiled, and finished the tune. He reached for his glass, bourbon and water, then placed it back exactly where he had found it. "Mac," he said to the man seated on the second stool on his left, "do us all a favor and don't sing along on this one. I can't see, and you can't sing, and since I'll never see again, why don't you match me and

129

never sing again."

Five pairs of hands applauded to the man's chagrin. "I'll have you know that at the Officer's Club at Pearl, I was known—"

"Ah, an officer and a gentleman. Navy?" Earl interrupted.

"Submarines." The man answered proudly.

"I didn't catch your name," Earl said.

"Tom. Lieutenant Commander Thomas Buck, and this pretty flower on my right is Terri Lynn."

"Hi, Earl," she said with a soft, breathy voice.

"Well, Lieutenant Commander," Earl said as he gently massaged the piano keys, "we could not have won the war without the subs. Say, isn't submarine duty known as the silent service?"

Terri Lynn, a platinum blond with voluptuous breasts, elbowed the Lieutenant Commander in the ribs as a hint to shut up.

Earl turned towards the recently filled seat nearest to him. "This one is for you, sweetheart."

'I can see my Stella beneath a moonlit sky...'

"Ouch, those last few notes were played by a blind man with a tin ear," Earl said. "Lieutenant Commander jump in here, I think I've found a spot for you."

"Hi, Earl," Stella said as she lit a cigarette. "That was great."

He replayed a few bars, finding his errors. "It sure beats playing in the day room. It was a swell crowd, the tips were lousy, but the acoustics will always have a special place in my heart. It sounded something like the inside of a submarine." He leaned back on his stool and called out, "Henry, bring the Lieutenant Commander here a drink on me. Stella?"

"How about a Tom Collins," Stella answered.

Henry, an amateur bartender at best, hadn't a clue how to make a Tom Collins. He looked at the long list of drinks waiting to be poured, or mixed, saw three more he didn't know, and tried not to look as out of control as he felt. Gibby should have been the one behind the bar, but he had insisted on working the floor. The bar hadn't had a crowd like this since before the war. No, not even then, that and there were still quite a few customers who didn't take kindly to Japs, even if they were Japanese Americans. Henry's eyes rested briefly on Stella. He wanted to apologize, it was his doing that had gotten her suspended.

Gibby saw the line-up of drink orders, stepped behind the bar, poured two beers and handed them to Henry. "Take these over to the bald guy and the floozy in the corner." He slipped a bar rag into Henry's apron pocket. "The tables over there" — he pointed at two tables recently cleared — "need wiping down. I'll work the bar."

He looked at the order forms and went to work. "Jesus, the help you get these days" he muttered loudly as he reached for a bottle. He missed the bottle, knocking it to the floor. "Damn, that's good money down the drain." He hadn't been able to quite grasp the bottle, his hand not quite registering what the brain was trying to tell it to do.

He knelt to retrieve the bottle, watched it drain. He massaged his hands trying to push the numbness in his right hand away. Christ almighty, what is happening to me? He left the bottle where it was, saw his face in the mirror as he rose. God, you are getting old, he thought as he wiped the sweat from his brow on his shirt sleeve. He poured a beer, which was out of the line of order, but the easiest task.

He worked the order list down, working it at Henry's pace, dropping two glasses, which broke, but managed to finish the evening without any more casualties. God, he was tired. His hand seemed a little better, but he still couldn't get the fingers to close all the way without some effort.

Stella stayed close to Earl until closing time.

Gibby came out of the kitchen with half a pastrami sandwich in hand and a dab of mustard on the edge of his lip. "Last call. If you can't drink it quick, don't bother." He stopped in mid-bluster, wiped his mouth, thought about picking up a couple of empty glasses, but decided to leave well enough alone. "Thanks, folks. Earl will be here for a while. Come back and enjoy some of his piano magic tomorrow night." He looked back as Henry escorted Earl back to the kitchen.

Earl put up his usual fuss, not wanting to be led but not familiar enough with the territory to negotiate it by himself. There was no way they were going to be able to close if Earl played, and as Gibby and Henry had learned, Earl would play into the wee hours of the morning if they let him.

"Earl never sleeps," Henry had told him. "He only naps, never seems to tire."

Gibby did sleep, and tonight he was bone-tired. It was taking some patience to get used to the radio blaring down-stairs while Earl learned new tunes and catnapped himself away from his dark dragon, but it was worth it. Henry was right, Earl was a gold mine.

Stella teased a sliver of ice in her glass as she remained seated at the piano. She hadn't felt this good in a long time.

She had so many questions. It was late, and tomorrow she would confront Mann, which would most likely get her fired. The longer she avoided going home, the further tomorrow seemed away.

Henry returned with Earl, who carried a plate of sandwiches as proudly as if he had made them himself.

"Here, Earl, let me take those," offered Stella as he found the piano bench with his knees. He sat. "Henry, I'm so sorry, I shouldn't have..." She said as Henry took a seat across from her. Gibby joined them, snatching a sandwich, before seating himself.

"Sorry for what?" Henry brushed her off, then continued before she could answer. "That hospital is a disgrace to medicine, one giant death ward killing the spirits of men who might otherwise survive. I really don't want time served there on my résumé. Fortunately, I got canned during the probationary period, so my dismissal can be considered no-fault. We didn't see eye to eye on a few things."

Earl listened and tinkered with a few piano keys as he downed half a sandwich with his other hand.

Enough said on that, at least for now, Stella thought, and she changed the subject. "How on earth did Earl get here?" She turned, reached out and touched Earl on the wrist affectionately.

"His majesty, the mighty Herbert Mann," Henry answered, "laid part of the blame for the party on Earl, and since Earl was Merchant Marine and for whatever stupid reason doesn't qualify for veteran's benefits, was force-marched to a cab and sent on his way. But not before someone ripped him off most of his back pay."

"Elroy," she fumed.

"Your guess is as good as mine, and in this case, I think I'll side with a woman's intuition." Gibby gave her a knowing eye, although he had never met Elroy. She tightened her grasp on Earl's arm. "Are you all right, sweetheart? You're not thinking about going back, there are you?"

"Only if you give me a gun to finish some unfinished business," Earl said wryly.

It suddenly dawned on Stella that it was Earl she had heard about in the news. "Oh, my gosh, that was you?" She looked quickly back and forth between Henry and Gibby. "Are you all... all right?"

"Fine," Gibby said as he massaged his hand beneath the counter.

"Although I feel a few years older, and none the wiser." The doctor had told him to expect some stiffness after his beating, but this wasn't that, this was a numbness, a disconnect between what his brain told his hand to do and what it partially wouldn't. He flexed his fingers, finding them slow to respond.

"Elroy." The softness in her eyes turned intentionally stone cold. "It's about time that slimy bastard got his up-and-comings." She blew out a stream of blue smoke. "I'll take care of him... soon."

Henry gave Stella an appraising eye and, for a moment, he almost felt some pity for Elroy. Almost. "Fortunately for us, Earl found his way here. He saved our hides."

"Earl here is a pistol-packing saint," Gibby said. "Four street punks who didn't like the color of Henry's skin followed Henry here. Next thing I know, Henry comes flying through the door, followed by these apes, who were high on

134

blood lust and God knows what else, who start kicking and punching the crap out of him.

"I got Earl safely behind the counter, grabbed Joe DiMaggio here," indicating the bat, "and went straight at them. Wham! I didn't have a chance. I go flying across the room, upturning tables and chairs along the way. I've got the wind knocked out of me, while Henry is kicked sense-less, and I can't lift a hand.

"The leader of this gang of hooligans, a mean ugly son of a bitch, now has my bat and makes to crack Henry's skull open with it. I've got to tell you, at that moment, I thought Henry was toast, and for my own chances... well..." He took a bite of the sandwich.

"Earl found the gun I had stashed behind the bar. Blamm! He took out two of the apes at point-blank range. The other two skedaddle out the back just as the cops arrive. So, I made Earl a deal he couldn't turn down." Gibby reached for another sandwich. "He gets free room and board in exchange for his music. I made up a room for him in the back."

Stella blew out a long appreciative whistle. "I knew there was something about you that I liked, Earl. Hero. Talent. Handsome. What other secrets are you keeping from us?"

Earl smiled, saving his answer for another time.

"Answer this for me," Stella asked Earl. "How did you get special privileges at the Veterans' Hospital when you had been a Merchant Marine cook? You were never an officer, yet you were given officer's privileges and veter-an's benefits that you were never entitled to — not that you don't deserve them — unless you served in some capacity you're keeping under wraps?"

"Earl," Gibby laughed, were you a goddamned spy; OSS?"

Henry looked long and hard at Earl and had to wonder.

"No," Earl answered, "nothing so dramatic. When the winds of war were first blowing across Europe, I figured it wouldn't be too long before FDR got us into the fight. I packed my bags and went down to the recruiting office. The Army and Navy both turned me down. They said I was too old.

"The Merchant Marine said they'd take me, and it wasn't long before I was baking up a storm on a Liberty ship on the Murmansk run. I was a ship's cook and never fired a shot. I had two ships sunk beneath me. The last, I was the only survivor."

"Is that where you lost your sight?" Stella asked.

"No," he answered and began to play a tune that reminded him of a distant place better forgotten. "What I'm about to tell you is classified." He put his finger to his lips. "Top Secret. If you tell another living soul, I'll disavow saying a thing and give your home address to Elroy." He ran his fingers long and hard across the keyboard.

"The war ended for me on July 5th, 1942. I was with the Merchant

Marine, convoying cargo to the Soviet Union. Of the thirty-three ships that left Iceland, eleven made it to Murmansk. The ship I was on is at the bottom of the Arctic Ocean. I was the only survivor. When they fished me out of the water, I had a busted ankle and a bad case of hypothermia. The nearest hospital was in

Murmansk, the coldest godforsaken place I've ever known. The hospital was short of skilled doctors, nurses, medicine and food. After ten days, and two botched operations on my foot, they said that they had done all they could. I was lucky to be alive."

"I spent the winter in a poorly heated dorm with eighteen other guys. We were all walking wounded, half of whom couldn't speak English. The cold was mind-numbing. The thought of spending another winter there drove me nuts. Three of our number committed suicide.

"In the spring I hitched a ride back to Iceland. I swore I'd never eat another herring for as long as I live." He turned towards where Gibby sat. "How about ordering in an anchovy pizza tomorrow?" After tapping three notes deliberately off-key, he continued. "From there I hitched a ride on a British freighter bound for Africa. There was plenty of work to do, but none for a cripple, so I just hung around waiting for a ride home."

Earl has a limp, Stella thought, *but it's minor, something a seasoned professional like me might recognize. At a casual glance, most people wouldn't notice it.*

"Thanksgiving Day, I reached Bari, Italy. Bari was one of the busiest ports in the Allied-occupied Adriatic. The harbor was jammed with ships. Most, when emptied, were going back to Africa, some to England, a few back to the States. I was on a waiting list. There was nothing to do but wait and keep out of the way. At least it was warm, the food good, and the wine plentiful.

"On December 2nd, 1943, I got word that I had a billet on ship leaving for the States. Three days and I'd be on my way home. After a celebration dinner and a bottle of wine, I went to the movies. That bottle of wine saved my life."

His finger hit a single dramatic key.

"I had to pee. While I was in the head an enormous

explosion rocked the building. Hell, the whole wall came down and left me pissing in public. When the dust settled, I could see that a massive chandelier that hung in the center of the theater had crashed down, crushing everyone below it — right where I had been sitting. The side of the building facing the harbor collapsed when a second pressure wave from an explosion in the harbor buried everyone else. I crawled out of the bathroom without a scratch.

"Out on the street I could see that the night sky was filled with white, yellow, and red ribbons of light. Hundreds of anti-aircraft guns were firing at the German planes, only there weren't any planes, at least none that I could see. It had been a small air raid, but a damned lucky one for the Nazis.

"Bari's old town took some serious damage, buildings collapsed, brick walls blocked the streets, windows were just gaping holes. A church tower collapsed on a neighboring restaurant - there were more dead than injured. All this caused by the first two gigantic explosions. I hurried towards the harbor to see if the ship that was to take me home was still afloat.

"It was far from over. More German bombs found targets in the harbor. What was left of the once mighty Luftwaffe, who were supposed to be fighting to the last plane defending the Reich, managed to surprise us; nobody expected it. We were caught with our pants down, and from what I could see it was worse than Pearl Harbor, only this time it was the Merchant Marine that took the shellacking.

"I heard a shrill, ear-piercing whine. Then a brilliant nova of light and flame rose a thousand feet into the night sky. That had been a fully loaded gasoline tanker, there one moment, gone the next. Any ships anchored nearby suffered the same fate. The John Henry, a freighter I had seen earlier in the day, was the next to go. I was blown off my feet. It was a cataclysmic explosion beyond anything I had seen. An unbelievable broiling cloud rose at least three thousand feet before slowly rolling inland.

"I lay stunned where I had been slammed against the wall of a school. The second floor of the building collapsed inwards from the impact of the explosion. My ankle lay twisted to one side, broken for the second time.

"That was the lucky part: this time the doctors were able to fix it right. A thick oily smoke stung my eyes and burned my lungs. That was the unlucky part, that broiling black cloud was the last thing I ever saw."

Stella reached out, her fingers resting on the top of his hand. Earl let her hand stay. There was visible tension in his neck, a slight tremble to his voice as he continued.

"I remember smelling garlic. When they found me, my scalp and neck were blistered. My ears were almost raw flesh. My eyes hurt something awful."

"No one knew what had been on the John Henry. At least, not anyone alive. There were thousands of dead, a lot more burned and injured. They tried to treat me at an Army Hospital, but they didn't know what they were dealing with. It wasn't until I got stateside, at Walter Reed Hospital, that I learned that the damage to my eyes was permanent. The cargo the John Henry was carrying was top secret. Far as I know, it still is. She was carrying mustard gas."

"Mustard gas?" Henry, Gibby and Stella repeated in unison.

"You heard right," Earl said. "Mustard gas had been packed into a hundred tons of artillery shells for use against the Nazis should they try to use chemical weapons on us. Had the doctors known, they might have been able to save my sight back at Bari. They couldn't because they didn't know. It was the luck of the draw." He took off his dark glasses, which he rarely did. The scars were evident. "Here's the rub: the ship that I was supposed to ship out on, once unloaded, was the John Henry. I was listed, prematurely, on the ship's register as being a member of the crew. I'm the only survivor of a ship I never set foot on, so the government thinks that I knew what made up her cargo. That's how I found out it had been mustard gas.

"The government still has a tight lid on what happened. They thought if they could bury me in the bureaucracy of a dead-end hospital, I couldn't do any harm, happy as a clam to have three squares and clean laundry. I guess Mann did me a big favor by booting me out of there."

"You going to blow the whistle on them?" Gibby asked.

"Can't say what I'm going to do, at least not yet. The fact that Mann contributed to Elroy's delinquency, that Elroy stole my money... I just may have to do something."

He slipped his glasses back on, then took a long pull of his drink. "Let's see if I can get this right this time," he said as he began to play Stella's song.

22
FAMILY

Stella stayed late, almost past her welcome - if that were possible. The truth was that she had not felt this close to friends or family in a long time. She did not have any living relatives, and her adoption of this oddball crew came without question or reservation.

Gibby reminded her in many ways of her father, a man whose heart had given out too soon. Henry, she had taken under her wings at the hospital, and had liked him from the start. He was courageous, smart as a whip, a guy with depths of compassion and who, despite his abilities, had to prove himself time and time again. She would never forget the compassion in his eyes the first time he had met Ivory Burch. *Take it easy fella, it's only a dream.* Sweet Earl, a gentle man who could bring tears to her eyes one moment or make her want to dance the next. She loved his stores, his music, and surprisingly enough his lack of sight. For some reason it brought out in him some qualities she had never connected with a man before. The man was a puzzle, and she was drawn to him.

"Sorry, kids," Gibby said, "we've got to wrap it up." He looked at the clock wishfully. It was close to three in the morning. "I'm not getting any younger, and neither is the morning. Henry, we'll clean up what's left before we open tomorrow.

"Earl, keep it down. You're like a goddamn rooster crooning. Just when I think I'm finally going to get some shuteye, there you are, crooning away. If we were nearer Chinatown, they'd string you up and make soup out of you."

"Not just yet," Stella said with a surprising level of motherly authority. "We've got one more thing to do, and I can't let it pass. Earl, you stink. You smell like stale beer, old socks, and cigarette smoke. There's another stench, but it would be unladylike to find the right description. Is that outfit you're wearing the same one we got you at the hospital?"

Earl lowered his head, sniffed, brought up his shirt sleeve, and sniffed again. "Sorry. Between the bleached bar rags, spilled beer, and tobacco smoke around here..."

"It's not your fault, Earl. You arrived here with barely a dime in your pocket and one shirt to your name; or so I'm told." She looked at Gibby and Henry, opened her palm and snapped a finger. "Your tip jar, gentlemen, all of it. We are going to buy Earl some decent clothes."

Gibby started to protest.

"I've got thirty bucks," Earl said as he searched his pockets.

Henry handed over the tip jar, which was reasonably full of change and one-dollar bills, then pulled out his wallet, which was thin. He had not yet been able to get a replacement check for his stolen wages, not that he ever would. Nevertheless, he took out a couple of dollar bills and added them to the pot.

"Jesus, I'm surrounded by saints and millionaires," Gibby grumbled as he opened the cash register, grabbed a few bills, counted them out, and tossed them onto the counter in front of Stella. He scooped up Earl's thirty bucks and stuffed it back into Earl's shirt pocket. "Earl," he said with a fatherly gruffness, "that is all the dough you have between Heaven and a rock and a hard place. Someday you may need it. Put it somewhere safe and keep it there, okay?"

Stella counted the cash and added a few bills of her own, then turned to Henry. "I'll drop by Accounting tomorrow, when I'm at the hospital, to see if they've been able to do anything about replacing your paycheck." She thought about that. She had better give Rose, in Accounting, a call first; that way she might be able to avoid another showdown with Mann. She needed to find out what time Elroy came on duty. After what had happened in the elevator, she did not want to be within shooting distance of the bastard. She gave Earl an appraisal. "Everything fit all right?" she asked. "Give me an honest answer."

"The pants are a little tight on the inseam," Earl answered.

Gibby threw up his hands. "I'm going to bed. Good night."

Stella got up, stopped at the door, turned and said to Earl, "Do a girl a favor and take a long hot bath. You're a bit ripe."

"Sponge bath?" Earl suggested with a puppy smile.

"Sure," she answered with a mischievous lilt. "Henry, help the man out."

"Come to think of it, a hot soak would feel right nice. Henry, do we have a tub around here?" Earl asked.

"Upstairs," Henry answered.

"Good, now use it," Stella said. "If not, I'll see that you do." She said as she closed the door behind her.

Henry locked the door. "Sounds more like a promise than a threat."

"That crossed my mind," Earl answered, and he played a few chords of Stella by Starlight. "Henry, would you mind setting up a hot tub first thing in the morning?"

"No problem," Henry said. "Get some shuteye. I'll see you in a few hours."

"It just might take more than one bath to get me smelling right," Earl said as he played a few keys at random. "See if you can find me some bubble bath."

"Bubble bath?" Henry asked as he left the room.

"That's what I said."

23
STEPPING IN HARM'S WAY

Stella slept like a baby for the first hour. After that, the worry goblins whispered in her ear. If she lost her job, which was the likely case, what could she do? Henry's paycheck? Earl's stolen pay? Reference from Mann — not likely. Elroy... Was she a fool for even going near the hospital? The man was dangerous. Brooks: bombastic and vulnerable. Her thoughts caught like so many leaves in a turbulent breeze.

When Stella arrived at the hospital, Rose told her that Herbert Mann wanted to see her in his office. Nothing was said about Henry's pay. Elroy would not clock in for an hour; she would have a little time to see how Brooks was doing.

"You wanted to see me?" Stella said with a tone less than respectful. She hadn't knocked on the door, which further irritated the administrator.

Herbert Mann looked up from his desk, greeting her with clear disdain: "No, Nurse Tate, seeing you does not brighten my day." He paused, allowing for the silence and his cold stare to dictate who was the boss. "I have summoned you, in my official capacity, to inform you that, despite your years of service, I regard you as an individual who has disgraced this institution, a troublemaker who has caused me a great deal of unnecessary distress. I said it before, and this time I'll make it official. You're fired, and don't expect any references." He pushed a small pile of documents across the desk in her direction. "There is two weeks' severance pay, which you don't deserve. But it is policy, and I have no choice. Now get the hell out of here."

"What about Henry Akita?" she demanded, her eyes burning holes in him.

"He gets no severance pay, he was a probationary employee. He's not even in the system yet. What he has coming he can collect from Elroy."

She stood there, her shoulders and neck tight, trying to hold back her rage. She knew without a doubt the sanctimonious son-of-a-bitch was complicit in the theft of Earl's back pay — and how many others? That Elroy had done it was without question.

Despite the NO SMOKING sign in the office, she lit a cigarette. "I think not," she said, and she deliberately blew a pall of smoke across his desk. She picked up the papers Mann had been reading when she had come in and, without another word, touched the red-hot tip of her cigarette to them until they ignited. She dropped the burning papers into a trash can. Its contents burst into flame. She turned and left, easing the door closed behind her.

"You're fired!" Mann shrieked. He poured the contents of his coffeepot on the fire and screamed at his secretary through the closed door. "Find Elroy and have him come straight up to my office!"

As smoke filled the room, he coughed, opened a window and leaned out into the breeze. "Elroy! Where the hell are you?" He cursed aloud. "It's a conspiracy! A conspiracy!" He slapped a tight closed fist into his open palm. "I knew it the moment that goddamned Jap arrived. It has got to stop, even if I must fire every one of them.

"This hospital has too many malcontents who do not understand that it isn't about medicine anymore. The doctors are all incompetent. They're as useless as the deadwood they send me. Deadwood.

"God, the money that could be saved by cutting out all the mollycoddling. This isn't God's little waiting room. Here we rack them, sedate them, then box them up in a bag when it's time to plant them in the ground. The best we can do is to keep them quiet, no unnecessary agitation. Elroy!" He screamed loud enough to be heard on the floors and the parking lot below. "Elroy!"

24
DESPAIR HAS LEFT THE GAME

Three, four beers, but who's counting? The strange sucking sounds that Brooks made as he drank through a straw were annoying to all around him. Brooks didn't care; for the first time in a long time, he was beginning to feel right with the world. Despair had left the game, no one dealt, while Complacency whispered vacant thoughts in his ear. Tedium, jealous for Brook's attention, bitched and moaned that it was all bullshit. Enough, at least until he relieved himself. The urge was there, not urgent, but being in a dark, foreign place, he had no idea how long it would take him to find a simple john.

He needed to gain someone's attention. Tap. Tap-tap. No, that wasn't going to do it. He rapped the head of his cane on the table. Whack! Whack! Whack! He could almost feel the cold stares around him grow frigid.

"What?"

He recognized the voice of the bartender. The son-of-a-bitch made Elroy sound like a choir boy. "You want more, then put up the money." He'd already charged Brooks four times the going rate for the beers. "Otherwise, get the hell out."

Complacency told Brooks to ignore the hostility and pay attention to what was important. "Your beer is swill," Brooks said. "I know you are a cheating SOB, and frankly I don't give a damn. You want the freak to give you a show? Fine, get me to a bathroom. I'm not about to pee in my pants for your sick thrills."

The bartender stepped back. This monkey has got to go. He glanced at two stevedores he used as bouncers and waved them over. They could take the freak for anything they could get, just if they took him out the back door.

Brooks stood. He rapped his cane once; hard. Then he sensed someone behind him, and he felt a firm, controlling hand on his shoulder. "Come on, pal, we'll help you down the hall." The offer wasn't exactly friendly, but what was he going to do? His poker pals had all called it a night, except for Despair, who was always nearby.

The next thing he knew he was strong-armed and force-marched, hoots and catcalls all around, out of the bar. A door opened. It wasn't to a john. It smelled of night air, fog, garbage, rank alleyway smells. His cane was torn from his grasp, and he felt hands searching his pockets. Then the air was knocked from his lungs as he was beaten by both men, lifted and thrown into a garbage dumpster.

A street bum, searching for food, stared down at the gauze-covered head of what appeared to be a man in a soiled tux. The dark stain that appeared to be blood soaking through the head bandage, near where a mouth should have been, told the drunk that whoever it was might still be alive. He stumbled to the street, hailed a cab, pointed and mumbled something unintelligible to the cabbie. Then he stumbled down the street, seeking as much distance as possible before the cops arrived.

The cabbie called it in.

The cops came. They knew the bar and didn't bother to ask any questions. Brooks was conscious, in some pain, and embarrassed, having peed on himself. He just asked the officers to take him back to the Veterans' Hospital.

25

TOO LATE

I'm going to regret this, Stella thought, as she gave Mann's secretary a conspiratorial wink and a smile. The secretary, with pursed lips, tried to ignore her boss's ravings from the next room.

Once out in the hall, momentarily free of bullies or curious eyes, Stella braced her back against a wall, as if by physical force she could take back her reckless response to the administrator. She listened to Mann's rants, it was becoming abundantly clear that the man was mentally unbalanced. How could she abandon her patients to some- one like him, to Elroy?

Her hands shook as she took a deep draw on her cig- arette, closed her eyes, and tried not to think about the future. As much as she hated to admit it, jobs were hard to come by, and she needed this one. She thought of the prior night, the time she had spent with her three grand men with their simple mastery of making the moment count for something special. If only she could grab a small handful of their stardust and just hold on to it.

Her cigarette finished, she gave in and let the wall push her away.Right now, she needed to see if there was anything she could do for Brooks. She had heard that Ivory had gone back to Oak Knoll. Brooks left alone to fend for himself, in his frame of mind, was a suicide waiting to happen.

"Elroy, get in here!" Mann continued to rage.

After what Elroy had done to Earl, to too many others, and had tried to do to her, she more than despised the rodent; she loathed him and wanted to see him squeal and twist in agony like a rat caught in a trap. But this rat had very sharp teeth and was dangerously cunning.

Fired or not, Stella had to stand her ground. She stretched her neck and shoulders and pushed open the stairwell door without looking back. The sound of her own footsteps in the empty stairwell sounded distant and foreign as she made her way towards the cavernous wards where the patients waited for care promised and rarely delivered.

The hospital seemed strangely silent, if not troubled. There was an unsavory stench, different from the smell of disease and corruption that she was used to. Something had changed in the few days she had been gone: too many of the patients were sleeping restlessly at the time of day when they were encouraged to rise, stretch, chat, play a game of cards, or work a puzzle. Staff? None to be seen.

The same was true of the second ward.

The day room was marked off-limits for patient use: STAFF ONLY. She pushed the unlocked door open. The room was bare-cupboard empty except for a mouse that scurried into the shadows at her intrusion. The music that had echoed from this room brought hope where there had been none; now the silence was oppressive.

She peeked into the staff lounge, where she found two orderlies staring at a checkerboard, coffee cups cold, empty, and stained. She noted the lockers on the far wall, five with doors open, empty, except one with a half-eaten sandwich lying open on its paper wrapper. "Simon, Alex," she demanded, "what the hell is going on here? This place looks and smells like the inside of a flophouse."

Neither man moved, neither spoke.

"Simon, answer me," she commanded.

Alex reached nervously for his coffee cup, pushed it away, then made an unconscious move on the checker board, which would cost him two pieces if Simon was paying any attention.

"Don't ignore me!" She grabbed Alex's cup and sniffed. Now she recognized the smell that permeated the room as that of men whose pores were clogged with poisons needing to be sweated out. The tell-tale stench the morning after a bad Saturday night.

Alcohol. Moonshine. It was the same unpleasant odor she had found in the wards. The hospital reeked of it. "My God, you're drunk?" She threw the cup across the room where it shattered with a loud crash. "Damn you! These men need you." Her arm swung up wildly, hand pointing out towards the wards. "How could you do this?" She cleared the checker board with one angry swipe of her arm.

Alex, his eyes bloodshot and rheumy, lowered his head in shame, his hand shook as he tried to reach out for her. "Stella, we thought you were fired like all the others. Elroy, he... he said we could stay on as long as we stayed out of the way. We don't have no choice. You know how mean Elroy can get. He's a mean son-of-a-bitch, pardon my French."

"We were stupid," Simon interrupted defensively. "We got into a card game with him, now we owe him big bucks."

The crack of her hand across his face was loud, her palm stung painfully, as she readied to strike him again. She saw crimson blood appear at the corner of his mouth.

She withdrew her hand as Simon brought his hands up to his face in shame and wept.

It dawned on her that she had not seen anyone working in the wards. "Everyone else? Fired? No." Stella raged as she found the coffeepot, added new grounds on top of old, filled it with water, then slammed it down on a hot burner. "Drink this, all of it," she ordered. "Take a hot shower with plenty of soap, then report to me out in the wards in half an hour."

She almost gagged on their putrid breath as she leaned in close and looked Alex and then Simon directly in their eyes. She said. "You think Elroy is a scary guy. You never know what he's going to do, or how far he'll go. If you are not scared of Elroy, you ought to be, but you had better be terrified of me. Now, move it!" She could feel her own heart race, Elroy was a scary guy, and she was a little more than scared.

Stella walked cautiously in the empty corridor, her soft footsteps disturbingly loud. Herbert Mann was unstable and mad as hell. He would send Elroy after her; not that he needed to: Elroy would come on his own.

If she were smart, she would leave the hospital post-haste, but she couldn't, because from what she could see, most of the staff had abandoned a sinking ship, leaving no life rafts for the patients.

Sudden movement made her heart jump.

"Stella, thank God. I was beginning to think there were only madmen left to run this charnel house." It was Irene's voice. She was coming out of a ward with a messy bedpan in hand. She was the image of exhaustion; her slumped shoulders seemed to have aged her a decade in little less than a week's time.

Stella took the bedpan from her and set it on an empty gurney nearby. She didn't have to ask: Irene was a Quaker and not one to tipple, let alone take refuge in strong drink.

Irene, a petite nurse, ten years older than Stella, began to shake as tears formed in her eyes. Stella took her in her arms and gave her a reassuring embrace. After a long moment, Irene pulled back, swept back a lock of unruly hair from her forehead, and feigned a smile. "I thought I was the last..."

"The last?' Stella asked.

"To take care of our patients. No one else showed up for this shift except for Simon and Alex and me, and I haven't seen them in hours. I suppose they're drunk like everyone else." Irene looked around hopelessly. "Everyone, except me. Father always said the devil was in the brew."

She looked painfully back into the ward. "The doctors are gone too, except for Doctor Garrity." She lowered her voice to just above a whisper. "The doctor, he's been drinking, like he always does. The poor man's hands shake so, he shouldn't be allowed in an operating room anymore." The concern in her eyes was palpable.

"I honestly don't know who is tending to any of the patients. This is my third shift. In the last couple of hours, the only one I've seen, besides you, is Elroy." She searched up and down the hall, her eyes wide. "He killed them, Elroy I mean, just as if he had put a gun to their heads. He's poisoning them with the devil's brew he's making from a still he has somewhere in the basement. I tried to stop him, all he did was laugh." Her eyes fluttered, then closed as she slumped from sheer exhaustion.

Stella caught her and eased her onto an empty bed just

inside the ward.

Elroy's heavy steps echoed, as he bounded down the steps in search of her. The stairwell door burst open. "Stella don't mess with me!" He was angry and sounded over the edge.

Stella stepped back against the wall as he leaned halfway through the doorway, scanned the ward, saw Irene, then scurried to the next ward in search of her. "Stella!"

A patient groaned as he turned in his bed. The smell of cheap alcohol, urine, and sour sweat hung heavy in the air. Stella was almost at the end of the ward when she sensed, in a moment when everything was wrong, that there was something worse. "Elroy?" she whispered, terrified that he might answer.

She slowly turned. The room was empty except for the patients and the night noises that accompanied them. "Irene?" She stopped next to an occupied bed. The name on the chart read: Burrell Smith. She took hold of his one good arm and felt for a pulse. The wrist was cold to the touch. He had been dead for some time.

"Oh Burrell, I'm so sorry. This should not have happened," she whispered as she let his mangled hand drop back onto his chest. Her foot knocked over a glass bottle at the foot of his bed. She bent down and found three empty quart-sized milk bottles. They smelled of moonshine. She followed a spill on the floor to an overturned cup. She smelled, then tasted the liquid with her finger. She did not need to guess any further: the gentle giant had died of alcohol poisoning. She looked with saddened eyes around the dimly lit ward and wondered who else Elroy had murdered.

"Irene," She whispered. Irene was sleeping. No need to wake her, Stella thought. Elroy has left her alone thus far.

The stairs at the rear of the ward took her down to doctors' row, the area of the hospital where the doctors kept their offices, where orderlies rarely roamed. Elroy would be least likely to look for her there. She wedged a chair beneath a door handle on the inside of the stairwell door in case she misjudged the thoroughness of his search.

Doctors' row was quiet. She opened one door cautiously, then another, another again. The offices were empty. Her fear mixed acidly with rising anger. She needed help. She knew she could not trust Simon and Alex, and the thought that she wanted to run like hell crossed her mind. Simon and Alex had bargained with the devil, and the devil is within Elroy. If they owed him money, then Elroy had them under his thumb.

She entered one of the offices, reached for the phone, and began to dial the police. At the sound of a cough, she hung up. The phone's dial tone seemed to be as loud as Henry's clarinet. She stilled, listened, her neck immobile with tension. Elroy? No. The cough came from an office two doors down.

Doctor Garrity sat alone in his office, a bottle of Famous Grouse Scotch open on his desk. She watched from the doorway as he poured two fingers into a glass. He looked up at her with heavy eyes. "Neat?" He pushed a glass towards her. She shook her head. "No, not that I couldn't use one." She rubbed the back of her neck, thought about a cigarette, and decided against it. "You know what is going on?" she asked.

Garrity took a sip of Famous Grouse and nodded. "Too much," he said. "You sure you don't want some? This day is not going to get any brighter."

"I need your help," she said, choking back her

desperation.

"I was afraid you were going to say that." He sat the glass down and rubbed his eyes. In the windowless yellow light of the office he looked a hundred years older than the forty-something years he rightfully owned. He held up his hands, examining his long narrow fingers as they quivered. "I was trained to be a surgeon. That was another time, another place, another life. Now, with these, I'm more likely to take a life than save one.

"My colleagues" — he motioned towards the offices that surrounded his — "are incompetent buffoons. That's why they work here. Just because they have medical degrees does not mean any of them are qualified to be real doctors. Mann has a file on each one of us. He can destroy a career with one phone call."

He gave a rueful smile. "The sky is about to fall on Mann's fantasy world, and no one wants to be here to be caught in the fallout." He tossed back a full finger of the potent nectar.

Stella looked apprehensively back out into the hallway.

"Elroy is a dangerous man," Garrity said. "I suspect the Nazis could have made good use of him: a man without an ounce of moral fiber. Our illustrious administrator understands this and has manipulated him magnificently. He thinks he's smarter than everyone else, and Elroy thinks he's smarter than Mann. They're about to turn on each other."

"Burrell Smith is dead," she said, the emotion heavy on her voice.

He looked at the contents in his glass. "Alcohol

poisoning?"

She nodded.

He picked up the glass and poured the remaining Famous Grouse in the trash. "I've been hiding in this for far too long. I was a ship's physician," he said matter-of-factly, "on a flat-top when it was hit by a kamikaze. The explosion ripped through a main fuel line and oil flooded the sickbay. I sealed off the hatch to prevent the fire from igniting the fuel. A second kamikaze finished the job. Every man trapped in the sick bay burned to death. I haven't practiced honest medicine since." There was no apology in his voice or his eyes. He was long past that.

He looked solemnly at the phone. "I had just hung up the phone when I heard your footsteps. Mann doesn't know it yet, but there is a time bomb in his pocket, and it is about to go off. The Regional Director for Veterans' Hospitals will be here first thing in the morning. I've already submitted my resignation."

He slid open a desk drawer and pulled out a thick file. "The evidence needed to lock Mann up for the next twenty years is all right here. As for Elroy, he's a dangerous man, and I suspect that he will go down fighting, and he won't hesitate to take anyone who gets in his way with him." He tapped his fingers on the envelope. "The police will be here soon, and that will be that."

"We — you — need to lock down the hospital section by section until the police get here. When Elroy becomes aware of what you are doing, he will go to any lengths to stop you." He pushed back his chair and tried to stand, his thigh cast made it slow and difficult. "I'm afraid I won't be of much help."

Doctor Garrity hobbled over to a shelf where he pushed

several medical books aside, retrieving a plump plain paper bag he had hidden there. He turned and handed it to her.

She took it. "What is this?"

"Open it."

She did. It was filled with rolls of dollar bills.

"Just over twenty-three thousand dollars." He said.

She pulled out a roll of bills and blew out a long slow whistle. "Twenty-three... Where?"

"I took it from Elroy's locker about an hour ago. I've been sitting here wondering what to do with it. Turn it over to the police, burn it, put it back? I suspect that it's the money that Elroy has stolen from the patients: booze money, money blackmailed from my so-called colleagues." He nodded. "That's right, me too." He fell awkwardly back into his chair. He did not look at her as he said: "Take it, and when this day is over, take it and go somewhere far away. Forget you ever knew this place. Get a fresh start."

"I... couldn't," she said, her hands gripping the bag tightly.

"You can, and you will. There is no way to give it back to those poor bastards upstairs. Many of them have passed on. The doctors... we don't deserve it. You do. If the police get their hands on it, I doubt much of it will ever make it to the evidence locker. Let some good come out of all this, Stella.

"Now, you had better hurry. Elroy will come here. He saw me snooping around, and I think he's smart enough to put two and two together."

"Come with me. I'll help you."

"No, Stella. It's too late for me. When the dust settles on all this, the least that will happen is that I'll be found criminally negligent in the death of Burrell, and God knows how many others."

"A fellow by the name of Raymond James is the Regional Administrator for the West Coast, Veterans Administration Hospitals. His brother Hank was one of the men I closed the door on when the kamikazes hit. Maybe today I can start to pay a debt I owe.

"Once Ray sees what is going on, he'll call in the Marines. I've already asked him to have all the patients transferred to other facilities as soon as Mann and Elroy are in handcuffs. There will be a full investigation, then we'll figure out if there is anything left of this hospital worth saving."

He gave her the best smile he could muster. "My career is finished, not that it hasn't been for some time. You've got guts, Stella, more than you know. Now, get this place locked down, then get out of here before the cops wonder what's in that bag."

With a heavy heart he watched Stella leave. Stella was no match for Elroy, that was given. Still, something had to be done. Garrity lit a cigarette and stared at the white wall through a blue haze of cigarette smoke as he waited for the axe to fall.

26
DARKEST BEFORE THE DAWN

Stella tried to wake Irene with a gentle touch and a whisper. "Sorry, girl, duty calls." Failing that, she gave Irene a firm shake. "Up we go. We've got to lock down the wards before Elroy can do any more harm. Doctor Garrity has called the police. Until they arrive, every person here is in danger."

Irene nodded sleepily that she understood.

Stella slipped Irene one of the master keys the doctor had given her.

"I need you to lock down the wards from the inside. All of them. Try not to wake any of the patients. If Elroy figures out what's going on, there's no telling what he might do."

"What do you mean?" Irene asked, as she gently slapped her own cheeks, bringing a flush to push the sleepiness away.

"There's no time to explain. I've got to see that Brooks is all right. I sent Simon and Alex to sober up in the showers. When they get here, don't let them in; they can't be trusted."

Elroy burst into Brooks' room, expecting to find Stella playing little Miss Nightingale. Brooks was sitting on his bed, his clothes soiled in more than one foul way, his head bandage looking anything but sanitary. Since his return to the hospital, no one had bothered to clean him up or see that his injuries were not more critical. His head down, a three-foot long strip of his head bandage drooped almost to the floor. The wrap, soiled and stained with his own blood, had not been changed. He smelled much like the dumpster he had been thrown into. His hand was shaking so hard that he was barely able to hold an empty tin cup.

Brooks turned, recognizing Elroy's gait. Elroy walked with a stride heavy on his left foot, always walking with a level of intensity and anger. His lips dry and cracked, Brooks spoke, his voice a rusty pipe. "Hah, my lord and master."

Elroy studied Brooks for a moment. There was something about the guy that bothered him. It wasn't the bandages that made him look like a freak; beneath the gauze and scar tissue there was something unsettling. He hadn't liked Brooks from day one, and nothing had given him reason to feel much different now. What bothered him this time was entirely different, and he almost gagged as his nostrils flared, rebelling at the stench. "Did you crap on yourself? Well, you're going to have to stew in your own shit, because I ain't touching it, and there's no one left around here who will.

"Oh, that's not quite true. I believe that Stella might be around. Why don't you come with me and we'll go find her?" He pulled a pint bottle of moonshine from his pocket and poured a third of it into Brooks' tin cup.

After a quick but loose rewrap of Brooks' head bandage, he pulled Brooks to his feet. "Let's find Stella, and when you're all cleaned up you can have the rest of the bottle. Hell, I'll let you have all the booze you want. Drink and be merry, for you, there should be no tomorrow. Drown your sorrows, friend, and be done with it."

Brooks tried to shake off the unwanted support as Elroy tightened his grasp and force-marched him towards the door. What the hell? They say it's darkest before the dawn, and it sure is dark. You are a murdering son-of-a-bitch, so go ahead, and, God willing, the fires in Purgatory will be bright and welcoming.

He gave a surprising sharp barking laugh, then raised his cup, spilling half as much as he was able to drink. *Thank you, you frigging bastard*, he thought as the liquid seared his cracked lips and burned down his parched throat.

27

DANCE WITH THE DEVIL

Dr. Garrity's eyes slowly moved from the closed door to the bottle of Scotch on his desk. He wasn't a brave man, and to step into this fight would be damned stupid. He had fallen, having drunk too much, and now that his leg was in a cast, Elroy could chew him up and spit him out without breaking a cold sweat.

So, what was he expecting Stella to do? Dammit! he screamed internally, as he pushed his chair back from the desk and brought his fist down hard on his cast. His eyes went wide with the unexpected pain. He hadn't meant to do that, at least not that hard. His eyes glistening with tears, his hand shaking so hard he could barely hold the bottle, he brought the Scotch up and took a healthy long swig.

"OK, Stella, let's dance with the Devil."

Another swig.

He locked the evidence file in his desk, keeping the bottle of Scotch. He limped to the hallway and locked the office door behind him. If he and Stella couldn't stop Elroy, Elroy would kill them.

Garrity did not have a gun, but he was beginning to work on an idea. After one last swig, he let the bottle drop in the stairwell. It rolled and dropped down a flight, smashing with a loud crash. That was not something a doctor would do, but far more than a bottle was broken here. He gripped the handrail, the pain in his leg be damned, and pulled himself forward.

Elroy squinted, not sure what he was seeing. Simon

and Alex had come into view at the far end of the corridor. Their uniforms appeared clean, their hair was wet and freshly combed. *The traitors are sober,* Elroy thought. *You're not playing by my rules, boys, so all bets are off. I'm calling in my chips.*

"Trouble," Alex warned. They stopped dead in their tracks, and with trepidation, they watched as Elroy quick-stepped Brooks towards them. Elroy's cold eyes were scanning their every move.

"Elroy?" Alex said, as his Adam's apple rose in his throat, wavering like a carnival puck hammered without enough force to ring the bell.

"We figured you were short-handed." Simon said.

Elroy pasted on his best carnivorous grin as he drew near to them. "Short-handed? Yeah, I can use a little help. Brooks here has messed himself and needs a little cleaning up."

The men moved to take Brooks from him. "No, this is women's work. Stella is the only one who can do it right. I want you to find Stella for me. And I'll caution you – you, worthless pieces of crap, don't take no for an answer. You find her and bring her to me. Now!" His eyes burned holes right down to their cowardly guts. "Oh, Stella!" he called out, loud and clear. "Stella, I've got Brooks, and he's been asking for you. It seems he needs a little help. Stella. He-he-he-Ha-ha-he..." His shrill Woody Woodpecker laugh echoed through the wards. "Stella!"

Simon and Alex stepped away. Elroy intended to hurt Stella, of that there was no doubt, and they wanted no part of it.

Irene, a wide-eyed, timid doe, watched from behind a door as she slowly closed it. That maniacal laugh had to be the Devil's own. With trembling hands, she found the key in her pocket. A patient moaned somewhere behind her, another coughed.

She sensed a presence, brought her hand to her mouth to stifle a scream. Her heart was pounding unnaturally. Please, God... She turned, knowing that the Devil can take many forms.

Dr. Garrity had entered the ward without her noticing him. He had opened a locked medicine cabinet and was standing with his back to her, working a large hypodermic he had taken from a drawer.

Upon seeing him, her heartbeat stilled just a little and she unconsciously tidied her hair. She asked in a whisper, "May I be of any help, doctor?"

Stella reached the second ward through the rear corridor just in time to hear Elroy call out her name. Brooks? Oh, no. He has Brooks, I'm out of time and options. She scanned the ward for help. It was wishful thinking. Except for the patients, she was alone. They were all asleep, most likely intoxicated, none able-bodied. This was the morgue, the ward where the worst cases came, the wait-and-see patients, and the poor stiffs whose cards were punched but who lacked a delivery date to either Heaven or Hell.

Stella reached the door. Instead of closing and locking it, she left it open just enough to see out into the corridor. Elroy was there, his back to the door. Brooks, his filthy head wrap partially unraveled, swayed unsteadily in Elroy's grasp. Simon and Alex looked like scared rabbits cornered by a snarling wolf.

"What are you two monkeys waiting' for?" Elroy demanded, his eyes hard, his grin cemented in place. "Find

Stella and bring her to me." He pulled a switchblade out with his free hand and sprang the glistening blade. "Do I sense a lack of team spirit? You're my hunting dogs, boys. Fetch."

The two men took three steps backwards, turned, and fled towards the door Irene had locked. "He-he-he-he-Ha-he..." he laughed loudly, an inch or so, from Brooks' masked head. He stopped abruptly, sensing he was being watched. He turned his head slowly towards the second ward. "Stella, sweetheart, come out and join the party."

Stella opened the door wide and stepped out, first one foot, and then the other, steps she was already regretting.

Elroy's eyes locked on the paper bag. His grin changed instantly to icy imperiousness. "What do we have here? Ahhh, I thought you were smarter than that." His undertone was menacing.

She watched in horror as Elroy brought the sharp blade of the knife to Brooks' bandaged cheek and scraped the bandage just enough to split the material, but not enough to draw blood. "Brooks is such a stinking mess it will take some scraping to remove all the crud. Now why don't you be a good girl and bring me what's mine. And I'll give you this worthless dung heap." The knife teased the tear in the bandage, drawing just a hint of blood.

Brooks flinched. "No!" His whiskey-burned voice was vehement, despite the obvious threat. His sightless eyes screamed No from within his cloth mask. Elroy scraped the blade flirtatiously across his bandaged cheek, drawing a thin line of blood. "Get out of here, Stella," Brooks pleaded. "I'm not worth it." The knife slid down to his throat. *This is it,* Brooks thought. *Elroy will do it. Fine, he will be doing me a favor, but I'll be damned before I let the* *bastard hur*t one hair on Stella's head. *If I'm captive, she's in danger.* "Go ahead, you miserable bastard, finish it." He tried to twist into the blade.

Elroy all but ignored Brooks. He fixed his full attention on Stella. She was close, almost close enough to grab. He wet his lips. *Revenge will be my sweet honey.* He laughed mockingly.

Brooks felt the blade slip slightly. He sloshed the booze that remained in his cup to see how much there was, then without warning smashed the cup into Elroy's face, stopping his laugh mid-breath.

"GAAWWDD!" Elroy screamed, and he raised both hands to his eyes as the alcohol blinded him. The knife clattered to the floor.

Brooks broke free and stumbled back. The searing pain was mind-numbing. Elroy threw a haphazard punch in Brooks' direction, a glancing blow, inflicting little harm.

Brooks fell.

"Enough!" Stella screamed as she threw the paper bag at Elroy.

Elroy turned, but did not see the bag in time to catch it. It bounced off him, tore, and dollar bills fell like so many autumn leaves.

Simon and Alex gasped at the sight of all the cash.

"No!" Elroy began to kick Brooks in his head and then his torso as Brooks tried to crawl away from the vicious assault.

"Stop it. He's blind, for God's sake." Without thinking of her own safety, she tried to pull Elroy away. She was no match for him and was thrown back when Elroy backhanded her with the entire length of his arm. Her head bounced with a loud thump as she fell to the floor. Dazed, she remained still for a moment.

Elroy, his vision still blurred, left Brooks cowering on the floor. He turned his wrath towards Stella. His eyes darted left and right as he searched for the fallen knife.

Stella tried to rise. She saw Elroy, then the knife. Her gaze told him where it was. She couldn't move fast enough before he had it. He turned, holding the weapon firmly in his right hand. "You want this? You can have it. Just a loan... I'll be needing it right back. Brooks wants to die, and what kind of a pal would I be if I didn't help him out?"

He eyed Simon and Alex who were skulking near the locked wardroom doors. The sight of the money was tempting, but their cowardliness was the better discretion. Elroy turned back to Stella. The look on her face was not what he expected. She wasn't quivering with fear. She was watching him like a cat, her eyes locked on his. Her lack of fear annoyed him even more. Perhaps she will make a fight of it? That could be fun, he thought, and he shifted the knife from one hand to the other. "You want it, you've got it."

"Ha-ha-ha-he-Ha-he..."

At the sound of Elroy's maniacal laugh, Dr. Garrity dropped the syringe. "Another, quick," he ordered, while he limped to the door. Irene filled a syringe and brought it to him. Garrity unlocked the door. Simon and Alex pushed though, the door slamming into Garrity's bad leg. The pain, an adrenaline cocktail, fired up his courage, when what he really wanted to do was race Simon and Alex to an exit.

Garrity took the syringe from the nurse, giving her a look that said God forgive me for what I am about to do. He could see that something had happened to Elroy. Brooks was down. Elroy was kicking him, while rubbing his eyes and screaming.

Stella threw the money bag, and that was all Garrity needed to know. When Stella attacked Elroy to save Brooks, he squirted a drop of morphine from the syringe into the air and moved as quickly as he could behind Elroy.

Irene, her small voice borrowing some of Stella's strength, snapped at Alex and Simon. "Hold it right there, fellas. You are going to be needed." They continued towards the rear entry. "I said hold it." Her authority was startling. They froze, bowing their heads, ashamed, and turned towards her.

Herbert Mann had grown impatient. He had ordered Elroy to find Stella and see that she was forcibly removed from the hospital. "Don't worry about being too gentle," had been his last words to Elroy.

Impatient, he wanted to see for himself. He took the back stairs, which led him through doctors' row. He saw Dr. Garrity. The doctor was acting strangely; Mann waited until he had gone into a ward before following at a discreet distance. He froze when he spotted Elroy, Stella, and Brooks. For a moment he thought that Elroy was going to take care of Stella, once and for all. He was wrong. Garrity stepped up behind Elroy with a raised hypodermic. It was already too late to shout a warning.

Elroy's eyes went wide, his back arched, the knife slipped from his grasp. Everything around him swirled into a white cyclone, the pain slipping away into nothingness. His lips shaped a round 'O' as a sense of nothingness overcame him.

Dr. Garrity held the syringe firmly in the nape of Elroy's

neck and forced the last drops of morphine into Elroy's spinal column. As Elroy slumped to the floor, Dr. Garrity turned to Stella with a pained smile. "I've suspected for some time that he had a drug problem. It is my medical opinion that he's died of an overdose. The authorities will be here any moment. There will be a full investigation." He saw Mann. "I'll do my best to see that Herbert Mann spends the next decade or so behind bars."

Stella didn't move.

"Pick up the money before someone else does, then help me get Brooks taken care of." He looked at Brooks and shook his head, as he knelt. "You took a big risk. If it hadn't been for you, this bastard might still be alive and Stella, dead."

He looked back towards Stella. "Is there somewhere you can take him? I don't think his odds are too good if he stays in the system. Let's get him cleaned up and give him something to wear. A little dose of dignity can go a long way."

He looked sadly at the hypodermic still lodged in Elroy's spine. Without a doubt the dose he had given was lethal. Elroy's breathing was slow and labored. Dr. Garrity looked at his watch. There was no need to take a pulse, it would all be over in a minute or two. "Simon, Alex," he called out, "get a gurney and take Elroy to the morgue."

"You heard the doctor," Irene told them. "Now snap to it."

28

SIMPLY WHAT FEELS RIGHT

Stella hadn't told Brooks where she was taking him. He was still rocky after the beatings and the abuse he had suffered. She had been lucky to get him cleaned up and out of the hospital before the police started asking all the wrong questions.

Once outside, Brooks rallied. Stella drove straight to Adam's Place and parked not far from the front door. She let the engine run and sat holding the steering wheel for a moment, asking herself why she had brought him here. Truth of the matter was — and she knew it — there just wasn't any room at the inn. Earl was a handful enough for Gibby. Still, what choice did she have? Dr. Garrity was right, if Brooks were left to flounder alone in another veterans' hospital, his life expectancy would be slim to none. He was suicidal and needed close supervision or he would find a way to jump off the proverbial cliff.

The San Francisco Veterans' Hospital would most likely be shut down until a full investigation could be completed and the hospital re-staffed. The patients would be shipped off to wherever there was room, and that would be the end of Brooks Weingarten, III.

She turned off the engine, then touched Brooks gently on his forearm. "Brooks, you stay right here. I won't be long."

"Where would I go?" he mumbled. He gave a short, bitter laugh and shook his head in exasperation. He hadn't said anything about his last adventure; she didn't need to know. Without Stella, his lifeline was a fast-burning fuse, and burning from both ends.

Stella thought about bringing him with her; she was afraid to leave him alone. At the door, she paused and listened to the warm bustling sounds of the tavern, the low murmur of conversation punctuated with laughter, and the bright clink of bottle glass. The smell of rank tobacco and stale beer threaded through the soft sound of a piano being played by Earl in the background. The door was open: inside she could see Gibby, and she felt bad for what she was about to do to his day.

"Stella?" Gibby looked surprised to see her. She hoped she didn't look as tattered and battered as she felt.

Earl played the first few notes of Stella by Starlight when he heard her name.

"Stella are you, all right?" Gibby asked.

"Couldn't be better," she said, as she faked an exhausted smile. *Couldn't be better for a girl who has just been through her own personal Pearl Harbor.* Her career as a nurse was over. Not that she couldn't get another job. She didn't want to; enough was enough. She was burned out, bone-tired from being a nurse. It was time to move on.

Elroy's ill-gotten cash would give her that chance. She needed the help, as did Earl. Part of the money was his, and now Brooks' as well. She didn't know what she was going to do. With all the troops returning home, jobs were not plentiful; especially for women. She would have to worry about that later. First, she had a blind man with one foot in the grave to take care off.

Henry stepped out of the small kitchen.

She gave Gibby a big, appreciative hug and whispered, "We've got to talk." She held the embrace for a moment, looked him in the eye with the look that only a woman can give a man that says. Here's fair warning sweetheart: trouble is coming. "First I need a drink. Henry. Gin and tonic. Double."

"Stella?" Henry and Gibby chorused in unison.

Earl stopped playing.

None of them knew Stella to be a heavy drinker.

"OK, gentlemen, gather round," she said as Henry poured her a gin and tonic — a single. "I'll tell you the whole story." She glanced apprehensively at the customers seated here and there around the room. None took any notice of her. Nevertheless, she lowered her voice to slightly louder than a whisper. "I've got Brooks out in the car." She spoke too softly.

"What?"

"I said I've got Brooks out in the car." This time they heard her, as did several of the patrons.

"The man finally grew some balls," Earl applauded. "Nice of him to drop by to say good-bye. OK, you all know that I've never liked the guy. He's a pompous ass. The man comes with a pedigree, and blind or not, he thinks he's better than the next guy. He's got a cushy place waiting for him back home. It's about time he got the goddamned courage to move on, pardon my French. Brooks checked himself into the place and setting your anchor down in that poor excuse for a veterans' hospital is a joke." He had to think about that for a moment. He chuckled at himself. Yeah, and I was almost a fool's fool. I thought I had it easy: three squares and a regular routine. When you're just beginning to figure out what it's like to live blind; that's not half bad. "So now he's come to his senses and is going home. Good for him.'"

"Balls! Trust me, Earl," said Stella, "you don't know the half of it. Down deep, Brooks has that special type of courage that can keep a man from drowning in hopelessness and melancholy. You found some of it in Ivory Burch."

I wonder what happened to the kid, Earl thought.

"Brooks is just now finding his own." *This could take some time*, Stella thought. *Time, I don't have.* "It's complicated." She let out a dramatic sigh as she searched for the right words.

She looked thoughtful for a moment, then spoke softly as if thinking aloud. "Gibby, I know your heart: you won't turn this man away. It's not just a roof, a bed, a meal that he needs; it's a place where he can reclaim his dignity. He needs you, all of you, if he's going to survive. He's like a plant: in the wrong soil he'll wilt and fade away in a slow and lonely death." She took a long draw on her gin and tonic then slid it over to Henry for a refill.

"Earl, he's not going home," Stella continued. "The only thing he will find there is rejection and ridicule," Her voice was a portrait of her soul.

"Burrell Smith is dead," she blurted out. There was no other way to say it; it hurt too much. "Perhaps others, I don't know."

She held her glass out impatiently. "Henry, I said a double." She took a deep breath. "Elroy poisoned the whole ward with bad moonshine. I tried to stop him. Brooks saved my life."

"What the hell are you talking about?!" Gibby exclaimed.

"Brooks?" Henry asked incredulously. A thought flashed

across his mind. "Elroy?"

"Elroy is dead," she answered with an odd catch on her voice. "How, that isn't important. What is important is that Brooks is waiting out there." She pointed towards the door. "The hospital will be closed, at least for the time being. He has nowhere else to go."

Gibby rubbed his chin thoughtfully, as he sorted through her story. "No." It was less a word and more a long sigh. He leaned on the edge of the bar for support, then dropped heavily onto a stool.

A bottle spilled.

He started to say something, then rubbed his face with his hands. When he took his hands away, his face was tired and ashen. He gave a bitter sigh that seemed to leave him deflated.

Tat... tat-tat... tat.... Liquor from the spilled bottle began to patter an irregular rhythm onto the floor. For a long moment only, the tapping of drops against the floor kept the silence at bay.

Earl's fingers hovered motionlessly above the keyboard.

All eyes on Stella. All except for Gibby, who seemed to stare down at his folded hands. When he finally pulled his eyes up, he tugged at his lip, then, frowned. "No way. Stella." Gibby's voice was sympathetic but firm, with a touch of desperation buried beneath. "I know you've got a heart of gold, but this just isn't going to happen."

Gibby's face took on an unusual beet red color. He raised both hands defensively. "No!" He could feel his heart pounding as he tried to fight the inevitable off. His expression grew anxious. "I've not got the money, nor the patience. Stella, I'm begging you, don't do this to me." He suddenly felt slightly nauseous and dizzy.

The next silence was longer.

Tat-tat... Tat...

Henry finally interrupted the silence. "Gibby's right. We can't take Brooks in, for the very reason you want him here. We can't. He's an emotional loose cannon and an alcoholic. Everything about it speaks of disaster. I..."

He focused his full attention on the old man. "Gibby, I hadn't planned to say anything yet, but... I guess this is what you might call a game-changer. Stella, dammit, you're forcing my hand. I've applied to Stanford Medical School under the G.I. Bill. If, and when, I'm accepted, I'll be moving to Palo Alto. I doubt that Gibby can handle Earl's needs. He sure as hell can't take care of Brooks." Henry could see that Gibby's blood pressure was off the charts.

"I can take care of myself," Earl said defensively. *Game-changer?* He admitted to himself, *damn if that isn't the truth. It's beginning to sound as if there is a mighty clock ticking. When it reaches the end of the twenty-third hour, this sweet little dream I've got could turn right around and bite me. With Henry gone, I'll just be in the way.*

Stella reached into her coat pocket and retrieved a wad of bills and slammed it angrily on the counter.

"Stella... I can't." Gibby pleaded.

"How much?" she demanded. "How much do you want?"

"For what?" Gibby asked. His heart was thundering through the ringing in his ears, and his chest was tight and uncomfortable.

"For the bar. I'll buy it," Stella said, as her eyes began to flood with tears. *What am I doing?* she screamed at herself.

Earl stiffened. This whole thing was going nowhere he liked. Dammit, Brooks, why did you have to come out of your alcoholic stupor and screw everything up?

"You'll do no such thing," said Gibby. "You don't know the first..."

Silence again filled the room as everyone struggled to find what to do or say next. The sound of the drip stilled.

Stella downed her gin and tonic, turned and left the bar. No one said a word as the door slowly closed behind her.

"Stella, God, I'm sorry," Gibby apologized. "If I thought there was a chance, I'd at least think about it." His words went unheard.

"You can't, and that's the end of it," Henry counseled. He poured Gibby a brandy, then counted the money Stella had left on the counter. He looked up with surprise, counted the money a second time. "There's over four hundred dollars here."

Where did she get that kind of dough? Gibby pondered, as his blood pressure began to fall with the brandy's heat.

Earl touched the piano keys lightly. The notes haunting. "To do what feels right or nothing at all?" he said. "A troublesome question." He didn't realize he was speaking aloud. "One bitch of a question, but it's the only kind that's worthwhile."

"You say something, Earl?" Gibby asked.

"Nothing important," Earl replied quietly. "I tend to think too much." Or not often enough. Either way, my best decisions come when I stop thinking and simply do what feels right. The question was beginning to nag at him.

29
AN INCONVENIENT PASSING

Officer Sam Newman was uncertain if he had a 10-8:
Possible Dead Body, or a 10-8-1: Person Down. Either
way, it felt good to get out of the car and stretch his legs.
There were times when a routine call was better than a jelly
donut.

The hospital was quiet, the main entry empty, no
patients waiting to check in, no nurses, orderlies, or medical staff visibly present. Still, this wasn't San Francisco
General, whose atmosphere almost always screamed
of chaos and human urgency. Come to think of it, the
Veterans' Hospital didn't have an emergency room. If
critical care was needed, the patient was usually rushed to
S.F. General. At least, the General had a decent cafeteria
and something that passed for a cup of coffee.

He had found the elevator and pushed the button to call
down the lift when a petite nurse came out of one of the
wards.

"Can I help you, officer?" Her name tag read Irene.
He pulled out his notebook. "Someone called in a report
about a body?" Hospitals have bodies, nothing unusual, he
thought. "A patient...?"

"Oh yes," she replied with a tired smile, "although I
don't know why anyone bothered to call it in. An orderly
— at least he used to be, overdosed. Dr. Garrity has already
signed the death certificate: suicide."

Suicide, that meant he had to see the body. "Name?" He
took a pencil out of his pocket and licked the lead point out

of habit.

"Irene Baker."

"No, miss, I mean the victim's name."

"Elroy. I think his last name was Hawks. I'm not sure. We didn't talk much. He was a vulgar, rude man, none of the staff took kindly to him. If you ask me... Never mind, one shouldn't speak ill of the dead, it's not polite."

He wrote down the name. "I'll need to see the doctor," he asked. This nurse has about as much personality as a librarian.

"I'm sorry, the doctor has left for the day."

He scratched off what he was about to write with a slight edge of frustration. "Mr. Hawk's body, where can I find it? You have a morgue?"

A male orderly came down the hall.

"Simon," she called, "would you please escort the officer down to the morgue. He's here to make a report on Elroy."

"Sure thing, officer," Simon said, motioning towards a stairwell. "Good old Elroy can't say anyone around here will miss him." He led the officer down three flights of stairs

"Elroy Hawks. Hawks was his last name?"

The orderly grunted in affirmation.

"He work here long?"

"Who?"

"The late Mr. Hawks."

"I wouldn't know," Simon said as they walked down a poorly lit hallway.

"So, you weren't a friend of his?" No one seems to know or care much about this guy, he thought. No small wonder if he committed suicide. 'If' is the operative word.

He was led to a gurney just inside the morgue. A foot, big toe tied with a toe tag, poked out from beneath a white sheet. He looked at the toe tag, confirming the name Elroy Hawks and the time of death. He never liked this part of the job but went ahead and drew back the sheet as far down as the cadaver's midsection. In life the man had been a giant, tall and muscular. In death he had a kind face. Officer Newman wrote in his notebook that the former Mr. Hawks was missing one arm and several fingers from his remaining hand. *Poor guy, no wonder he committed suicide.*

"Will there be anything else, officer?" the orderly asked as he pulled back the sheet.

He wrote down Simon's name. "No, that will about do it," Officer Newman said, satisfied with the cause of death. "Send the death certificate to me soon as possible. Here's my card. Thanks."

30
A SPECIAL COURAGE

Stella felt her anger rise close to her breaking point. Gibby had turned her down, and Henry had supported it. She yanked open the car door and threw herself into the driver's seat, fumbled in her purse for the car keys, which weren't there. Unable to find them, she pounded her fist onto the steering wheel, causing the horn to blare. "Dammit!" She dreaded going back into the bar in search of her keys. The soft rustle of Brooks' head bandage as he turned his head towards her brought her rage to a sudden embarrassed stop.

"I concur," said Brooks, sounding like he meant it.

"Oh, shut up," Stella responded. She meant it. She gave him the Don't you say another word look as only a woman can do. It was wasted effort.

"Yikes don't nip at my hemorrhoids, woman, it makes me grumpy."

Stella spat out a laugh, then dropped her eyes, feeling properly chastened. After a moment she looked at Brooks and realized that her look meant nothing to this fragile man who sat across from her. His mask could never deliver a human expression. The eyes just inside the slits that she had cut to allow for air could not see her. No judgment made. For a moment she felt small and self-centered. I couldn't do it, she thought, then finished the thought aloud: "I couldn't do it, Brooks, because it's not up to me."

"I don't understand. What isn't up to you?" he responded, confused.

"There's no going back, only forward. And the only one who can take you there is you, Brooks. You showed a whole lot of courage back at the hospital. You may have saved my life, and that is something I will never forget. Whether you like it or not, you are going to need to find that strength one more time." She looked at Brooks and wondered if he could do what she was asking.

"Courage? Me? That's where you've got it wrong, sister, I'm the cowardly lion and the scarecrow all wrapped up in one confused mess. If you try to tell someone different, I'll laugh in your face," Brooks said with a wry tone.

Stella got out of the car, went around to the other door, opened it, and took his hand. "Out," she said as she gave him a directive tug.

He groaned as he struggled out of the car. He was bruised, stiff, and not exactly glad to be alive. If I had ten cents worth of courage, he thought, I'd have taken myself out a long time ago.

A cool breeze felt good as it brushed against the eye holes in his bandage. He hated the damn thing, it was hot and uncomfortable. Then again, he would be mortified to be seen without it. "Where are we?" he asked, shifting his head from side to side as he tried to catch the breeze again.

"We're just outside Adam's Place."

He cocked his head thoughtfully. "Is that the place Henry's at?"

"Yes," Stella answered. "Earl, too."

"Earl, I'll be damned, I thought I was done with that obnoxious warbler. Say, isn't Adam's Place a bar?" He gave a short barking laugh. "Lead on woman. You've just made my day." He forgot all about the courage business and whatever point Stella was trying to make, as he heard the alcohol calling. *Come on Tedium, Mr. Dark, it's been one hell of a day. Drinks are on me... Hell, the drinks are on Earl.*

"Hold on Brooks, you need to know something. I've asked them to take you in. And you are about to give them every reason not to."

Brooks gave an incredulous laugh. God, he hated it when a woman was right; they never let you forget it. "You've asked them to take me in, as what? A circus freak?" He paused as if he were considering his next words carefully. "I'm sorry, Stella, you didn't deserve that." He let out a breath emotionally and self-consciously. "I don't deserve your heart." He wanted to say more, couldn't, and let his words fall silent. *Shut up, Desperation, I'll let you know when you're needed. OK, come to think of it, now is a good time.*

"What are you afraid of?" she asked softly.

"Afraid?" He tried to brush the word aside but couldn't. "Sure, every waking moment. Only priests and fools are fearless, and I've never been on the best terms with God. If there is a God, he's a mean bastard with a wicked sense of humor." He half-expected a lecture but got none.

She listened in all the right ways.

"Dammit, you're right, Stella. I was about to go in there and make a pompous ass out of myself. That's one thing I'm good at. Right now, I'm a homeless, angry, pompous fool. I need a place to be — and a bar — what better place for me? And I'm about to blow it."

He straightened his shoulders and held his head high as if his Humpty Dumpty mask could disappear and he could become that handsome man on the celluloid screen one more time. He found the door. Stella tried to help. "No," he said, "this is between me and them." Anxiety and Despair crowded him. *Back off, you assholes, I'm perfectly capable of screwing this up all by myself.* Brooks felt the rough, weather-worn wood of the door. Beyond it, he could hear a piano and Earl singing*: " I can see my Stella beneath a moonlit sky".*

"It would take some doing," Earl said and continued to play. "I mean..."

Gibby studied the peanut shells on the floor with tired hound dog eyes as he argued aloud with himself. "Stella put up a good argument. But not good enough. She lost. We can't, and that is all there is to it. There is no way — no how." He looked at Earl for support but didn't get any. The front door slowly opened, and, at his first sight of Brooks, he let out a long-agitated sigh.

"Sounds like you've made up your mind," Henry started to say. "What if..." Then he stopped short as Brooks slowly made his way into the room. Stella followed behind at a respectful distance.

"God help me." I should be saying God help him, Gibby thought. He had never set eyes on Brooks before and was taken aback by the startling tragedy of the man. He could almost feel the scars and pain hidden just beneath the harsh white cloth that wrapped his entire head. His clothes, an old wrinkled tux, dirty, and possibly bloodstained didn't help with his image. "I can't," Gibby moaned. He leaned his face onto his arms on the counter, not wanting to hear or see what was about to happen. The pressure built in his chest, the tingling numbness in his hand again, only this time a little farther up the arm. "No," he cried to himself, "I just can't."

Earl played the first few notes of *Oh, Look at Me Now*, a

tune he had recently heard Frank Sinatra sing on the radio.

Brooks stopped, cocked his head towards the sound of the piano, then looked down with unseeing eyes to the floor, where he kicked around a few of the nutshells he had heard crunch beneath his feet. *Better shells than peanut butter.* He was uncomfortable as hell, his throat dry, palms clammy, the sweat on his brow beginning to soak through the mask, his stomach churned. Despair teased him with the thought of a double shot of bourbon. He blew out a long low whistle, the drink his motivation. "Earl, you're tone-deaf, and the piano is out of tune." Not a great start.

Earl stopped playing and for a moment the only sound was the soft crunch of peanut shells as Brooks slowly maneuvered around tables and chairs towards where he had last heard Earl play. The aroma of burley tobacco that hung in the air reminded Brooks of the pub in England. His sense of smell hadn't been much use since the bomb took his face, but there it was, the delightful aroma of tobacco. *Has the beating I got from Elroy somehow triggered this?* Even through his bandage the aroma seemed intoxicating. This renewed sense stirred his courage.

Stella stayed back by the door, her fingers crossed, breath held.

Earl touched a key or two as he listened for the crunch of peanut shells. He flexed his fingers, then swept into a song so gently everyone was listening before they knew it had begun. "Lady and gentlemen," he said, his words close to the melody, "we have a poet in the house — Brooks Weingarden, the Third. God isn't one enough?" He briefly played a curious melody before continuing. "A poet, you see, is a musician who can't sing. Words have to find a man's mind before they can touch his heart, and some men's minds are woefully small targets. It's been said that music touches their hearts directly, no matter how small or stubborn the mind of the man who listens. Sadly enough, Brooks rarely listens, and the words he chooses are usually wrong. If only he would let his fingers do all his talking, the world would be a better place. Unfortunately, he isn't much better on the piano."

"Ouch," Henry said aloud.

Gibby sighed as he cautiously raised his eyes as would a child playing hide-and-seek.

Brooks edged towards the bar where he had heard Henry. "Henry, pour me a double anything, something that will go well with the crow I'm about to eat. Stella?" He called out softly. No ears showed through his whole head wrap as he listened for her response. "You still here?"

"Yes," she said as she stepped forward just enough to crunch a peanut shell or two.

"Good." He found the bar, then the bar stool, but didn't sit. "I'd best stand for this one. Thanks for the words, Earl," he said with a slight catch to his voice, "I heard them. Bastard." He laughed quietly to himself. His pals, Desperation, Despair. Self-Pity, and Mr. Dark, stood right by his side. He nodded, acknowledging his bond with them. Tedium stood to the side, feeling somewhat out of place, but Brooks knew that he would belly up to the bar in his own good time.

Henry tapped the bar with the bottom of a whiskey glass then slid it into Brooks' hand.

"Bourbon," Brooks said as he took a long drink. "Only, next time I order a double I don't mean half water." He took another drink, then pressed ahead with the dogged persistence of the wishfully inebriated. "I'm a self-centered prick. You all know it. Now that I've said it, we can all agree on something. For too long I've been stewing in my own self-pity... It's time to let some pity out of the pot; so here goes. I'm a self-centered bastard, who hasn't cared a lick about anyone but myself for as long as I can remember. There was a day when I thought I had it all. Whatever I had I threw away long before a buzz bomb in London blew away my face and any dreams I might have had. If I could see myself in a mirror, I'd put a gun to my head and pull the trigger."

He let out a short bitter laugh and shook his head in exasperation. Desperation gave him a pat on the back, while Self-pity beamed with a self-centered grin.

Earl played 'Blues in The Night', soft and mellow.

"I'll never look in that mirror, and if I could I wouldn't have the courage to even pick up the damned gun." He held up his glass and listened to the ice crackle. "This here is my bullet." He opened and closed his mouth a few times, at a loss of words.

"The worst has happened," he continued, his voice a river of emotion, choked back by the same stubborn streak that held back his old pal Denial, "and it's been a lot harder than I ever dreamed. I've become a mean and nasty drunk, comfortable only with my own company, and I can't stand the insufferable son-of-a-bitch any more than Earl. Hah!

"Stella, you're one tough broad and an angel. You peeled me from my nightmares and freed me from that cesspool they call a veterans' hospital and brought me here. Why? I don't know. But since it's a bar," he raised his glass in salute, "I'm grateful. She's told me she's asked you to take me in. Hah! That would be a damn foolish thing to do, now wouldn't it. That's a statement of fact, not a question.

"Mister Gibby, I don't take you for a fool. No, sir. But" — he paused, giving anyone an opportunity to contradict him — "I'm asking." He took another drink, his pride hurting like an impacted tooth. "There is one thing worse than the dark pit I've been dwelling in, and that would be living alone with my disagreeable self until I die. I... I can't do that... Earl... Henry... I need your help." His voice broke, no longer able to hold back the desperate sob that had been building within him. "I'm asking." Desperation couldn't have been prouder. Brooks silently told him to go to hell.

I'm sunk, Gibby thought as he let out a dramatic sigh.

Stella quietly stepped behind Brooks and gave his shoulders a gentle hug. "You did good," she whispered. "You did good."

Henry poured Brooks another shot. No water.

Earl took a deep breath. He did not like it one bit, no, sir, not one bit, but he knew that there were times when you just did the right thing, like it or not. He threw his head back, and music began to pour out into the quiet. His fingers danced, intimate and quick. The music moved like a spider's web stirred by a sudden breeze and changed like a leaf twisting as it falls to the ground.

His hands moved until he couldn't handle the strain. Finally, they slipped, and the music fell to pieces like a dream on waking. He rose, pushed back the piano bench, and felt his way to the back-storage room he called home. After he made sure that the door was securely closed, he sat on the edge of his cot, put his head in his hands, and wept.

It was the first time he had let his emotions overflow since he had been scared to death on a sinking ship. Since he had lost his sight, he had held it together like a rock.

Now that rock was riddled with cracks and beginning to crumble. He wept because he did not want to do what he was about to do.

Humbled and chastened, Brooks stood alone, as Mr. Despair whistled sour notes in his ear. Brooks tried not to listen. But he did, and each note seemed to suck a little of his life away. His knees quivered beneath his own weight as he waited for the verdict.

He knew that many things in life were not fair, that justice was blind. At least there was irony in that. Deep down he did not expect any reprieve. Despite Stella's heart, he had made one too many deals with the devil, and his chips were about to be called in. He listened to the sounds coming from behind a closed door and understood that his judge was trapped in the same darkness, that the one to decide his fate would be Earl.

Earl's sobs brought Stella up short. Behind that closed door he sat alone in the dark, his pain carrying away the silence that had followed his impassioned refrain. Her eyes met Henry's as she searched for permission to run to Earl and take him in her arms. To somehow absorb his pain, pain she couldn't guess at or understand. If she had known the sacrifice she was asking, she wouldn't have... Yes, she still would have, and there was the tragedy that tore at her heart.

"Is there anything I...?" Gibby started to ask.

"No, just give him some time," Henry said to both.

A sudden gust of wind seemed to come out of nowhere, as if a storm had suddenly burst with no warning. Earl's sobs grew quieter as the front door swung shut behind a retreating customer who wanted no part of the story unfolding inside.

The gray cigarette smoke swirled and seemed to settle in front of the storage room door. The brownish gray curtain parted as Earl opened the door and felt his way to the bar without a word. The breeze had blown nut shells into his path, and they crunched loudly with each step.

The scar tissue behind his dark glasses seemed redder and more prominent to Stella as she watched, her breath catching with the cannonade of each flattened shell. He didn't say a word. When he got behind the bar he found a cloth, draped it over a forearm, and then cautiously began to feel some bottles.

"Earl, what are you doing?" Gibby broke the silence.

"Gibby, have you ever been annoyed and amused with yourself at the same time?" His voice seemed unreasonably calm under the circumstances. "It's an interesting feeling. Your gut squeezes the breath from your lungs as you struggle to laugh and cry simultaneously." Earl caught a bottle just as he was about to tip it over. He felt around until he found a shot glass, raised the bottle, then tried to pour a measured shot. The liquor spilled over before he could stop it.

He smiled slightly as he allowed for a moment of silence.

"A blind man walks into a bar with his Seeing Eye dog." he said with his best storyteller's voice. "He lifts the dog up and swings him around over his head by the tail. The bartender says, 'Hey, man! What are you doing?' The blind man answers, 'Oh, I'm just looking around'."

No one laughed at a joke that might have been funny another time.

"Back before the war, I was a bartender at a country

club in Tennessee. I used to be good at this." He placed a finger just inside the shot glass. "I'm willing to bet I haven't forgotten how." He held a glass up as if he were inspecting it for spots. It may take me a while to get used to handling these, but I can still banter with the best, and that is half the trade.

"Have you heard this one? A string walks into a pub and orders a drink. 'Sorry, we don't serve strings,' says the barman.

"'What? That's discrimination,' says the string. The string walks into the bathroom and ties himself in a knot and messes up his end. He comes back out to the bar and again orders a drink.

"'Aren't you that string I just refused to serve?' asks the barman.

"'No. I'm a frayed knot'."

Earl smiled, his jaw slightly working as if he were chewing on a word until it was just right. "Brooks, you're right. You are an unbearable prick. I'll say it to you straight: you are not a nice guy, and I've often wondered if you ever have been. Like it or not, Stella has dropped you off at our miserable little watering hole."

"Say, wait a minute," Gibby interrupted.

"No offense intended," Earl countered. "I owe you more than you can ever understand, Gibby, but for now, do me a favor and shut up. I'm drowning here and don't need any extra rocks. Now, as I was saying... Brooks, you've made your case, sad and true. The more one thinks about it, the more reasons we can come with to say no. Have you ever thought about something so hard you can't remember what the question was? Now I'm even confusing myself."

He turned, took a few short steps forward to the bar

where he thought Brooks might be, found the iced, weeping glass in Brooks' hand and touched it. "One could almost believe that on the other end of that hand lay a person of some sort. A person who has bared his soul and asked for help. Gibby, of course, you have the final say. Me. I've decided, against my better judgment, to take the risk." He paused with a slight catch in his voice. "Brooks?"

Brooks touched Earl's hand with his own then withdrew it. "Does this mean we're engaged?"

Earl snorted.

Stella put a finger to her lips to stifle a laugh and came up with a sob instead.

An ice cube sounded as loud as a calving glacier in Brooks' glass in the brief silence.

Earl reached into his pocket and took out a small wooden metronome that Henry had purchased from the front window of a pawn shop and placed it on the bar in front of Brooks. At Earl's release it began to tick, its swing sounding a perfect measured cadence. "I want you to have this — on loan. You're going to need it more than me. From now on, it's your ass that's going to polish the piano bench. You are going to play. Maybe you can improve, which I doubt. It's up to Gibby how long you're allowed to stay. Play, my friend, and play well. But for God's sake, please don't sing."

Earl let loose of Brook's hand, turned back to where he had over filled the shot glass and tried again. "We'll earn our keep with the price of admission. Gibby, you should charge a premium for the entertainment: a blind bartender and a tone-deaf crooner. What a side show." His tone changed to that of a good friend giving sage advice to a drunken fool. "Brooks, you and I are both on a short lifeline. Adam's Place is a swell place to be. Don't screw this up. There are no second chances."

"Stella, it will take a good twenty years or so to forgive you for this setup, but, hell, if all goes right, we'll have the time to work it out."

"Gibby, if it's all right with you, we'll just take it one day at a time." He paused, sounding for a moment as if he wanted to take back his words, then repeated them. "One day at a time, if that's all right with you?"

"Gibby? Please," Stella said in a soft whisper with an edge of a prayer in her voice.

"Oh, brother," Gibby said as he raised his hands in acknowledged defeat.

Earl dropped a glass of Scotch in the sink water.

"God help me, I'll be bankrupt by week's end." Gibby frowned; the numbness in his arm reminded him that he had greater worries.

"Henry, help me out here. I think I need a bottle of water for this," Earl said as he attempted to fill another shot glass. "I'm wasting too much good booze; take it out of my next paycheck. Oh, that's right, I don't have one."

Henry caught Stella's eye and smiled. The kind of smile that says, you got us into this, so you had best stick around.

Brooks wanted to cry but couldn't. He dabbed at his mask with his sleeve, took the metronome gently in hand, careful not to disturb its cadence, and moved to the piano with Stella's help.

"Stella," Earl said, as he turned and smiled at where she had been. "I took a hot bubble bath while you were gone. It felt right fine. I didn't get much done with my hair though." He waved his hand through the hair on the side of his head. "It feels like I still have a regulation hospital perm. The world's one and only blind barkeep ought to have a little more style, don't you think? Henry offered to help. I liked your offer better." He then sniffed his shirt sleeve. "Say, where are the clothes you promised?"

Stella's laughter rang bells.

Brooks found the piano, sat and began to play, self-consciously at first, timid, until his pals Tedium and Boredom whispered in his ears. Then, he let loose. Brooks had a bright, reckless, alto voice that seemed to wander off, looking for notes in all the wrong directions, just as Earl had promised.

"Christ," he heard Earl swear. Brooks stopped, then laughed at himself. "Earl, the next time I go astray, help me out here. I'll play, you sing." This time there was no conceit about him.

Earl hesitated. God knew he wanted to sing, as did Stella and Henry. He took a stiff drink of rye, thinking it was bourbon. His grimace said it all. "No," he rasped, "Brooks, you go ahead. There is no one here who hasn't heard you caterwaul before. The question is whether I can learn to pour a proper drink before you can learn to sing. Time will tell..." He hummed quietly to himself as he practiced his new trade.

Without being asked, the last customers left. Gibby nodded and smiled, knowing they would be back. He got up, walked over to Earl and watched with a father's patient gaze. He placed the bottle of water Henry had filled in Earl's right hand. "Easy does it. Measure with your little finger to the top of the nail. Oops! Try again."

He looked over at Brooks who seemed to be struggling a little in finding the keys. Brooks' full-head bandage still bothered Gibby; it would take some getting used to. He turned back to Earl. "You didn't just give Books a lousy piano bench, did you?" The question private, between men.

Earl shrugged, bringing his shoulders almost to his ears and back down. "You've got a big heart, Gibby, so I'll tell it to you straight." His voice lowered for a private conversation. "If I could kick myself in the ass for doing this, I would kick hard. I very much regret it, but it's done. Is it the right thing to do? I don't know. What I do know is: if I could see Stella, I couldn't stand the hurt in her eyes if I let her down."

He filled a shot glass with whiskey, downed most, spilling the balance on his shirt. For a moment his whole body drew up into a tight knot of emotion held back, he had already cried once too often. He shook with it, holding the glass so tight Gibby grew afraid that it might shatter. With a long audible hiss that rose from deep within, Earl released the glass onto the counter top. "I can do this," he whispered to himself. "I will do this."

"Gibby" — Earl's voice sounded rusty from whiskey and strain — "my number came up twice during the war, and I cheated the Devil. It has been music that has given me a second life. I'm a jealous lover. I can't stand to be near music; being a part of it, controlling it — it's passion with me. Not to be in control would be like listening to the woman you love bed down with another man. The French have a term — let's see, oh yes — ménage à trois." There was a profound sigh that seem to start down low, then rose until there was nowhere else to go. "Brooks and me," he continued as the last of the sigh masked his words, "are going to have to learn to share her. That is, if she'll have us both." A single tear slid out from behind his dark glasses. He tipped the bottle up and took a sip of water, then he filled the glass again to overflowing.

Gibby, who had lost a wife and a son, thought he could understand Earl's pain. Earl's music was something to be felt, it was within his soul, his breath, and no one could feel the music as Earl did. He was just beginning to get a sense of that. Go ahead, son, take it back, this here fellow — Brooks, can find his place somewhere else. He wanted to say that, but it was too late, what was done was done.

Gibby placed a warm hand on Earl's shoulder and said, "We'll find a way to make it work, somehow. Right now, I haven't a clue where to begin. As for you giving up your music, I can't see that happening. You said that music was your mistress. It might help, if you showed her where your heart is, that your voice is a more passionate lover than Brooks' fingers can be."

Earl thought about that, set the bottle down, turned and made his way to the piano where Brooks played. "Brooks," he asked curiously, as he heard the last note echo and fade away, "did you ever see The Wizard of Oz? That's right, you were an extra. A Munchkin. No, wrong size, right voice. Well, I'm about to take you on a little road trip. Give me an E-flat major and follow my lead." Earl gently bumped Brooks from the piano bench, found the keyboard and began to play.

Earl sang colors to the blind man, with a startling passion. And in the end Brooks could see them: red, green, gold, all the hues in the rainbow. Music was Earl's mistress, and he seduced her with no questions about his intent. Brooks had just been put on notice that he was lucky to be along for the ride.

Henry polished bar glasses as he watched and listened. Earl's was a rare talent, and music was a gift that had never really blossomed until he had had to confront the dragon he feared the most, alone in the unforgiving and terrifyingly personal dark.

Henry had not seen his mom and pop since 1942, when his people, the Nisei, had been imprisoned and he had joined the Army. He had planned on paying them a visit before he went off to medical school. Now that would have to wait. Things happened for a reason, and for the moment he was needed here.

"I believe this is yours," Henry said, as he pushed the four hundred dollars across the counter to Stella. His eyes asked the unspoken question. Where did you get that kind of cash?

"It's a long story," she said with an evasive smile. She took the cash and became immediately uncomfortable with the thought that she had left the rest of the money in the car. "Gibby, you have a safe? Would you mind if I put something in it for a short while?"

"Why don't you just prepay a bar tab, and we'll call it even." He thought she was referring to the four hundred dollars. He chuckled. "No problem."

She went out to the car and returned with a rolled-up pillow case. Three hundred of the four hundred dollars she added to the case, rolled it tight, wrote her name on the outside, tied it off with some string, and handed it to Gibby.

"Good grief!" Gibby exclaimed. He couldn't even guess at the amount. "How...? Where...?" He rolled his eyes as he took the pillow case, giving it a curious squeeze. "Never mind, I don't want to know." The tightness in his chest came back, constricting his breath. He felt a little dizzy. No more surprises tonight. Please. "I'll see you in the morning.

Henry close up, will you please? Good night."

He took the pillow case upstairs, put it in the safe, then lay on his bed without even taking off his shoes, and listened uneasily to the voices and music that leaked up from the bar below. What was done was done; somehow, they'd make do.

What troubled him now was the tightness that pressed down on his chest, a haunting specter he didn't want to face. It wasn't that he was afraid to die; it happens to everyone. But now that he had been dragged kicking and screaming into taking in first Earl, now Brooks, he couldn't just check out, somehow that just didn't seem right. He closed his eyes and let sleep push that question into tomorrow.

Stella took a gin she hadn't asked for from Henry and sat down at the piano, her eyes moist, a little blurry. It had been one hell of a day, both terrifying and glorious, one of the most topsy-turvy, confusing, and surprising days she could remember.

She laughed to herself as she began to realize that she was falling in love with these two blind men: one, a desperate alcoholic afraid to live; the other, a man so full of surprises he would keep her guessing until the end of her days.

The evening ran long, a wonderful blur of emotion; warm with a tinge of bitter.

31

FOUL BALL

"No. No more!" Ivory blubbered as a flashback plunged him into sudden panic. In his mind he saw "Foul Ball," the Japanese prison camp guard, move into his pitching position. The prisoners had nicknamed the short, pudgy, malicious guard "Foul Ball" because of his sadistic interest in baseball. Ivory had been called to batting practice, where he was forced to take on the unbearable Ofuna crouch, where he was forced to stand on the balls of his feet, knees half bent, arms extended over his head, as he waited for Foul Ball to pitch a baseball at him. Then, and only then, was he allowed to try to catch the ball. If he moved before the ball was airborne, he would be beaten. If he fell, or otherwise moved out of the crouch, he would be beaten.

This was Foul Ball's fourth pitch. The first had given him a close shave. The second he had caught in his bare hand. His little finger, swollen, wasn't broken, but he hadn't the flesh or the strength in his hands to catch it again. It was the same finger that he had injured the last time he had been called to "batting practice." The third pitch had driven into his forehead, stunning him. Now as he waited for the next pitch, his vision swam, his undernourished legs shook beneath him. He begged, "No more," knowing he would be punished for being weak. Punishment came at the end of a bat. Foul Ball wound up and let loose a fast ball...

Ivory woke. He fell from the wheelchair, crawled frantically on his one leg, then curled into a ball, hands over his head, to protect himself from the beating that would come.

He flinched when Dr. Fryback bent down and gently

touched Ivory's hands as if soothing a frightened dog who, while whining and shaking from fear, could turn, lash out, and bite without warning. Slowly, tenderly, he separated Ivory's taut fingers, aware that his patient was caught on a treacherous tightrope from which he could fall back into the dark memories lurking in his subconscious. Or he could reach out to his helping hand to firmer ground.

Each staggered breath represented a thousand days of captivity, a thousand nightmares, and the repressed memories of the men who had suffered alongside him, been dead and buried, stripped of all hope and what little remained of their dignity.

Fryback was second-guessing. Working with patients suffering from war neurosis was a new science; no one had any real expertise in it. But the cause — the horrific experiences men suffered in war — was nothing new.

Homer's Odyssey described the psychological travails of Odysseus, a recent veteran of the Trojan Wars, who was returning home. His problems included flashbacks and survivor's guilt. The symptoms included restlessness, aggression, depression, memory impairment, sympathetic overactivity, concentration impairment, phobia and suspicion. Ivory, who was weeping before him, was much like Odysseus, or so Dr. Fryback suspected. Odysseus had no helping hand, as Ivory had now, if he would accept the help. The degradation and horrors he had suffered as a prisoner of war would be with him every day for the rest of his life; nothing could change that. He might manage to live with his neurosis and the mighty ghosts that haunted him.

"Ivory, it's Doctor Fryback." He leveraged two of Ivory's fingers and gently lifted. "You are home, son, safe;

no one here will hurt you. The camp, the guards are all in the past. Foul Ball is dead. Send him to Hell, where he belongs. He can't hurt you anymore. Ivory... it's only a bad dream."

Ivory flinched, and started to recoil, at the sound of a door closing somewhere nearby.

"Ivory don't go there," Doctor Fryback said with as much reassurance as he could muster. He squeezed the fingers he held in his hand. "Ivory, it's only a dream."

Somewhere, Ivory had heard those words before.

32

OMAHA BOUND

Irene, her eyes downcast, was nearly disconsolate at what she had done. It was her sin; no one had asked her to do it. She needed repentance, to ask God to forgive her. She had sinned by borrowing a few moments of Burrell Smith's death to hide the truth. She had lied to the police. She compounded the sin by not having the courage to speak up while there was still a chance to stop the evil, before it was too late. She had involved Simon and Alex in a despicable charade. As for God, it might have been His will that Elroy be given his ticket to Hell, but she had taken it upon herself to interfere. Now, instead of going to Hell, he was Omaha bound.

Irene found Dr. Garrity in his office, packing a few personal items in a cardboard box. She couldn't miss the open bottle on his desk. "Dr. Garrity, I'm surprised to find you here, considering everything that has happened." Her heart went out to him. The poor man thought he had committed murder.

He did not answer.

"I'd like to talk with you, if you have a moment." Her voice faded to an insecure whisper, her eyes still low.

"A sad little hope," he answered without expression. "You should aim higher." He stiffened, sighed, open and closed his mouth a few times. He took a cigarette from an open pack on the desk, lit it, his hands shaking. Blue-gray smoke wafted across the desk, its irritant slowly forcing Irene to raise her eyes.

"There's not much to say," Dr. Garrity continued. "Elroy

— Mr. Hawks — left us no other option. When you look at the damage that has been done, I can only wish I had acted earlier. It's done now, and wishful thinking can't change that." He poured a touch of the Scotch into his glass. "Care for some? No, I thought not." He looked at the bottle. It was almost empty. "The police will be here soon. I thought I had best pack a few things."

"A policeman just left," she said. "Simon took him down to the morgue. I don't think there will be any further questions. However, the officer did ask for the death certificate."

Doctor Garrity stopped and stared into the box. Until that moment, he had been certain he was about to be arrested or at least taken down to the station for questioning. When he had plunged the needle into Elroy's back, being arrested didn't seem to matter much. While waiting for the police to arrive, Dr. Garrity had grown more apprehensive. The news that the officer had come and gone brought on a physical sense of relief. A long gray finger of ash caved from the cigarette.

"The death certificate." He repeated Irene's words. "Yes, of course." His cigarette was still in place. "It must be around here somewhere. Where did I put it?" He glanced randomly around the office, his eyes suggesting that he had already forgotten what he was searching for.

Irene slowly dropped her gaze back down to the floor and began to speak. "It wasn't Elroy's body the officer examined. It was Burrell Smith's. We — Simon and Alex and I — switched the bodies. When we took Elroy down to the morgue, he still had a pulse. I thought it best to not risk complications."

She smiled, as might a child about to reveal a special

secret. "Elroy is on his way to Omaha." She glanced at the clock. "The train left about five minutes ago. Alex went with him to make sure he got on board without anyone asking too many questions. You authorized... I... I signed the transport requisition for you authorizing a private sleeping berth.

"There is a veterans' hospital in Omaha, but Elroy wasn't a veteran. Alex will take all of Elroy's identification and transfer papers with him. He asked if you might see that his last paycheck is forwarded once he gets off the train in Denver and gets settled.

"When Elroy arrives in Omaha, he'll just be some nameless John Doe. He'll be in hospital blues, no identification, no money, and no one will have an idea of where he came from, or where he's going. I think the authorities in Omaha will think he escaped from a mental hospital." She giggled.

Doctor Garrity's expression changed by degree, first from puzzled, then confused, surprised, confounded, as he began to understand what she was telling him. After half a breath of silence, a little sparkle seemed to come back into his eyes along with a grim little smile. "Omaha, but of course! Why didn't I think of that? It could have been Topeka or Grand Junction. It doesn't make much difference, does it? Very clever. Very clever indeed."

Lacking an ashtray, he set the cigarette on the edge of the desk. He found two shot glasses in his box and poured a Scotch for himself and Irene — neat. "Are you sure you won't have one, to toast Elroy's bon voyage?"

She shook her head and whispered a polite "No, thank you."

The hospital might not have to close after all, he thought

as he emptied both shot glasses. Quite a reversal. Perhaps, with a little luck... Who knows?

Sweet, Alex thought as he unlocked the ambulance doors.

They had arrived at the train station at the busiest time of the day; the depot was filled with people arriving and departing, announcements were blaring, people were saying goodbye, others hello. At first, unloading Elroy from the ambulance unnerved Alex. He didn't want anyone to ask any questions; questions he couldn't answer.

If Elroy had possessed the decency to die when he was supposed to, it would have made things a lot simpler. If he were dead, he'd be in a box, that was a whole other type of paperwork. Putting a dead man, not in a box, on a train, would bring questions that could only lead to trouble. Since Elroy was still breathing, things were easier. If Elroy somehow manages to survive, he's going to be one pissed-off asshole. Don't even think about that. He mentally crossed his fingers that Elroy would continue to hang on to life just long enough to be tucked safely on board and for the train to get under way.

The first complication had come with the train schedule. To get to Omaha, they would have to change trains in Oakland and Denver. If Elroy expired, changing trains would be out of the question. The next best option was a train that went through Los Angeles, Santa Fe, Kansas City, to Omaha and beyond. The route took an extra nine hours, but there were no transfers. Once Elroy was on board, all Alex wanted was to get off the train without questions.

"Would you mind?" Alex touched his shoulder gingerly,

as he asked two Marines about to board the train for help. "I can't take the weight until my shoulder heals a bit more. Okinawa. My buddy here celebrated being back in the States for the first time in four years a little too much. I'd sure hate to see him miss the train. He pissed his pants, and I borrowed the hospital blues from a laundry truck. When he wakes up I'll get him squared away and back into uniform."

The Pullman porter had seen more than one soldier all liquored up, especially since the troops had started coming home. He didn't blame them. Who could? They'd had a hard time of it. He was more than happy to guide the two Marines as they shoulder-carried their pal towards a reserved sleeping berth. They helped tuck the inebriated man into a bunk and then made their way towards the bar car.

A civilian whom he hadn't noticed before showed him two train tickets for the berth and tipped him fifty cents, a pretty good tip. He asked that they not be disturbed until an hour before they got to Omaha. "Yes, sir, no problem," the porter said with a broad smile, flipping the fifty-cent piece in his hand. Man, oh man, he thought as he made his way towards the next car, that poor boy is stewed. He's sure going to feel it in the morning.

Alex glanced at Elroy, who remained alive for the time being, resting beneath a blanket on the lower bunk. Alex looked at his watch and yawned. He looked out the window as the train pulled out of the station. It would take just five hours to get to Los Angeles.

The constant rocking of a train in motion had always made him sleepy. The bunk above Elroy was inviting, but not when you knew that a man beneath you was about to die. He opted to stay in the seat nearest the window and nodded off.

Elroy sensed the first jerk of the train as it began to move.

33

ON THE CONNING TOWER

'*Three days passed like a spring rain, a kind of squall that refreshed the air, pushed the winter blues aside, and then was over all too soon.*' Stella finally finished reading Miracle of the Bells, which by the end had her both smiling and crying.

The story line was about Catholics. Stella wasn't one, but it didn't matter, because what little faith she had left her feeling a lack. It was a great book for someone who had fallen off the path and no longer believed that good still exists. It gave her a lot to think about.

When she left Brooks to make his own way at Adam's Place, she deliberately left all the questions on her front porch to be scooped up with the morning paper, when she got around to it. She had not left her apartment for three days, nor had she thought about the questions she had put off, until now, when they were knocking demandingly at her door.

There were hard questions with no easy solutions. Had she done the right thing bringing Brooks to the tavern? Could Brooks pull himself together? How was Elroy's death going to complicate things? The money — oh Lord, the money — how much was there? Should she return it? If so, to whom?

All the what's and ifs began to nag and make her restless. Then there was Earl, sweet Earl. Here she allowed a little more access: there was something warm and comfortable in that, but she still tried to wrap herself in a protective blanket. Earl was a complicated man and, blind or not, he always seemed to find a soft spot in her defenses and show up with a smile as sweet as a Sunday picnic and a fresh berry pie. Sweet? He also was beginning to arouse her as no man had ever done before. Damn you, Earl Crier.

It was starting out to be a perfect warm sunny day, so common in stories and so rare in the real world. Stella started the day with coffee and pastry at a little bistro on Union Street. After that, she went shopping, first at a specialty shop, where the choices were bewildering. Finally, she found what she wanted at a secondhand store.

It only took about an hour at her sewing machine to fashion the silk she had purchased into a special gift for Brooks. It was the least she could do after what he had done for her. She held up her creations, smiled, packed them into a paper bag and set off for Adam's Place.

The door to Adam's Place was open: fresh air in and stale tobacco smoke out. Although a smoker herself, she appreciated the fresh air. Old bars smelled like old men who could no longer take care of themselves, and she appreciated that Gibby made the effort. She entered with a jaunty, convivial step and a smile, which quickly turned into a silhouette of a frown. The air, just inside, tasted heavy of worry. "Oh Brooks, what have you done?" She whispered aloud as if that might appease her anxiety.

Gibby looked up from a table where he was counting receipts. She found his etched frown unnerving. He gave a sigh that hung somewhere between annoyance, frustration, and anger.In three days, he seemed to have aged, changed from a pudgy curmudgeon with a twinkle in his eyes and a winning smile to a pale, worn-out old man whose beefy jowls pulled his mouth down into a melancholy frown.

He slowly plucked his spectacles from the tip of his nose and set them on the table. He rubbed his bloodshot eyes, then tapped his pencil repeatedly as he stared back at her.

Earl stood behind the bar practicing his pours. If nothing else, he was tenacious. She had to stifle a laugh because he now wore a yellow rain slicker, proof that he wasn't exactly mastering the craft.

"OK, guys," she asked, "what gives?" Earl did not respond to her voice, and she found that disquieting. While away, she had missed his deep seductive tone, her male siren beckoning to her with *Stella by Starlight.* His silence weighed on her as she slowly took in the room.

Brooks was sitting at the piano, plucking randomly at the keys, deep in his dark thoughts. She wondered which of his imaginary pals were sitting around the piano: Self-Pity, no doubt.

Henry, who was sweeping under a table at the rear of the bar, looked up and smiled halfheartedly. At least he smiled.

Gibby's expression had not changed. She had gotten him into this and it pained her to see him so unhappy. The silence was emphatic as he sat there staring at her.

Stella chose the lesser of evils and sauntered over to Henry. "Someone die?"

Henry gave her an inscrutable smile. "Your good intentions."

"Ohhh?" She sat down at a table, rested her chin in one hand. "Tell me all. I'm a big girl."

"After you left, Earl stayed up, played and sang, as if he would never be able to again. He was loud, brilliant, off the wall, and a sleepless night for the rest of us. The next morning, I found Brooks crocked with an open bottle of bourbon half-empty, not half-full. When I asked what was going on, he clicked his fingers and told me to piss off.

"Earl was behind the bar practicing his new trade. I watched him pour six shots in a row without spilling a drop, but when he knew that he was being watched, he over-poured the rest. If you ask me, Brooks is developing a little paranoia about playing whenever Earl is around, which, as you know, is most of the time. If Brooks were to find that rare moment where he might be able to play, Earl would hear and be on him like a hungry hawk.

"Once Brooks knew I was going to stick around, he tried to play. He tried. The alcohol didn't help, but at least he tried. Earl struck hard and fast, driving up the tempo. I've never heard him sing better.

"In no time at all Brooks' playing began to sound like a bad rendition of chopsticks compared to Earl's raw talent." He looked over at the piano where Brooks sat, a pathetic Humpty-Dumpty, waiting to fall.

"We are talking about grown men here, aren't we?" Stella shrugged. "Maybe we should take away their allowance." She couldn't repress a slight smirk.

Henry smiled. "Gibby cut them both off. No booze. Earl doesn't seem to care. Brooks is as miserable as he looks."

"I see," Stella said as she tapped her nails against the table. "And the raincoat?"

"He's got only one set of clothes. I brought out the raincoat. Look, Earl had good intentions, but giving up his spot at the piano was never really in the cards. The man sweats music. Music is as much a sense to him now as hearing and touch.

"When he thought that he could at least take a step back from center stage, he set out to prove himself by becoming a blind bartender. You must admit it would bring in the curious. Now he's convinced himself he can't do both, and he's rapidly becoming the clumsiest blind bartender he can. Which reminds me, have you done anything about extra clothes for both Brooks and Earl?"

"I've got a secondhand tux out in the car. I've got something for Earl, but it needs some alterations."

Henry glanced at the clock. "It's been a good two and a half hours, and no one has said a word. Brooks just sits there and hits random keys, while Gibby fumes. And Earl is behaving like an eight-year old splashing in a rain puddle." Henry studied Stella's eyes, which had not grown dark with the news but flickered as a thousand thoughts dashed around her mind.

"I see," she said thoughtfully to Henry. "Brooks lost more than his sight when the Nazi rocket blew the hell out of that London pub. He lost his face. I did not mean that as a pun. That once-handsome man hides behind his horrid bandages, afraid that someone might discover what a pathetic, ugly monster he has become. He has little dignity, no self-respect, and little hope.

"For a moment I thought we might have stumbled on an answer; at least temporarily. I hope your game, because I'm going to need your help. If we don't find some answers soon, Gibby will kick the two of them out, and I wouldn't blame him.

"Earl and Brooks may not like each other, but events beyond their control may have made them inseparable. Earl is defending his first love by trying to drive Brooks away.

Every time he takes a jab at Brooks, he takes a chip out of what's left of Brooks' dignity. It won't be long until there is nothing left to chip away at. Earl will have his piano back, but Brooks?

"I can't see Earl singing 'Pencils for sale' at the corner of Powell and Market. I can see Brooks stepping in front of a moving bus. Looking at him now, that thought may be crossing his mind. We have to discover some workable options soon, or all we'll have accomplished with our good intentions is to throw them both into quicksand neither can climb out of."

Henry gave a grim, frustrated chuckle. "So now we are the blind leading the blind. Great. Any ideas?"

"As long as Earl is throwing a little water at the fire, let's see if we can warm up Brooks." She leaned forward and pushed towards Henry a small bag she had been carrying. "I've been working on an idea, and now is about as good a time as any to try it out.

"Henry, will you please get the tux out of the car, and then take Brooks into the back and get him dressed. Take off those awful bandages he's wearing and dress him in one of these. I'll take care of Mr. Crier."

Henry opened the bag and found three silk masks; white, light brown, and black. They were soft to the touch and could easily be slipped over Brooks' head. The open end would slip down to his shoulders. The white and brown masks each had a black stripe sewed across at eye level. The black mask had a white stripe. There was a hole for the mouth and a pull string near the shoulders to help keep the mask in place. The cloth was light and cool, allowing for easy breathing. In comparison to the stiff bandages that Brooks now wore, the masks were good-looking. They added a dash of mystery where pity had once ruled.

"Oh Stella," Henry said as he held up the black mask, "if only Brooks could see this."

"He'll feel it," Stella said, "and that's something. Now we've got Earl. Sweet Earl. If he has one constant, it's his ability to resist change. That's not quite true is it? Somewhere down deep he wanted to help Brooks, but not at the expense of surrendering his music. They just can't work together."

Henry took Stella's car keys and left to get the tux.

Stella had heard the front door open and close but paid no attention until she noticed a man standing next to her. "Oh, hello, Commander. I didn't see you come in."

"May I?' The Commander held up one of the masks to the light. "Classy." He looked over at Brooks, who was banging out a single annoying note three times running. "These are for him?" He spoke softly, not sure if Brooks could or should overhear.

"Don't worry, Commander. Brooks is currently playing a duet with Self-Pity and is tucked away in his own little world. He can't hear us because he doesn't care what we have to say."

That bad, the Commander thought. *Too bad*. Then he turned back to Stella. "You made these? I've got an old Chief Bosun's mate on the boat with a puss ugly enough to scare away a school of hungry sharks. Could I talk you into making one or two for him?"

They laughed.

"Too bad about the poor sod at the piano. It must be rough. I couldn't help but overhear your concern regarding

Earl. Earl is a bright and talented guy. Maybe I can help."

"Oh? How so?"

"In a submarine, we're all in close quarters, where there is no room for childish behavior or jealous grudges. You might say we're all in the same boat.

"I remember one cruise where I had two sonar men who were always on each other's case. Their section chief wrote them both up on charges and brought them to me for disciplinary mast.

"One had served with me on three cruises; the other was on his first cruise. The more experienced man was one of the best sonar men I've ever had the pleasure to serve with. The other, okay, but just okay. The problem was that the more experienced man would never let the other forget he was inferior."

Stella offered the Commander a cigarette, which he turned down. One thing she would miss about the war were the men in uniform: handsome, rugged, ready to test their mettle. She would never miss the wounded, though she could never forget them.

Submariners were one of a kind, with foolhardy bravery tucked neatly into a tin can. She studied the commander; he was wearing an air of confidence that intrigued her. "What did you do?" she asked, truly curious.

"What I wanted to do and what the Articles of War would allow me to do were two different things. I opted for the middle ground. I could have docked their pay or canceled their next liberty, but that seemed counterproductive. I had a boat to command, in wartime conditions. I needed a quick fix for bad behavior.

"I set my sights on my senior sonar man, who should have known better. Long story short, I surfaced and sent him to the top watch position on the conning tower." He paused for effect. "Then I brought the boat down until his feet were treading water. The poor guy didn't know if we were submerging under pending attack or if we had forgotten him.

"It wouldn't be the first time that a sub had to leave a man topside to save the boat and the rest of the crew. Scared, you bet, but he learned quick about the value of being one of the team. Out there you need to forget about personal agendas and petty differences. We all sink or swim together."

"You are a hard man, Commander, but I get your point."

"I lost one boat back in 1943. We were on the surface, and a Jap patrol plane came straight out of the sun. We should have seen it, but someone was not on the ball. One mistake cost fourteen men their lives in a matter of seconds."

He cast his eyes up towards that blazing Pacific sun burned into his memory. "They couldn't get out in time. The boat went down like a rock." He sucked in a breath as he made a silent whistle. "Every man is on duty every waking moment on a boat, and regardless of the tedium they've got to be one hundred percent focused.

"As the boat's skipper I had to have a zero-tolerance policy. We were there to win the war, we were expendable; the rules were being written as we sailed."

Stella could see the unspoken pain in his eyes.

"Sending the senior sonar man up to the conning tower was only part of the lesson. Once we brought him back on board, I had my section chief run him through the numbers: a tough life-or-death drill, the survival of the ship dependent on keen ears, good judgment, where the clock is ticking faster than you can think.

"He didn't pass. He wasn't meant to. He was good, very good, but not good enough. We drilled him again and again until he got better.

"Once he got it right, I tasked him with bringing the junior sonar man up to the next level. They became a team any skipper would be proud of."

Henry returned with the car keys. "New?" he asked Stella, nodding toward the car to indicate the tuxedo.

"I borrowed it from a friend, but I'm thinking of making an offer." Stella was lying; she had spent a little of Elroy's money on the suit. Her eyes flickered with sudden intensity. "Henry, after you get Brooks into his tux and ready for show and tell, would you bring out your clarinet? Brooks can whistle up a storm with lots of high notes that I doubt Earl can hit. Let's give Earl a run for his money."

Henry didn't have to be asked twice. "Earl sings sweet and low, but he does struggle a bit with high notes. I think Brooks and I can take him for a ride."

"That's the ticket," the Commander said. "Maybe I can be of help?"

Stella took a second to ponder his offer. "No conning tower here, Commander, but as you can see" — her eyes directed his attention towards Earl in his yellow rain slicker — "our sonar man is currently a solo act, not exactly a team player."

"At your service, ma'am," the Commander said with a sly smile, followed by a slightly theatrical salute.

You go for it, Commander, Stella thought. "You won't be too hard on him?" She wore her nurse's heart on her sleeve. "Earl has amazing strength, but as you can see..."

The Commander gave her a reassuring smile. "He'll be

fine, just fine. If the man wants to play in the water, then play he shall."

The Commander remembered that Earl had a voice like Frank Sinatra's. Once you heard him sing, it stuck with you. Earl Crier was as pigheaded and stubborn as the day is long, but he was likable. The Commander did not have much respect for Sinatra; in fact, many in the service scorned him. They considered him a 4-F crooner who stayed home, screwing someone's girlfriend or wife while they were risking or giving their lives a long way from home. They saw Sinatra as flaunting his philandering, which many men in uniform neither forgot nor forgave.

The Commander had to laugh at the first time he had met Earl. Earl had asked him not to sing, to honor the "silent service." Well, blind or not, Earl was about to become the student, and he, the teacher. Under normal circumstances, he would start the lesson without warning, but Earl's blindness required some accommodation.

Earl poured water into a shot glass until it overflowed, then began to fill a second, only more slowly; he was trying to determine who had entered his space. The sound and smell were that of a stranger, but this person had ventured behind the bar, which meant he had Gibby's permission. Not knowing who it was put Earl on edge. This time he stopped as the water neared the top of the glass. Perfect. He was looking for acknowledgment, a voice or clue. Whoever it was remained silent. "I've heard your sound and smelled your presence before, and you are not a woman; so that narrows the field."

The bar was his safe-haven. He knew most of the regular customers by voice, smell, or the way they walked. None were allowed behind the bar. The fact that someone had crossed that line prickled the hair on the back of his neck. "Stella?"

No answer.

"Henry?" The silence was alarming. "Gibby?" He set the glass down and reached for a bottle, his grip firm on its neck. "I don't know who you are, friend, but I suggest you back away before you regret it. Now." His voice lacked the authority he tried to muster.

"Earl, we've met." The Commander edged slowly closer to Earl. He could see that Earl was agitated by his presence.

"Commander Buck, United States Navy Submarine Service." His tone of voice changed. "The last time we met, you made a point that I can't sing; point taken. You, on the other hand, can give that bastard Sinatra a run for his money."

"I wish I had his money." Earl relaxed his defensive grip on the bottle, though something still told him that everything wasn't quite right. "What can I do for you, Commander?"

"For me, nothing." He saw the spritzer hose and settled on the lesson plan. "I do have one question. What's with the rain slicker?"

Earl patted the slicker with both hands. "Oh, this little thing? Why, it's the latest rage in uniforms for blind bartenders. Do you like it?"

Earl's smugness forced the Commander's hand. "One of a kind, just like you. Do you know the words to Here's That Rainy Day?" The Commander slowly lifted the spritzer nozzle and aimed it.

"Sure, that's an easy one."

"Sorry, Earl, but I'm about to rain on your parade."

Earl heard a slight hiss. "What the hell?" He sputtered

as a stream of spritzer hit him straight in the glasses. He was cornered, floundering like a fish out of water, shot glasses flying off the counter, and the Commander gave him a thorough soaking.

* * * *

Earl spat out wretched, oil-tainted sea water, and another frigid wave slammed down on him. The star-studded night sky turned upside down. He was pulled under then twisted about, saved only by the buoyancy of his life jacket. His ankle was broken. He screamed. It felt as if the sea would tear his foot off. He felt himself being pulled under as his cargo ship sank into the dark depths of the Murmansk Sea.

The cold felt like a thousand needles. He screamed, retched, and gagged on another mouth full of oil-fouled water. A patch of oil was burning on the surface close by; the heat was no comfort, and the smoke obscured his possible rescue. Another wave turned him head over heels in the dark, deadly ocean. There was a rescue ship nearby, but he never felt more scared, alone, or close to death. His head surfaced, and he raised a hand as another mountainous wave bore down on him. "Here... Over here... help."

* * * *

The Commander changed positions, continuing the soaking. Earl sputtered as a stream of seltzer caught him open-mouthed. He fell to the floor, his scared sightless eyes wide with panic. "Here... Over here... Help!"

"Enough!" Gibby barked. "What kind of man are you,

can't you see he's had enough?" Before Gibby could say another word, Stella was on her feet, running to Earl.

The Commander did not have to be told twice. He shut the spritzer hose off and threw it back towards its cradle. He had gone too far and triggered a traumatic memory. Having survived two boats sunk during the war, he did not have to guess what was going on in Earl's tortured mind. He grasped Earl's hand reassuringly and pulled him to his feet. "Easy there, you're on dry land, easy."

* * * *

In the dark, as the serpent nudged him, testing for his soul, Earl felt a human hand pull him free just as another wave crashed about him. He remembered being pulled out of the frigid water into the sanctuary of the rescue boat. He caught his busted foot on the side, but the onset of hypothermia numbed most of the pain. He heard the words: "Easy, we've got you... easy."

He was soaked through, and they wrapped him in dry blankets. "Can't do much until we get you aboard ship. Wrap your hands around this." The coffee cup was scalding hot, his hands shook so much that he spilled most of it. "There's more where that came from but give yourself a moment: that coffee is hot enough to crack nearly frozen teeth." A towering wave nearly capsized the rescue boat as they turned back towards their mother ship.

* * * *

The raging sea disappeared as the dragon reeled. He was

wet, chilled but not cold.

"I'm sorry... I'm so sorry, Earl." Nothing ever sounded as sweet as Stella's voice as he found himself cradled in her arms, his head nestled against her breasts where he felt and heard her heart. "Are you, all right?"

The panic and anger drifted away with it, the dragon, its power spent. It was then that he knew that he needed this woman, that he loved her, and that if she was by his side he would fear that dragon no more. He began to sing sweet and low. *"Oh, my Stella beneath a star lit sky, where have you been all my life..."*

The Commander found Earl's glasses and gave them to Stella. His hands, held open, said the same as his eyes: I'm sorry. We shouldn't have gone there.

Brooks held the silk mask in his hands, squeezing it lightly. He touched the rough bandage that enveloped his head and began to unwind it. His head free, the air cool on his ruined face, the scar tissue hurting just a little. He held the silk to what remained of his nose and inhaled.

Henry had described the colors to him. He whistled to himself Stella by Starlight as he slowly slipped the black and white-striped mask over his head until the silk drifted softly down to his shoulders.

He continued to whistle as he rose and stood in front of an imaginary mirror, positioning the comforting silk just so. He felt for and found the slip-on bow tie Henry had put on him, straightened it, then found the drawstring and ever so slowly drew it closed, allowing for his new silken image to settle in place. His shoulders seemed to square as he stood tall. He had not felt this good since the last time he had felt the gentle caress of a good woman. He sighed with pleasure and mouthed the words 'Thank you, Stella' as he felt his way towards the door.

"What was that all about?" Earl asked as he slipped his dark glasses back into place.

"Believe it or not," Stella said. "something about learning to work, live, and survive together." She looked at Gibby, then at Henry, who was standing with his clarinet at the ready. Brooks felt his way out of the back room wrapped in a new cloak of dignity. "I guess that means all of us," she said.

Henry raised his clarinet and began to play: Let the Angels Sing. The high notes were clear, crisp and above Earl's range.

Gibby shook his head at the mess, then poured a beer on the house for the Commander.

Brooks sat at the piano and played, matching Henry note for note, with his amazing ability to put his lips together and whistle. Beneath that mask, it was a wonder that he could whistle at all, but he could, and the silk mask fluttered as he did.

Earl smiled as he felt the dragon drift farther away. He knew what they were doing and why. *Never again will I be that childish,* he thought as he felt the music and his woman. He tried to ignore Brooks, but he had to admit the man could whistle.

"Come on, handsome," Stella said. "Let's go find you some dry clothes."

"This is what I've got, sweetheart, unless you've got something in the car."

"My place," she said as she led him away. Stella had

bought Earl a white tux when she bought Brooks his.

After a bubble bath, where more than the bath water was shared, they dressed. "Where's the mirror?" He found her face and gently moved his hands, his fingers taking everything into measure. It was the first time he had done so. She kissed his fingers as they caressed her lips. "There's my mirror, and I can tell exactly how good I look by the smile on your face."

"That's some smile you've got, handsome." How fast he bounced back, the drenching the Commander had given him all but forgotten.

"That's because now I know how beautiful you are."

"All dressed up and no place to go," she said as she adjusted his hat. "When was the last time you went out on the town? I'm buying."

Earl came up a little short on words. The last time he had been "out on the town" was in Italy, the night the lights went out for good. "I... I'm a little short on cash."

Stella sensed his embarrassment. "It's all right, I picked the Commander's pocket. The least he can do is buy us dinner. The Cliff House has a great steak." She took him by the arm.

"Is that the place overlooking the ocean? If so, I think I'd prefer to skip it. I've had enough salt water for a lifetime."

"Mayes' Oyster House is good. Have you ever had abalone?"

"Can't say that I have. How about Chinese? I hear San Francisco has a great China Town." He reached up and tapped the rim of his dark glasses. "Ever since I've gotten these, I've been wanting to try my luck with chop sticks."

34
DON'T COUNT ELROY OUT

Elroy woke in a fog, not knowing where he was, or how he got there. He could move his eyes, but there was a disconnect with the rest of his body. He tried to call out but couldn't. The back of his neck hurt like hell, and the pain was deep.

It was the pain that drew his memory back to the hospital. The memory was fuzzy, but he was able to piece some of it together. He remembered having the blind joker in a death grip and threatening to kill him if Stella didn't give him back his money. That was all he could remember. Had he killed either or both? Where was his money? Where was he, and why couldn't he move? His eyes moved slowly around the room, his vision still swimming. The room was small. He felt movement: it was the room. Was he on a train?

He felt a nervous tic in his left hand and found that with a little effort he was able to move a finger. He felt a cramp in his leg; at least he wasn't paralyzed. Panic overran any relief, and he felt an urgent need to get the hell out of wherever he was. He did not know what had happened, but figured he was on the run, which meant the cops were looking for him. He forced his hand to move while screaming Move... move... move in his mind and trying to stir some life into his feet.

"I'm really not all that hungry," the woman said to her

husband as she glanced at the menu.

"We won't have time to find anything in Omaha, not if you want us to get to your sister's farm by five. The blue-plate special looks pretty good for train food. I'm hungry. I'd like a beer, too." Her husband sounded a little annoyed.

"I'll just have the soup," she surrendered with a sigh.

He raised a finger to get the waiter's attention. "Oh hell," he said as he patted his coat pocket. I left my wallet in the cabin. "Go ahead and order. I'll be right back. And don't forget my beer."

Elroy managed to sit up. He moved his legs to the edge of the bunk. He felt unsteady. He ached from head to toe, and it didn't help things that he felt like puking. He rose, leaned against the compartment door for support, as he tried not to vomit on his hospital blues. Blues? Where the hell did I get these? He had no pockets. He knew that he had no money and no identification. He couldn't jump the train until he had some real clothes and a few greenbacks.

He heard the heavy metal door at the end of the car open and close. He slid open the door just enough to see a man about his size coming his way. When the man was just in front, he opened the door. "Hey, pal, can you lend me a hand?" He slumped back into his compartment drawing his victim in.

Elroy didn't have much strength, but surprise was on his side. He forced a washcloth into the man's open mouth, used his weight to hold him down, and held his nostrils closed until the man stopped twitching.

The Pullman porter knocked on the compartment door for the third time as the train pulled into Omaha station.

He knocked a little harder. "Sir is everything all right?" He looked at his pocket watch. The train was running fifteen minutes late and needed to make up for lost time. A sick passenger always added unnecessary delay, and today was not a good day for that.

It was Thursday, and Emma was adamant that her pot roast be served at a precise moment and temperature. The last three Thursdays he had been better than an hour late, and there ain't nothing worse than a woman's scorn served along with cold pot roast.

"Hell's bells, what mischief has the jackanapes brought me today?" He searched the large key ring attached to his belt for the compartment key and slipped it into the lock. The train whistled its arrival as he slid the door open. "Sir, we's in Omaha, time to get up and off the train." Something wasn't right. Two men had checked into the compartment and only one was here, still in bed. He kept a close eye on the comings and goings of his passengers and hadn't seen anyone come out. He knocked on the small lavatory door. "Sir, it's the porter, we's in Omaha. Is you all right?"

The door easily opened to an empty toilet. *Oh, Lord what trouble has come my way?* He slid open the shade to the compartment window and turned to wake the remaining passenger. "Sir... I..."

The man in the bed wasn't sleeping, wasn't moving, and didn't look like he was even breathing. The porter touched a limp wrist protruding from beneath the blanket. The man was dead. He stumbled back from the body as if death were contagious. "Oh Lord, this train is nowhere bound. There will be no pot roast tonight, and no understanding."

He sucked in a cold breath then reached down and pulled the blanket back to see who it was that had up and died on him. What he saw caused his dark face to turn gray. The body was stone cold dead, but it didn't belong to either of the passengers who should have been there. "Today is the day I's going to retire," he said and pulled the emergency cord to call for help.

35
A DAILY DOSE OF MUSIC

Ivory Burch was a rare kind of patient. After all the years, the long hours, the sorrow that the doctor held tucked away in a private place for all the ones who didn't make it, Ivory made it all worthwhile.

Dr. Fryback stood silently in the door way and studied Ivory, who was sitting on his bed strumming his guitar. Ivory was the most unusual patient he had ever encountered. He had called Stella and listened with amazement as she told him the remarkable story of the two blind men and a Jap that Ivory had spoken about when he had first been readmitted. After that, the doctor wrote a prescription allowing Ivory a daily dose of music: medically necessary, as often as needed. No one in the ward complained if he wasn't too repetitious. Sometimes he sang, but mostly he just played. Ivory couldn't read a note of music but what he made up sounded damned good.

Dr. Fryback took one last look at Ivory's chart, then closed it. In the few weeks that Ivory had been here, he had put on enough weight that he no longer looked like a dead man walking. Considering the menagerie of jungle diseases and parasites that he had played host to, he was in remarkable shape.

Ivory played a few bluesy notes. "Hey, Sarge, it's Doc Fryback and, what do you know, he ain't got no damn needles in his hand this time."

Dr. Fryback chuckled. Ivory frequently spoke to the phantom Sergeant Ware as if he were recuperating in the cot next to him. When Ivory concentrated on the strings, he didn't think about the past. The dead didn't whisper in his ear, except for Sergeant Ware, who sometimes sat just on the edge of his consciousness wishing him well. Getting things straight with the sarge had taken some doing. "Old sarge here has got my backside covered," Ivory had said. If one friendly spirit, out of a thousand unfriendly ones, could help him overcome the guilt of surviving when they hadn't, that was just fine.

Dr. Fryback looked at the bed next to Ivory and wondered if Ivory thought he saw the sergeant. Dr. Fryback nodded towards the empty bed.

"Sergeant, as always."

Ivory strummed out a few more bluesy notes.

"Well, Ivory, it's been a long time coming. Are you ready?" The doctor peered through the top of smudged spectacles. "Son, are you really ready? Once we start, there is no turning back. The first amputation and for, what it's worth, the second were classic field hospital butcheries, cut out the bad, pack it with sulfur powder, sew it up, allow for drainage, then ship the patient back to a rear area hospital or hospital ship where a clean saw can be used. You got a rotten deal."

He shook his head apologetically. "You've had two brushes with gangrene, and the risk of infection is too great. That's why we have to take off three more inches." He reached down and touched Ivory's stump and could tell by Ivory's face that his light touch had drawn pain. He gently rested his palm over his patient's kneecap. "Six months ago, we might have been able to save your knee. Now, we just can't risk another infection." He gently moved his hand forward and drew a line with his finger. "Here will be the first cut." He moved his finger up another inch and a half.

"And here the second. The remaining healthy flesh and skin I'll fold over the stump and graft it together. With time, patience and hard work, and a little luck, we should be able to fit you with an artificial leg. With some real sweat and tears on your part, you could be walking with only a slight limp by this time next year."

"Doc?"

The doctor took off his glasses and pretended to clean them on a handkerchief. "The pain? I'll give it to you straight. There will be some pain. At first it will hurt like a sonofabitch, but you'll get through it." He closed the chart. "Are you sure?" he asked, knowing what his patient was about to go through.

Ivory's Adam's apple rose as he sighed. "Nothing will ever hurt as bad as it did when that Army corpsman cut my leg off. He didn't have any morphine. He said if he didn't take the leg, I'd be dead by nightfall. The next morning, I wished I was. Let's do it, Doc, before I change my mind."

The doctor patted Ivory's shoulder. "Tomorrow morning then. Anything I can do for you in the meantime?"

"How about a big fat medium rare steak with all the trimmings?"

The doc smiled. "Sorry, it's Jell-O tonight."

"Fruit?"

"No, hospital plain. All you get is a choice of color: yellow or orange."

Ivory started to play again. "Give my steak to the sarge. He's looking a little rawboned. And Doc, you've got one thing wrong: I'll be walking inside of six months."

36

CHANGES

When you are blind, time is damned elusive. Earl marked his time by the usual sounds of the world around him. Delivery men on their regular rounds. Henry's tea ceremony when he first rose in the morning. Gibby's assorted noises when he arose stiff and tired, not having slept well; he never did. "Old bastards like me don't sleep well or long," Gibby would grumble when asked about the start of his day. Earl learned early on to stop asking.

Early afternoon came when Brooks staggered from his bed, which he rarely did prior to noon, usually closer to one o'clock. Stella came around five; her smell and the sound of her voice brought the promise of a good evening.

Now all that had changed. Henry had left for medical school three days ago. He had gone with few words, a brotherly hug, and a final handshake. Earl felt the mixture of sadness and relief in Henry's voice when he wished them all well. When the door closed behind him, the room fell deathly quiet, the only sounds the monotonous tick-tock of a clock and Gibby's labored breathing.

Then, for a moment, from out on the street, came the sweet sound of Henry's clarinet as he faded from their lives, playing for the last time Stella by Starlight. It was as if some of the heart had left the room.

Earl had not thought about it then, but Stella had not been there to see Henry off. When he tried to add the days up, Stella had not come around for six, perhaps eight days. That was when Earl tasted the saltiness of his own tears and wondered if Stella had deserted him. It wasn't just Henry's leaving that had changed the atmosphere, it was something else, something the damn clock punctuated with each tick: all was not right and might never be again.

Gibby had started sleeping late into the mornings. Once he was up, he was mostly silent, holding back his anger, no matter how many glasses Earl broke or drinks he spilled.

Brooks, on the other hand, had begun to rise early, tinkering earnestly on the piano, while trying to draw Earl into conversation he really did not want. Five o'clock came and passed, then eight, ten, and closing time,

Earl listened to the clock tick. Time was becoming elusive, and it scared the hell out of him.

"You got a forwarding address for Henry yet?" the postman asked, as he dropped a stack of bills on the bar.

"Haven't heard word one," Gibby groused. He picked up the bills, opening the first one. "You'd think the guy would be a little more grateful." He looked around the room at all the things that needed doing. Things he had neither the time nor energy to do anymore. He knew that Henry was not coming back, but he couldn't seem to get around to putting the Help Wanted sign in the window.

Earl, with a little help from Brooks, had transformed the old bar into a happening place. Word was out that there was a blind bartender in town, and that he could sing the socks off Sinatra. He brought in the cash-paying customers night after night. Gibby couldn't keep up with it, and as each day passed he seemed to get farther and farther behind. He was tired, and there was no telling him what to do or not to do.

"Ouch." The postman winced. "You're being a little hard on him, don't you think? If it hadn't been for Henry, you wouldn't have found Earl. Without Earl, this would just be another run-down bar in need of a neighborhood drunk. Now it's a cash machine."

"Don't I wish," Gibby said, and he tossed the rest of the bills, unopened, into a drawer.

"Where is Earl?" the postman asked as he searched his mailbag for something.

"He's back in the kitchen, breaking something."

The postman laughed. "Well, tell him I said hello... Oh, I almost forgot: I have a letter for Henry. There is no return address, so until you get a forwarding address on the guy, this here is what they call dead mail."

Crash.

"That must be Earl," the postman said as he turned towards the door.

Gibby tossed Henry's letter into the drawer with the bills and turned towards the kitchen door. "Christ Almighty, Earl, I'm going to have to raise the prices around here just to pay for the damage. You're like a bull in a china shop. A blind bull."

37

LAST CALL

Stella sat at the kitchen table and stared at the pen that lay on the piece of stationary in front of her. Her tea grew cold as she sat and stared at the pen as if it might jump up and bite her.

When she had gotten a call and a job offer at the Naval Medical Center in San Diego, she had taken it, wasting no time in catching the next train out of town. She thought she was done with nursing. She had enough money to retire. She was in her early forties, too young to retire and too old to start a family.

And she had been single for so long that she really did not want a man in her life. That was until she started to fall in love with Earl. She had gotten too close, too fast, that was why she had run away. Loving one man would be difficult for her; a blind man was something else altogether. So, here she sat, alone and unhappy in San Diego.

That was why she stared at the pen and paper, because she couldn't just run away. She needed somehow to say goodbye. "Dammit, you're blind. It's so complicated." She had put the miles between them, but her heart was with him, and he wouldn't let her go. Tears ran down her cheek as she picked up the pen and began to write.

Dear Henry,

I writing to you because I know that you will understand and not make a girl feel worse than she already does.

This letter is for Earl...

The evening started out good, quickly shifting to bad.

Earl's ill-gotten fame as a blind bartender had attracted the attention of MovieTone News, which showed up ready and eager to film with no prior request or invitation. The MovieTone van parked out front drew immediate attention throughout the neighborhood, which packed the place with the curious. Brooks played. Earl poured as best he could while chatting it up with his fans. Gibby took orders, served, cleared tables, and tried to seat more people than the place could handle.

The drinks fell behind when Earl started singing, which meant that he was not paying attention to his bar keeping. This mess soon added to the frivolity of the evening. All of which was captured for movie audiences far and wide.

The bar was noisy, crowded, cigarette smoke thick enough to cut with a knife. To add to the confusion, Brooks was trying to sing above the clamor. Gibby needed to be in four places at the same time. There was a line at the door, and he couldn't get there to move it along. Half the crowd hadn't given their drink orders, and he hadn't delivered most to those who had.

Earl was spilling much of what he poured. And a woman with a perpetual frown whined that either the toilet had overflowed, or someone had peed all over the floor. His first thought was, Brooks again. Only Brooks hadn't left the piano since Earl had started playing to the cameras. The bar only had one public bathroom, so he couldn't let it go. "Goddamned inconsiderate S.O.B.s," he muttered to himself as he tried to push himself through the crowd.

"Hey, waiter, where are our beers?"

"Coming right up," Gibby answered, suddenly feeling a little nauseous. He set a tray of drinks down on the wrong table, the weight suddenly too great for his hand. The numbness he had begun to feel a few weeks back had never gone away - tonight it was almost debilitating.

"I demand..." the woman with the frown screamed into his face.

"Hold your water, lady. I'm gettenaire." Gibby did not notice that his speech had become slurred as the room seemed to swim around him.

"Order up!" Earl cried out. "Six to go." He slid six beers cross the counter, the last knocking the first to the floor. "Oops, make that five." The phone rang. Earl answered, leaving the beer tap running free.

"Hey, Gibby, looks like Earl needs some help," someone called.

Gibby leaned in, with a long reach, between two customers at the bar to shut the beer tap off. He couldn't quite reach it, but neither could he close his right hand, if he did reach it.

Earl hung up the phone.

"Eur, for Chrissake, remem shuh off the eer tap."

"Mister, the restroom please. I've been waiting for—"

"Lady, will you shuh da el." *Where's the mop?* he thought as the pain grew in his chest. The room swam as he staggered through a rear door, not remembering where he was going, or why. Once inside he leaned against the wall, brought his left hand to his chest, and a pained "Ahhhh... no" became his last breath as he slid to the floor.

"Ladies and gentlemen, Mr. Earl Crier," Brooks crowed as he yielded the piano to Earl.

Earl splashed his way out from behind the bar. He was tired of mixing, pouring and spilling. He was ready to fawn to the cameras with his music. With that thought in mind, he paid little heed to Gibby's absence. "A fellow by the name of Como recently released this little number. It's currently number one on the hit parade. Here is how it ought to be done."

'Alone from night to night...

The crowd made its own noise. The camera crew was packing up to go. They had come to shoot a blind bartender, not a crooner. Everyone wanted service that wasn't to be had. Earl could feel that he had not captured the audience, the noise and vocalizations told him that folks were not happy. "Okay? That one did not rock your boat. That's okay. Let's put a little life in the party." Earl ran his hand along the keyboard, and partially stood, as he floated a little more energy into the room.

He failed to engage the audience again. He could smell trouble but could not figure out why. NUTS! Gibby is going to skin me alive for this one, but what the hell, the night is not one to be forgotten. "Okay, folks, in honor of the MovieTone people and my sudden fame, the next round of drinks are on the house."

The place erupted with a cheer.

What was lacking was Gibby.

Beneath his silk mask Brooks held a rare smile. The place was jumping, alive, and he for once was beginning to like himself. Of course, Mr. Dark was always with him, but Desperation and some of the other unsavory characters were off irritating someone else. He listened to Earl crank up the volume and thought, go ahead, Earl, there is nothing you can do to ruin my evening.

He smiled to himself as he sought his hidden bottle of rye he had stashed in the back room. His throat was parched, his whistle dry, his addiction in need of a fix. Gibby cut him off when he was at the piano. If he had a drink, he was offstage for the rest of the evening. Some nights that was okay by him, but not tonight. Tonight, he needed to loosen up, because tonight he was going to go back to that damned piano and whistle up something for Earl to chew on. So, Gibby be damned, *I'll have a drink when and where I want one.* He felt his way, touching familiar things, knowing exactly where he was going, the bottle of rye he hidden behind an old bag of flour. No one baked, so God only knew how old the flour might be, which made it about as safe a place to hide a bottle in a bar as there might be.

He counted the steps. At fourteen, he found something unexpected. He leaned down and felt what was blocking his way. It was warm. It was a human body. Brooks found a shoulder and shook it. "Hey, buddy you can't sleep it off here. Say, wait one moment? Oh my God..." That was when he found the eyes, and nose. The eyes were open, there was no breath. That was when he knew it was Gibby and that Gibby was dead.

All right, Earl thought, *I have them now. It's a tough audience, but damn, when you hook them, they usually ride the wild train right to the station.* "Okay, folks, here's one I think you will really like." His fingers hit the first three notes...

"Earl, it's Brooks." Brooks whispered loudly in his ear. Earl felt Brook's hand fumble to find his shoulder, his grip unusually tight with nervous tension. "We've got a sonofa-bitch of a problem. It's Gibby. He's... he's..."

Earl's fingers froze a fraction of an inch off the ivory keys. "What?" Earl demanded in an impatient low whisper. *Brooks is a guy who can blow a hangnail into life-threat-ening surgery.* But something in his voice told Earl that yes, indeed, there was a sonofabitch of a problem. "Take a breath, old buddy, and tell me in a word what's going on. I'm losing the audience here."

"I was in the back room, working my way to my stash. You know. That was when I almost tripped over him."

"Who?"

"Gibby."

The noise in the bar was wrong. The voices, loud, people were not happy. Through the cigarette smoke Earl smelled trouble. He was losing the audience again. He blocked out Brooks briefly as he listened to the room:

"Come on, Herbert, we're leaving."

"Mildred, we just got here. We've got drinks on the way."

"Good luck, pal. I ordered mine ten minutes ago."

"The bathroom is filthy. I've got to go."

"Shut up, lady. Gibby's working on it."

"Well, I never... "

"You got that one right ..."

"Anthony are you going to let this hooligan insult..."

It was the same across the room. Earl blew out a long breath. Frustration drew him to speak a little too loud as he focused once again on Brooks. "Gibby, what the hell are you talking about?"

"Gibby," Brooks answered, "he's dead." His breath whined like an ill-gotten wind as he spoke.

Earl fell silent. His hands dropped down to the keys with a resounding off-key clink. After a moment he gave a great sigh that seemed to leave him deflated. He started to say something but couldn't find the words.

"Hey, asshole, shut up." Someone swore from across the

room at a rowdy drunk.

A woman stood up nearby. "Hush, everyone," she demanded with genuine concern.

"Earl, what's going on?"

The audience grew quiet.

Earl started to say something but couldn't quite find the words.

Brooks stood silently behind him, looking every ounce the beaten man.

Earl's finger slowly started to play the first notes of Sentimental Journey. "I can't see who is here, so would anyone who has known Gibby for a long time, please come forward? Lloyd? Jake? Paul? Please?" The soft strains of Sentimental Journey held everyone in silence as Earl waited. "Someone please," Earl asked again as the melody continued to waft across the room.

Jake McClintic, a friend of Gibby since before the war, rose and made his way to the piano. He looked around the room, saw faces he knew, many more that he didn't. The one face he could not find was Gibby's. "Earl, Jake McClintic here. What's the problem?"

Earl motioned with his hand for him to come closer. "Earl?"

"Would you mind following Brooks into the back room? It sounds like something has happened to Gibby." Earl touched a key, it's one single note caught within the sudden silence of the moment.

"What is the problem Earl?"

"Jake, just do me a favor, and follow Brooks. I don't want... Please just go." Earl's voice trailed off with emotion as tears began to slowly edge their way from behind his dark glasses.

Jake followed Brooks.

Earl started to play *Tangerine* but couldn't find the notes. *Serenade in Blue* came next, mixed with the missing notes from *Tangerine*. Energy and passion from deep within his soul poured through his fingertips as he played and waited for Jake to return. His voice was rich, if not mesmerizing. He shifted uncomfortably on the piano bench as he heard the door to the back room open and close.

Jake's hand on his shoulder confirmed what he already knew in his heart had happened. "I'm sorry," Jake whispered, "Gibby is gone."

"Is there a doctor in the house?" Earl asked the room.

No answer.

Earl turned towards Jake's hand. "Would you mind making the call?"

"Sure."

"Thanks," Earl said as he tried to hold himself together. "Brooks, do us both a favor. Pour me a double of what you're having, pal. Keep yours a single. We've got enough problems without you getting pie-eyed, okay?" Earl's hand ran all the keys in a loud roll. He then bit back his tears and sang. It was supposed to be a

Humorous, lite and gay, but it rumbled with dark clouds and a soul struggling with loneliness. "Last call, ladies and gentlemen. Last call," Earl called out abruptly. "Last call."

Earl stopped singing and played one lonely note slowly repeatedly as he spoke. "Ladies and gentlemen, I said last call. If you have a drink, please raise it high; if you don't, I'm sorry, this bar is now closed. Its last drink is poured and raised now in memory of Edward Gibson, Gibby to his friends, who a few moments ago, passed on."

The cacophony of voices dropped like a rock into a pool of silence. The silence following was long and deep until it was broken by a single voice.

"What?"

"No."

The single note Earl played echoed throughout the room.

"Please, finish your drink if you have one; it's on the house. And quietly, with respect, please leave. Adam's Place is now closed." With that Earl played Moon Glow which he knew to have been one of Gibby's favorites. It had been he and his wife's song.

The bar quietly emptied with many a sad eye cast back.

Earl played until the bar emptied. He played until the police arrived. He played as the scream of an ambulance shattered the night. He played as Gibby's body was taken from his home of thirty-plus years. He played until only he and Brooks were left alone, the tick of the clock the only sound left at Adam's Place. They had lost a good friend, and they had lost a good home they would now be forced to leave.

But to where?

38

DON'T BE A FOOL, STELLA

San Diego was nice, it didn't have San Francisco's bone chilling fog, but neither did it have its charm.

Stella smiled at the man who sat across from her at a quaint little bistro she had discovered near the hospital where she worked. Lieutenant Colonel Marcus Jennings Drake, M.D., formally Chief Surgeon U.S. Army Medical Corps,

Okinawa. He'd been there, and seen it all, including first-hand medical observations at Nagasaki. He was forty-five years of age, handsome as the day was long, single and interested in her.

Don't that beat all.

He wasn't interested in raising a family, and neither was she; that time had come and gone, at least as far as she was concerned. He was career Army with a short ticket to General. Rumors were that he was top of the short list for command at Fort Sam Houston in San Antonio, the new site for the U.S. Army Medical Field Service Training School.

Why this man was interested in her was beyond her understanding.

Nevertheless, it made a girl feel good; well, a little better than good under his watchful sky-blue eyes. God, his eyebrows are sexy. She had all but forgotten about Earl — almost. The music playing in the background reminded her of how close she had come to him; that same feeling was beginning to curl her toes now as Marcus slid his hand across the table towards hers. They touched.

She smiled.

He responded.

She slowly pulled her hand back, hesitated.

He withdrew his. "Another?" he asked, meaning her Scotch.

"Please." She lit a cigarette. *Too fast?* She thought. *Don't be a fool, Stella. Don't let this one get away.*

39
THERE IS NO WE

Earl had slept at the piano, not that you could call it sleep; bad dreams had clouded his mind. Not war dreams, nor the one he had of being a child and trapped underground in what had been a poorly covered well. No, these dreams were new, terrifying and undefined, fleeting thoughts about the dark roads ahead.

Life had been sweet at Adam's Place. Stella, Henry, Gibby, and even Brooks. They had become a family of sorts. He had beaten his serpent, at least so he thought. He had played and sung to his heart's content, and then some. No doubt he had walked a little on the edge learning to bartend — a legend in his own mind. Hadn't that been a hoot, the best of times. He had fallen in love with Stella, his nightingale. Then she was gone, without word one. Gone. Not a whisper. Not a note.

Sometimes life deals you a bad hand, and you just must grin and bear it. He had survived the loss of his sight and adapted. Things happen in threes. First Henry left, then Stella disappeared. Gibby died. Damned inconsiderate. He felt abandoned, alone, adrift in a pitch-black whirlpool without a lifeline. Earl had spent the night drifting back and forth caught in this whirlpool of hopelessness, his chin resting on his hands as they pressed heavily down on his faithful ivories. What next? The word he did not want to think, let alone speak, Homeless. And so, the ivories had remained silent. At this moment he could find no music within him, not even the blues.

"Earl?" Brooks tapped down three times on a piano key near where he had heard Earl snoring. "Earl?"

Earl wasn't asleep, he just didn't want to face the waking world. He especially did not want to answer Brooks. He knew what Brooks wanted to ask, and he hadn't any answers.

"Earl?" Brooks found his shoulder and shook it. "Earl, damn you. I've sat here all night, without one drink, waiting for you to tell me what we are going to do. Earl, what are we to do?"

We? Earl thought with a certain amount of anger. *We?* He lifted his head, neck stiff, fingers almost numb. His mouth dry as cotton and tasting of things he did not want to contemplate. "We?" he flared. "There is no 'we', you bloody moron. It all ends here. I am not and will not be your keeper. I have my own goddamned problems. So... so... go drown yourself in as much booze as you want." Earl waved his hands wildly in the air. "There is plenty here, pal. Don't let it go to waste."

Brooks stepped back, barely resisting the need to smack Earl upside the head. Instead, he quietly walked over to where he knew the cash register to be, rang it open, and took out a handful of bills. He did not know what they were, but what the hell did it matter? He found a pint bottle and stuffed it into his coat pocket. "You're a sorry bastard," he muttered as he shuffled his way towards the front door. The only sound that marked his exit was the soft crunch of peanut shells. Outside, the fog was cold and bitter. Couldn't have asked for better, Brooks thought as the door closed behind him.

Which way are we going? Desperation asked.

Does it matter? Mr. Dark laughed.

Not one damn bit, Self-Pity piped in.

"Shut the hell up," Brook demanded. "I don't need nor want help from any one of you, especially that miserable prick Earl Crier. The next time I see him, if he is frying in the fires of Hell, then the trip will have been worthwhile." The wind ripped at his silken mask. He shivered as he brought a hand up to keep the cloth from sailing off. For a moment he thought of going back. The thought flickered and died like a moth in a flame. "No, sir, it ends here," he said with little conviction. He took five steps forward.

"Hey, watch it, asshole!" He heard someone scream as a deafening shrill of a car horn threw him back. Stumbling, he fell, landing painfully on his left hip against a cement curb. Desperation and Self-Pity mocked him as he screamed out. "Can't you see I'm walking here? Goddamn that—"

The screech of car brakes interrupted his thought as he struggled to find his feet. Another car honked, only farther away. A car door opened. A hand toughed his arm. "Hey, Mac, are you, all right?" The supporting voice added strength to the grip that helped him to his feet.

"That was close. Did you get the license? Jesus..." Brooks heard the man gasp as he most likely saw his mask. "What the hell? I mean—"

"It's OK, mister, I'm blind. It was my fault. It was" — he laughed at his own expense — "it was my fault. I didn't see it coming."

The man helped Brooks to his feet. "Where are you headed, pal? I've got a car and plenty of time." He steered

Brooks towards the car.

Brooks did not argue but he did have to think for a moment about where to go. He dusted off his tux. "Well, I'm all dressed up, so I might as well go to one of the best gin joints in town. What do you recommend?"

"The Tonga Room is always jumping. Perhaps the Top of The Mark? The Mark Hopkins might be better for you, it's a little less crowded, has a great view, and great music."

"View, you say?" Brooks chuckled. "That would be nice. Do you know if they might have a piano?" Brooks stretched his fingers. "I think I'd like to play."

40
IT WAS GRAND WHILE IT LASTED

Earl listened to the crunch of the peanut shells as Brooks left. They had never sounded louder or harsher. He knew that the next time he heard the sound, it would be from his own feet as he left this place and everything behind him. He thought of Gibby and felt resentment. He thought of Henry and smiled as he almost heard Henry's clarinet in his memory. He thought of Stella and brought his fist down on the piano keys. Twice. The echo from the strings hidden within the old piano resounded like a flock of crows battling it out with drunken seagulls.He could wait around until some lost relative claimed the bar, but that was unlikely. Or until the creditors came to claim more than they were entitled to. For once, the bastard is right. Hell must be freezing, and the fat lady has stopped singing. Damn that bastard, whoever he is.

He found his way to the cash register and took the remaining cash. What little he had didn't matter. It was just time to go. He heard the shells crunch beneath his feet as he found the door, paused and remembered the fateful day he had arrived. Time to go, he thought as the door closed behind him. It was grand while it lasted. He left as naked as they day he had first arrived, only a little richer for the memories. If anyone was listening they might have heard him whistle Stella's song as he walked away, the click of his cane almost in tempo.

Brooks knew the future was bleak, but for now he was

not going to dwell on that. There was one positive in this sea of carp, once and for all: he was rid of Earl Crier. No one was looking over his shoulder telling him what he could or could not do. The silk masks that Stella had made for him worked wonders for his self-confidence. He was headed to the Mark Hopkins Hotel, one of the most prestigious places in town. Top of the Mark. Yes, sir, why not?

This is it, old boy, Mr. Dark whispered. *Gloom and Despair missed this ride. They're yesterday's fair-weather friends. You got no future, so why the hell not enjoy today before you cash in your chips? Take a room at the Mark; room service, if you want it, and charge all the booze to the room. When they get wise, what will it matter? You went out on a high note. Yes, sir, if you've got to go, you might as well go out in style.* Brooks laughed aloud. "Why the hell not?"

"What's that pal?" he heard his host and driver ask.

"Nothing, nothing at all. I appreciate the lift." Brooks introduced himself. "The name is Oscar, Oscar Brandt."

Oscar Brandt was a pretty good piano man he had met back in Hollywood before the war. He rarely worked the club circuit, did mostly movie scores and studio work. He had heard that in late 1945 Brandt had died in car accident.

Rumors were that he had jilted his wife for a platinum blond twenty years his junior. Either way, he had a recognizable name that just might get him a suite at the Mark Hopkins without too many questions asked.

"Saul Feldman," the man answered. "Holy cow! Did you say Oscar Brandt? And you play the piano? You're not...?" he asked incredulously. "I heard you were dead."

"Almost." Brooks answered. "It's a long story I don't care much to talk about." He brought his hand up to his silk mask and left it there long enough for the driver to see in his rearview mirror. "After my accident, I've been taking things slow, one day at a time. I couldn't take the quiet anymore, so I thought I'd step out. To think that I came this close to being squashed like a bug, gives a guy pause to think. I sure appreciate you being there."

That a boy, Mr. Dark, whispered, *just don't lay it on too thick.*

"I came in on the train this morning," Brooks continued. "The cab driver thought he could pull a fast one on me just because I'm blind. He ripped me off for eighteen bucks then left me off God knows where. When we get to the Mark

Hopkins, it would be my pleasure to buy you a drink."

"Mr. Brandt, I couldn't..."

"I won't take no for an answer. Besides, I'd appreciate a friendly hand checking into the hotel. If you will help me find the piano at the Top of the Mark, I'd be pleased to play you a tune."

"Before the war," Saul said, "I used to do a little studio work, played the oboe. Boy, oh boy, this is going to be a day I'll never forget. You wrote three or four of the scores I had the pleasure of working on. I'd be honored, Mr. Brandt, you just name it."

41

JOHN DOE

Elroy stared at his gatekeeper, a woman whose ample breasts brought little charm to her matronly girth. She was a gorilla, a ball-buster. Elroy could sense that she enjoyed inflicting pain as much, if not more, than he did. They stared at each other through the barred glass of the ward door's window. Her emasculating stare unnerved him, but that was her intent. Elroy knew that, and he refused to blink. He wanted to pounce on her and tear her limb by limb, but he couldn't because he was afraid of her. Here, she held all the power, and she bought none of his lies. And it was his lies that kept him here, safe from the cops and a long-term prison sentence he knew waited for him if the truth were to be revealed. He needed to bide a little more time, wait for her to let down her guard for just a moment, and he would make his escape. He stared at the bitch. It wasn't her he wanted - it was Stella.

Nurse Moldawsky was about to start her usual rounds, which usually meant the patients deemed to be a threat to themselves or others were to be removed from the common area and secured back in their cells. St. Joseph's Hospital had been founded in 1887 as a pest hospital, the cells designed to separate those with tuberculosis, cholera, and smallpox. The hospital had come a long way since its founding, but these few remaining cells were ideal for keeping the criminally insane from harming one another.

The patient she watched, one John Doe, was without a doubt one of the more dangerous she had ever encountered. Her problem was that she could not get rid of him. He had been delivered to her custody without an identity. He had been arrested for armed assault and robbery with a broken bottle. His victim had suffered multiple lacerations, and it had taken three policemen to subdue the man's assailant. Without some proof of identity, they could not file charges. He had no identification and, since his arrival, he had refused to speak to her or to any of the doctors, at least not in a civil way. He was hostile, violent, and silent. They did not have enough to hold him or to release him. Was he insane, or just trying to outsmart the system? It was the latter, she thought.

She watched and waited. OK, Mr. John Doe, today we will see who is smarter than who, she thought as she waited for Doctor Weber and two of her strongest orderlies to arrive. One of the original arresting officers stood behind her. Today John Doe would not be returned to isolation. She wanted to push her John Doe to the limit, to show his true colors, in front of an officer of the courts, and a trained psychiatrist. Their eyes locked.

43
WHAT'S IN A NAME

Brooks passed himself off as a celebrity recluse to the Mark Hopkins. They bought the story, and they treated him like royalty. Everything was first-class, which suited his temperament just fine. He knew that one day the bill would come due, but until that happened, he was going to just keep on charging everything he needed to the room he couldn't pay for.

One day it came to him, while he was having a manicure, that he need not give all this up; all he needed to do was play the recluse con at a higher level. He half expected Mr. Dark or another of his poker pals to tell him that he was a fool to try but, come to think of it he hadn't heard word from any of them for a couple of days. Perhaps the Mark Hopkins was too highbrow for the likes of them. He laughed at that one, and then thought, *I laughed, now that's something.*

After a tall gin and tonic in the bar at the Top of the Mark, he dealt his first card. "Al," he called out to the bartender, he called all the bartender's Al. This one's name was Alan, who never answered to the name Al. Alan was also the assistant manager, who usually did not work behind the bar. The regular guy was off for some reason, and that, as far as Brooks was concerned, worked in his favor. What he needed couldn't be provided by the hourly-rate hired help.

"Good afternoon, Mr. Brandt. You're looking well today," Alan lied. The blind recluse gave him the willies. The silk mask, with the mouth hole that fluttered every time he spoke, was downright creepy. He told himself that accidents can happen to anyone and thanked God for his own good health, but that didn't change the way the masked ghoul gave him the creeps. The only difference today was that the silk mask was white with a black sash, which was less unnerving than the black mask with a white sash that he usually wore. "Another tall gin and tonic?"

"Please," Brooks answered. "Al, I've got a small favor to ask..."

"Just name it, Mr. Brandt, and I'll do my best to see that it happens."

"I appreciate you letting me play the piano now and then. The truth is that I'd like to play a little more often, say on a nightly basis. I know that you've got some swell headliners performing here regularly. It is the Top of the Mark, as they say. I was just thinking that it might be fun to fill in between sets, play for the late afternoon crowd, or perhaps the late-night crowd at the lobby bar downstairs." He flexed his fingers. "It feels good to play again, and I can sing a little too."

Alan thought about that, it would be a great draw to have a major talent like Oscar Brandt as a regular. The creepy mask might just add a little spice, a little mystery to the act. He poured the gin and tonic, then followed the blind man to the piano. He set the drink down in the exact spot where the blind pianist knew to find it. "I'll take it up with the boss and see what he says. Personally, I think it's a great idea."

"Thanks Al," Brooks said as he began to play. "Under the circumstances, I wouldn't want to go by my real name. I don't want folks feeling sorry for old Oscar Brandt, most think I'm dead anyway. So, if we can work something out,

I'd like to go by the name Oscar Katz. You won't have to pay me much, perhaps we can work something out with the hotel on a trade basis." With that said, Brooks began to whistle while he played. In no time at all he attracted an appreciative crowd.

44

FOLLOW YOUR HEART

Stella had been in San Diego for just over three months and had barely given a thought to family: Earl, Brooks, Henry, Gibby. She had been wrong to leave them. Now she sat in the small departure lounge at the San Diego airport, chain-smoking, and worried. She had never flown before, but that was not what bothered her. She felt... well... she didn't know what she felt, only that she was devastated by the news that she had only learned a few hours before that Gibby had died and the bar was closed. As for Earl and Brooks, that was the question that drove her nuts.

She had been waiting at her favorite café for Marcus, who consistently set new standards for being late. She was beginning to think she might marry Marcus, if he would ask her, not that they had known each other that long, but sometimes a girl just knew these things. She thought she had come to terms with being an old maid — a spinster — for the rest of her life. Then Marcus had turned her world upside down.

She ordered a second martini, a drink she was beginning to appreciate, when she spotted Lt. Commander Buck on the sidewalk just outside the café. She knocked on the window and waved.

The commander smiled, glanced at his watch, then joined her in the café. "Well, Commander, what brings you to town?" she asked as she lit yet another Camel cigarette.

"I was about to ask you the same thing." A waiter

arrived just as he sat down. He waved him off.

"Are you sure?" Stella asked.

"I'll have to take a rain check. I'm due at the Officers' Club for a wake."

"Oh, I'm sorry, someone died? You served together?" Stella felt suddenly uncomfortable.

"No. Just the opposite," the Commander laughed. "When an officer resigns his Commission to return to civilian life, it's a wake-up call. One last drink to remember those who we served with who will never come back."

"Oh, I see..."

"After 1900 hours today I'll be a civilian." He looked at his watch. "Enough about me. What are you doing here? A well-earned vacation? If so, I'll be in town for a couple more days." He grabbed his hat and pushed his chair back.

"Vacation?" She looked at the blue sky and remembered the cold fog in San Francisco. "I guess you could say that. I've been here close to three months. I'm working as the head nurse at..."

The Commander suddenly sat back down almost before he started to rise. "Then you don't know, about Adam's Place, I mean. Let's see, it's been two months." He looked at her, not sure how to break the bad news other than to just blurt it out. "Gibby had a heart attack, he didn't make it. I'm sorry. With Henry gone, there was no one left to run the bar. It closed, and about a week later someone broke into the place, accidentally started a fire, and that was it. Ashes."

Her heart lurched. Her cigarette slipped from her fingers, landing with a silent hiss in her martini. Tears welled up in her eyes. "Oh, poor Gibby. Earl?" His face, voice, his music, his smell, his laughter, everything she could

262

remember seemed to race through her brain all at once. "Earl? If I hadn't left..."

"Earl." The Commander filled in the blank to the question she couldn't quite find the words for. "Earl and Brooks..." He shrugged his shoulders and reached across the table to take her hand.

She did not take it.

"They left shortly after Gibby passed on. Where? I've asked around, but no one seems to know, with the bar burned and all, if they had left a note, anything... I haven't a clue."

The Commander glanced at his watch. "Stella... I..."

"I know," her voice barely a whisper. I'll be fine."

The Commander left, with an awkward glance back, as he left the café, hat in hand. Stella sat there, her mind numb, not knowing what to do. Finally, she silently reached into her purse, found a couple of dollars, paid for her drinks, and rose from her chair. Her legs were unsteady, but she was determined. It did not matter how, she was going to find him. *Earl. I'm coming.*

45

CRAZY AS A WOODPECKER

Elroy, a.k.a John Doe, had passed all his tests. It had taken a while because the authorities needed some level of cooperation to evaluate his mental stability. Finally, out of a combination of boredom and a strong desire to get out of the loony bin, he had given them enough cooperation to certify that he knew right from wrong, was a skilled con artist, and career criminal. Crazy? No, but all the certifying powers agreed that he should be locked up for a good long time. Now he sat handcuffed and chained to a bolted-down chair waiting for his ride back to Omaha and ultimately to the city jail where he would be held until his trial was set for aggravated assault and attempted murder. Once Elroy had determined that it was impossible to escape from the insane asylum, he needed to be transferred elsewhere. The hospital in Omaha was just as escape-proof, and he doubted that the Omaha City Jail would prove to be any better. Here he was, waiting for his ride to Omaha, and with any luck he would never see the city limits; somehow, he would make his escape. He had never given anyone a clue as to his real identity. Once he was out of the state, he would be a free man.

The chair was uncomfortable, and he shifted the best he could. The guard gave him a rap on the shoulder with a billy-club just in case he was thinking of trying something foolish.

The door opened and to his surprise in came the ball-busting nurse he had wanted to strangle back in

Omaha. He read her name tag. "Ahhhh, Miss Moldawsky, how nice to see you again. Moldawsky? Polish? It's a shame the Germans didn't get a chance to finish their work. Oh well, perhaps another time."

"Are we ready, Mr. Doe?" she asked with a curt nod. "I'm afraid the paperwork requires that you pass one more time through my care before you are officially handed over to the police."

"Please, call me John," Elroy said to the nurse. "I've had some time to think since we last met, and I'm pleased that we've got this final time to talk, heart to heart, so to speak. I do hope you don't think I'll of me?"

She remained silent as the guard stepped forward to unlock his chains.

Elroy's eyes widened as he looked up at the guard, whose expression changed to a shadow of a smile, as Elroy began to sing, his voice high and theatrical as he mimicked the cartoon character Woody Woodpecker.

'*Everyone thinks I'm crazy*
Yesiriee, that's me... '

"Oh, you are good, John, very good," she responded with a voice as friendly as burnt toast. "But not good enough. Today they are going to come and take you away, put you behind cold steel bars, hopefully for the rest of your life."

"It's nice to finally have some validation." Elroy cocked his head, giggled, as he mimicked the actor Vincent Price. "I'd like a couple of hamburgers, and I want them raw." He licked his lips slowly and deliberately. "It's amazing how long a chap can live with his skull smashed in. Would you like to try an experiment?" The woodpecker returned with a long unnerving laugh.

She stared at him and wondered.

"In my dreams you're dead. Dead. Dead. Dead. It is such a pleasant dream." His voice sounded much like Vincent Price's again.

"Time to go, John, or would you prefer we call you Woody?" The guard yanked up on Elroy's chains and directed him forcibly towards the door.

This time Elroy yanked back, nearly pulling the guard off his feet. "If you must know," he said, sounding quite sane, "my name is Elroy, Elroy Hawks. Come on flatfoot, let's get this show on the road."

46

VINEGAR AND SUGAR

There was nothing but a vacant lot where Adam's place had been. It had burned, and the blackened ruin had been knocked down and carted away. Stella's thoughts were mixed as she stared at weeds wrestling for control of the barren earth. Her eyes glistened as she thought of Gibby. If he hadn't taken in Brooks and Earl, he might still be alive Was his death partly her fault? On the other hand, thank God she had taken the money from Gibby's safe, or she would have lost it all. Now, somehow, she felt obligated to use the money to see that Earl and Brooks were taken care of. That is, if she could find them. She hoped they would be still together. She had to laugh at that. These two men really did not like each other; vinegar and sugar. But they needed each other. Two blind piano players shouldn't be that difficult to find, especially with Brooks sporting his silk mask. Where to start? Neither would be wanting to wander off too far. The logical place to begin her search would be in the neighborhood. After that, the Tenderloin, where there were plenty of single-room occupancy hotels.

Stella spent three fruitless days searching for the two blind crooners. She covered three dozen bars, some not in the best neighborhoods, and two downright scary ones. She asked at the front desks of a dozen tenement hotels and got nothing, which came as no surprise; the gatekeepers were usually tight on information about their guests. She tried slipping a few of them a couple of dollars to loosen their tongues but got nothing for nothing.

She went to every piano bar in town, or at least she thought so. The bartender at Jack's Top Hat remembered a blind man who had come in applying for a job. There wasn't one, and he had not left a phone number where he could be reached. He was colored, so that ended that.

Foot-tired and heart-weary, Stella returned to San Diego with nothing but a deeper sense of guilt. She returned to San Francisco again a month later with no better results.

47

AN AFFECTATION MOCKING VICTORY

There had been no chance of escape on the ride back to Omaha. Frustrated and angry at himself Elroy sat in a featureless cell and waited; his one shot in the dark was gone. Now he expected prison time. They had him tied and hamstrung three different ways with buffalo-sized cops watching his every move. Waiting was a bitch. Waiting, for what?

He had expected to be held at the Omaha hospital only a couple of hours. The cops were eager to get custody of him. He shouldn't have pissed them off; now it would be payback time.

The thing he most regretted was giving the bitch his real name. Talk about stupid. If they linked him to the guy he had killed on the train, he could get life. *Does Nebraska have the death penalty?* He didn't know. *And what about San Francisco? Did I do someone in there?* He hoped it was Stella. *Who had put him on the god-damned train in the first place? It's all that bitch Stella's fault, if only she hadn't pried into my business and stolen my money.* If he ever got out of this jam, he knew exactly what he was going to do with Stella.

The door swung open.

OK, show time, he thought as he held out his handcuffed hands. It was Nurse Moldawsky, and she did not look very happy. "Well, well," he sneered, "don't tell me you're going to miss me." Two orderlies stood behind her. No cops. The last time he had to deal with these gorillas, they had been none too gentle. The fact that there were no cops raised the hairs on the back of his neck. Are they going to send me back to the nut house? *It might be better than death row*, he thought.

"On the contrary, Mr. Hawks, or Woody. We will miss you. Your dream about me being dead was in error. You're the one who's dead. You died by a lethal injection in San Francisco. The chief physician at the veterans' hospital, and a police officer has certified to your untimely demise." She gave a curt nod to one of the orderlies, who stepped forward and roughly grabbed Elroy's handcuffed wrists. "The man you assaulted died two days ago. Apparently, there is no way to say that his death was immediately caused by your assault. There are no witnesses, and since you're dead, all charges have been dropped. It seems that it is very difficult to sentence someone to life in prison when he's already deceased."

A key clicked, and the handcuffs slid from his wrists.

"Good day, Woody. Mr. Hawks."

Elroy smiled, an affectation mocking victory.

48

BUBBLE NAKED

Earl waited behind the curtain to be introduced. Not that he needed an introduction, most of the gals who frequented the bar at this early hour were regulars. He fidgeted with his wig, which didn't quite seem to want to slip into place. He had been working on a new novelty tune and ran the lyrics through his head. It was a song about chickens. *Maybe he should throw this one away to caution. It was cute but stupid; maybe he could jazz it up a bit*. He began to sing with little affection. "Nobody but us chickens… ducks. The piano went quiet. "Flying squirrels, who gives a damn."

"Earl, you've got a phone call," the bar's owner whispered in his ear. At the same time the curtain began to part.

"Ladies, and those of you who wish you were men, here's our favorite man, Earl Crier. Trust me girls, there are not enough Earls to go around." He clutched his boss's hand who then motioned for the curtain to be closed.

"Earl, you OK?"

"No. No one I know has a phone, so who the hell is calling me, and why? The show will have to wait. Take me to the phone, and don't stop to flirt with anyone along the way," Earl demanded.

"Meow – you're testy today."

Earl put the phone to his ear. Who the hell even knows I'm here? "This is Earl." He recognized Brook's' voice right away.

"Earl, it's Brooks, guess who's in town?" He did not give Earl a chance to guess. "Stella. It seems she's got fliers all over town that say that she's looking to hire a blind bartender." He chuckled as if they were old friends. "And that ain't me, brother."

"Brooks, how the hell did you find me? Where are you? Never mind, where's Stella?"

Earl caught a cab, paying extra to break all the speed limits in getting him to the address Brooks had given him. He had never felt so nervous and hadn't bothered to change out of costume.

"Is this the place?" the cabbie asked.

"How the hell should I know?" Earl answered a little tersely. "What's the sign say?"

"The only sign I can see is a closed sign in the window. You sure this is the place?"

Earl fell back into the seat like a deflated balloon. He must have gotten the wrong address and he had not asked for Brooks' number back. He slammed the end of his cane against the far window in the cab. "Damn, not again!"

"Hey, watch it, Mac, my boss will bust my balls if you break that window. OK, so you got the wrong address, you got another, or shall I take you back?" The cabbie snickered a little as he eyed Earl's costume and wig through the rearview mirror.

"No," Earl answered without an apology. "Just help me to the front door of the place, and we'll see if anyone's home."

Stella lay submerged in the bath in her upstairs apartment above the bar. The water just right, the steam warm, the bubbles soft. She wondered for the millionth time if she had been a damn fool for buying the bar. Odds were

that she would never find Earl, and without him it made no
sense.

The bar, rumpled, dusty, and warn, she had purchased
for Earl; hope works better when fed. She had fixed it up,
adding a woman's touch. The bar was stocked, the tables
ready, each complete with a bowl of peanuts in the shell. A
new baby grand piano sat ready in the center of the room.
But the place was as empty as the day she had bought it.
She reached for the glass of Scotch she had sitting by the
side of the tub. She took a sip and closed her eyes. She
often remembered his voice. The way he sang. Sometimes
it seemed so real.

"I can see my Stella beneath a moonlit sky…"

Real? Her eyes opened wide as she sat bolt upright,
her glass splashing into the tub. Real! It's Earl. How…?
She splashed out of the tub with little concern for the floor
around her. She grabbed a too-small towel. Wrapped in a
blanket of bubbles and not much else, she rushed to the top
of the landing. "Earl?"

"*I think of you every…*

It is him!

Dream of you…."

Stella took the steps, hesitantly, one at a time, afraid that
she might wake up from a dream. At the bottom, the door
open, she saw him as he sat at the piano in a sequined tux
and a strange Victorian snow-white wig. She brought her
hand to her mouth to cover what started out to be a giggle
but came out a whoop instead.

She did not see the cabbie standing just inside the door
as she approached the piano, barefoot and bubble naked.

"Oh, my gosh." Surprised and embarrassed, the cabbie

turned to leave, but not before taking one last peek.

Stella stepped behind Earl and wrapped her arms around him. He felt her nakedness and the wet of bubbles and leaned back to meet her kiss. "Now that is one fine way to dress for dinner," he said as their lips met.

50

A BLIND MAN AND A CLOWN

Stella had wanted to call the bar Earl's Place. Earl argued that it made the place sound like a cheap gin joint. They settled on Stella's Starlight Lounge. With Earl's crooning and magic on the keyboard, Stella's soon became a popular night spot. Their location in the Cow Hollow neighborhood just off the Marina was a natural.

Three months passed, with eleven bartenders come and gone; they were happy but overworked. They only needed two good employees, and that was the problem: they couldn't pay enough to keep quality help, and without quality help they couldn't grow enough to be able to afford paying them. The problem in finding good help nagged at them daily.

Earl muttered to himself as he washed glasses in a sudsy sink. He hated the dish detail. His left little pinky stung from a small cut when he had broken a glass. He kept his hands near the surface knowing that there was broken glass beneath that he could not see. Being a blind bartender had its challenges; washing the glasses he preferred to leave to the sighted.

The last bartender had lasted about as long as his predecessor, and he had lasted less than a week. It was Friday afternoon, only a few hours away from their busiest night of the week, and the *Help Wanted* sign still hung in the window. Stella had gone to the store for last-minute shopping. The bar needed stocking, tables cleaned, floor swept

— a game Earl reluctantly called blind man's bluff. "Nuts," he swore aloud, "nuts, nuts, and more frigging nuts."

Tired, short, pudgy, and mostly bald, Stub Wilcox, was frustrated, hungry, and depressed, having lost three jobs in a week due to no fault of his own. He could not help being the way he was. His curse had come to him when he had been an early teen.

For years he had lived with his mom and pop in a small apartment above the bar his dad owned. He had managed his condition, had hid it the best he could, until his pop had grown too old to run the bar. Stub had tried, but the stress had been too much, in time he had lost the bar. The hurt in his pop's eyes he would never forget. Mom had just rocked sad-eyed as she watched their life's work slip away.

He struggled to just find good honest work. The Army wouldn't take him, even in the desperate years, and now the veterans had first shot at most of the jobs.

The afternoon was succumbing to the early shadows of evening, and Stub did not have dime one to his name. A day's work with a few tips might get him a room for the night, a half a loaf of white bread with some Spam.

He sucked in his pride along with his gut, pasted on a good bartender's smile, waited for his tic to pass six times, then pushed open the door as he took the sign out of the window. "It says here that you are in need of a good bartender," he announced with determination. He tossed his head suddenly to the side twice before regaining control of his seizure. "You can stop looking, I'm your mah... man."

"Who says?" a man asked from behind the bar.

Stub noted that the man had not turned in his direction,

hadn't seen his tic. Yet. Grateful for an unprejudiced introduction, he answered. "My name is Stub, Stub Wilcox, and
a better man for the job you will never want." His right arm
rose high above his head, his fingers mimicking a bird as
he lied, "I just got in town from Chicago, couldn't stand the
winters. The Windy City's loss is your gain. Is the boss in?"
His arm dropped down with a resounding slap to his thigh.

Earl turned at the unusual sound. "At the moment you
are looking at him." Without thinking Earl's hand slipped
too deep in the water. He barely felt the cut as his hand slid
across broken glass. "Wilcox? I knew a Harry Wilcox from
Chicago back when I was in the merchant marine. Any
relation? No, I suppose not. How long have you been bar-
tending?" *The guy has a good voice,* Earl thought, *friendly,
good-natured, someone you can share your thoughts with.
That there is the makings for a good bartender. What the
hell, I'll give the guy a shot. Stella will be happy as a lark
we've got someone for tonight.* He heard peanut shells
crunch as the man stepped forward.

"I started in my pop's bar back in 1919, poured more
than my share, even during Prohibition, not that I would
admit to nothin' in front of a flatfoot." He noted the dark
glasses. "Say, wait one moment. Well, I'll be darned... you
are..."

"Blind," Earl finished. "And you are hired. My name is
Earl." He held out his hand, a little bright red blood dripped
noticeably from his cut.

"That must hurt."

"What, being blind?" Earl absently scratched his cheek
leaving a livid red stain.

"No, your finger, you've got a nasty cut. "Stub threw
his neck back as far as he could to the left, then slapped his

face as he bit down on each repeated word. "Cah... cut... cah-utt... utt... cut."

Earl missed the relevance of the Stub's repetition as he tasted his injured finger, then pulled it sharply back as his tongue pierced the wound. "Damn, now I've gone and done it. I've sliced the tip of my finger off. Damn that hurts." He shook his finger in pain, marking glasses and a few nearby bottles with speckles of red.

Stub stepped quickly forward, crunching peanut shells with each step. "Hold... stah... still and let me take a look at that." He grabbed a bar rag as he held Earl's finger up for inspection. "That, pal, is going to take more than a bandage." He wrapped the cloth around the finger and pressed down. "Got a First Aid kit?"

Earl shook his head. Stub found a strong rubber band, took off the towel, and slipped it over the bloody finger, rolled it tight enough to cut off the flow of blood, then secured it with a toothpick. "Hold this tah... tight while I see how bah... bad it is."

Without much concern for pain, he washed his new boss's finger under cold water and held it up for inspection.

"Sonofabitch, that hurts," Earl grimaced as he let the pressure slip from the rubber band.

"I said, hold that tigh... tight." Stub opened a few drawers, found a rubber glove, cut off the first two knuckles worth of a rubber finger and slipped it firmly over Earl's throbbing digit, the pressure of the rubber bringing the raw edges of the wound together. A second rubber band tightened it down to stop most of the bleeding. The rubber band was loosened, the toothpick slipping silently to the floor, as Earl felt the makeshift bandage.

"Hold that in an ice buh... bucket for about ten minutes,"

Stub said, "and you should be-be-be fine. I'd leave that on until morning just to be-be safe." He filled a bucket with ice and water, put Earl's hand in it, grabbed an apron, and started to clean up Earl's mess.

The finger throbbed, but the ice helped with that. "You're not bad in a pinch," Earl said, grateful for the help. "Were you a medic in the service?"

Stub left the question unanswered.

Earl sat and listened to Stub go about his work. The new man worked fast and efficiently, asked few questions as he explored the setup behind the bar. Yes, sir, Earl thought, Stella will be pleased. His smile slowly disappeared as he thought about the evening. Friday night was the busiest night of the week, and he was going to have to play second fiddle. A one-handed bartender was about as good as a Kentucky mule in a brewery. He pulled his hand from the ice bucket testing his finger. Ouch! Playing the piano is going to be a little more than a challenge. *Damn fool, Earl, why can't you be more careful?* He chastised himself.

Most of the bars that Stubs had worked at had a stocking and supply system that was everywhere much the same: booze that moved was usually placed front row, easy to reach, with extra bottles behind. The more expensive, exotic liquors were well-lit on a high shelf to tempt those with thicker wallets. Not here. The gins and the bourbons were not together. It was almost as if the bottles were arranged by height or shape.

"U... U... Eureka," he thought aloud, "this here bar is set up for a blind man." He turned and looked for a moment at Earl with admiration. He had never heard of a blind bartender. A blind bartender, now that took some doing.

And then it came to him: if there was ever a watering hole where he could hang his hat, it just might be here.

U... U... Eureka. Earl had heard that before: the stutter. He thought it strange that he hadn't caught it earlier. He held his finger up as if he could see it. He had been distracted, but perhaps the time was good to explore this a little more. "Do you prefer to go by Stub or by another name?" he asked.

Stub spoke before Earl could finish. "I prefer to go by Stub... prefer to go by Stub... prefer... go by Stub ... prefer to go by Stub... another name... nah... prefer nah... name."

"What the hell?"

"I'm sa... sorry." Stub implored, as his head arched back, his hands hitting the beer tap multiple times splashing the area with suds. "I've got a handi... cah... handicap that is hard to con... con... trol. I'm worse with str... streh... stress." He looked long and hard at his new boss, thinking all the while that he was about to be canned. "Once given a chah - chance, I'm still the bah... bah... best bartender you'll ever hire." His voice quieted as he struggled for a little dignity. "Second to you, that is. I've got to admire whah... what you have accomplished."

The short silence that followed was as thick as molasses. Earl laughed with a deep guffaw as he remembered someone with a similar condition back at the veterans' hospital. For the next few minutes their brays mimicked each other until they almost collapsed in hysteria.

Stella heard them from the street. Her eyes went wide with surprise as she entered to find Earl practically rolling on the floor, his hand shielded in part of a rubber glove held high, matched only by a stranger who seemed to mimic Earl's every move. Her eyes wild with curiosity. "A blind man and a clown," she said with a haughty air. "Earl has got that covered on two accounts. And who the hell are you?" she laughed.

A week passed, and Stub still held the job. It didn't take long for him to endear himself to the regulars. Whenever Earl played *Stella's song*, which he opened with every night, the notes would trigger Stub's tic. Stub's arm would fly up and whatever drink he was tending would rain down. Stella bought him a yellow rain slicker, and an opening act with a few friendly ribs back and forth between Stub and Earl was launched. Stub managed to do the work of two bartenders even on the busiest of nights. He didn't care about the pay; he had finally found a home and a family.

53

STELLA'S STARLIGHT LOUNGE

Earl sat at the piano playing nothing, softly and gently.

Stella sat at the bar with her back to the door, struggling through the bills and paperwork she never could seem to get to during the week.

Stub busied himself cleaning and polishing the bar and everything in it. Sunday afternoons were usually quiet. This one was dead.

Stella had thought about closing the bar on Sundays, but what would they do? Since opening the bar, Earl did his best to avoid the outside world. She couldn't blame him; the world was a big place, and she could only imagine how difficult it must be to navigate through it without sight. At least she knew where he was and that he was safe.

She wanted to keep him close, never wanting to risk losing him again. Still, she got bored, needing a little fresh air, a night out on the town, a picnic on Mount Tam, a walk on the beach. Last week she had escaped for a couple of hours by taking a ferry boat ride over to Sausalito and back. She enjoyed the fresh sea air, the cry of the gulls, wind in her hair, laughter of children, and the view of the city she called her home, although she did not get to see much of it these days. She marveled at how much her world had changed, but to love and to be loved was all she really needed.

"What do you think about serving food on weekends?" She asked Earl. "We have a big enough kitchen. Nothing fancy, mind you, cheese trays, cold sandwiches, perhaps some soup."

"Frah... Fry... fried... chic... chicken," Stub threw in hopefully.

Earl knew where Stella was coming from; something was needed to stir up some business on days like this. He didn't answer right away and thought it over. He heard Stub splash a little in the sink and couldn't resist a playful tease as he played the first stanza of Stella's song.

As if on puppet strings, Stub's arm flew up over his head, dumping the contents of the glass he had been washing. "Dammit, Earl," he sputtered, more annoyed than angry. "I had me a pint glass of soapy water in my hand, and no slicker."

Earl chuckled.

Stub followed with his own laugh.

Stella smiled.

"The way I see it," Earl answered, "if we were to serve food, we either have to go all out or not at all. Someone must fix it. It's got to be served, and someone's got to clean up. If it's not good, then why bother?

"On a day like today, it's no big deal, but when we're busy, we'd just be creating a whole new set of problems. We either have to sell enough of it to hire someone to take care of the mess full-time, or not do it at all. The kitchen is small; we're not likely to do fried chicken with all the trimmings," he added.

"How about the fried chi... chicken ju... just for us?" Stub volunteered.

"I can see my Stella by the moonlit sky…"

"Dah...da... dammit, Euh... Earl!"

Stella laughed at their boyish behavior. "Earl be nice." Of course, she knew he was. A lot of people were cold-hearted when they picked on Stub. In the short time Stub had been with them she was amazed at how well he took it.

Earl's stomach had a mind of its own and grumbled. "Speaking of food, do we have anything interesting in the kitchen?"

"Oh, I think I can come up with something you'll like." Happy to push the bills aside, Stella got up and headed towards the kitchen. "Stub, we still have all the empty bottles. Will you please take them out to the alley?"

"Now is as good a time as any," Stub answered as he dried his hands and followed Stella into the kitchen.

54
A CRAZY WOODPECKER

Elroy Hawks pole-danced on one of the side bars of the cable car as it clanged its way down the steepest hill. When one passenger complained, Elroy pitched his hat into the wind. When the conductor approached with a reproachful look, Elroy did the same to the conductor's hat. In his Woody Woodpecker voice, he sang a new Tex Williams tune about a woman that will drive you nuts.

That's right, Stella, I'm back in town. His maniacal laugh sent chills through most of the remaining passengers as Elroy took flight before the cops could be called.

55
IVORY

Ivory Burch stood on his own two good legs. One could hardly notice that one leg was prosthetic. He had earned this day. It wasn't that long ago that he had been shipped out to the Veterans' Hospital with pretty much a death sentence over his head. And he hadn't given a damn. Then a Jap, two blind men, and a nightingale came into his life. How would he ever really be able to thank them? It had been a long, hard, steep road he had to climb, and now that he had walked out of the hospital, he felt for the first time whole again. Well, as close as he could get. He had promised himself that once he got out the first thing he would do would be to look up Earl, Stella, Henry, and Brooks and buy them all a drink. He never would have had the guts to beat this thing without them. It was hard to describe how he felt. Whatever it was, it was nothing short of exhilarating.

Ivory had heard about Stella's new joint and given her a call. She had offered him a job on the spot. With guitar in hand, he was on his way. He blew out a loud shrill whistle as his hand went up and he practically stepped in front of the cab. "Taxi, right here."

He gave the cabbie the address, then looked back one last time at the hospital. For a moment he thought that he could just make out a wave from one of the windows near where his room had been. "Sarge, you take care," he whispered. "It's not like I'm going to miss your sorry ass." *Stand at ease, private. You've earned your liberty,* he heard the sarge say. He could almost see the Sarge smile — almost, because Sarge rarely smiled. "See you around, Sarge."

56

CRISIS

Earl pushed the piano stool back, rose, and counted the steps to the back of the bar. It was time to sort the marbles. Stub had come up with the idea to use different-sized marbles to indicate to him which beers to pour. When they got sticky with use, Stub soaked them in a bowl of soapy water. Earl dried and separated them into small glass bowls that Stella kept on a tray near the beer taps.

He turned the radio on as he worked. The Hit Parade had just started with Vaughn Monroe crooning *Let's Get Lost*. Earl sang along, memorizing the lyrics and the notes, which is why he did not hear the front door open. He was clueless as to who was now sitting at the bar.

Elroy sat at the bar, his ferret eyes taking in everything. He reached over the bar for a glass and poured himself a beer. He plucked a hand full of maraschino cherries from a bar bucket, popped one in his mouth, and then began to flick them one at a time at Earl's back. A Colt .38 Super Pistol with nine rounds lay on the bar, cocked and ready.

The door to the kitchen opened.

Stub came out of the kitchen with half a ham and cheese sandwich in hand, the other half stuffed in his mouth. What he saw scared the hell out of him. He chewed and swallowed as best he could but was unable to swallow fast enough in time to give Earl a warning.

Elroy was itching to use his new toy. He had expected Stella to come through the door and was somewhat disappointed, but it did not matter. He was here on an agenda, business was business. "Earl, my man, long time no see."

Earl didn't recognize the voice, but the Woodpecker laugh that followed he had heard before. His hands almost went numb as his heart dropped all the way to his toes.

Elroy reached for and aimed the pistol as he gave his trademark Woodpecker laugh. "Guess who?" The bar resonated from the explosive blast at close quarters. Stub took the round in the chest, not far from the heart, and was flung backwards through the swinging kitchen door.

Stella screamed from somewhere behind the man he had just shot. "Oh baby, come to Papa, we've got some unfinished business, you and me," Elroy cackled.

Earl dropped the bowl of soapy marbles, the bowl shattering as his hands flew up to his ears as he stumbled back, his hearing temporarily deafened by the blast. His feet rolled on the marbles and he fell.

"I knew we had something in common there, partner. It appears you've lost your marbles." Elroy brought the gun up and held it steady as Stella appeared at the door.

Strella couldn't quite fathom what was happening. As soon as Stubs had taken his sandwich out of the kitchen, he was catapulted backwards through the door and now lay on the floor with a large crimson stain spreading on the front of his shirt. She knew that she should try to help him but was gripped with only one terrified thought: Earl... how? Earl? Please, God, not Earl!

Elroy pulled the trigger again. "That's all folks," he screamed out in his cartoon voice. The woodpecker laughs followed long and cynical as a bottle of Scotch exploded two feet from Stella's head, a shard of glass suddenly drawing a red line across her cheek.

As Stella saw Earl go down, she reached out for him in

terror and panic. A third shot shattered a row of bottles, the debris and liquid raining down on Earl as he tried to roll into a protective ball. The nearby radio was playing *Peg of My Heart*. He listened, needing the distraction.

"Stella... tsk... tsk... Stella," Elroy chuckled, "I'm hurt. Is that any way to greet an old flame?"

Stella's ears were ringing, and smoke from the pistol swirled through the air, stinging her eyes. She could see Earl's mouth open and close, but there was no cry of terror. She could only read his lips as he cried out her name. The shrill ring in her ears cleared. "My God," she mumbled beneath her breath as she stared at Elroy in disbelief, "I thought you were dead."

"Not quite, sweetheart." His sudden laugh brought shivers. "As you can see I'm very much alive." The gun swung towards her as he pulled the trigger, and for that brief second, she thought she was dead. She turned as if she already felt the impact and saw Stub, who had somehow struggled to his feet, take the bullet in his right shoulder. As limp as a Raggedy Ann doll, he collapsed, blocking the kitchen door and any retreat.

"No!!!" Helpless to do anything for Stub, she turned back towards Elroy. A shrill wail and cattle bells were all she could hear. He was saying something, but she couldn't hear a word.

"I came for my mo-ney." The word was pronounced with a smacked lip into two distinct syllables.

Earl found it hard to focus. His mind wanted to spiral back to the painful memories of the explosions aboard his ship in the Murmansk Sea. He shook his head and tried to focus; the nightmare at hand demanded his full attention. He heard the word "money," and now knew where Stella had gotten the money to buy the bar. He did not need to see what had happened to Stub to know that Elroy planned to kill them both. He needed to focus, to overcome the helpless terror that tore at his heart.

'Peg of my heart, I love you.
Don't let us part, I love you.
I always knew it would be you,
Peg of my heart...

Elroy motioned with the pistol for Stella to come to him. She backed away. "I said come here. Don't make me ask twice. That will really piss me off." He pointed the gun down towards Earl and started to pull the hammer back. No, I may need you for a couple of minutes more, he thought and pointed the barrel back at Stella. "I said I came for my money."

'Since I heard your lilting laughter,
It's your Irish heart I'm after.
It's your Irish heart I'm after,
Peg of my heart.

Earl sang softly, slowly folding the layers of darkness until he sensed everything immediately around him. Stub moaned and moved just enough that Earl knew that he was still alive. For how long? A serious clock began ticking inside his head.

He searched with his mind to remember the exact placement of everything behind the bar: marbles, broken glass, lemons under the bar in a plastic container, and a slicing knife. He prayed that Elroy could not see much of him from where he was standing.

'Since I heard your lilting laughter

It's your Irish heart I'm after.

It's your Irish heart I'm after…

He sang a little louder as he reached out for the knife, rolling marbles as quietly as possible across the floor towards the service entrance to the bar.

'Peg of my heart,

Peg of my heart,

Peg of my heart…

Stella tried not to glance down for fear that it would draw Elroy's attention to Earl. She saw the marbles roll and the knife as Earl slid it in his sleeve. As much as she wanted to run, she knew that she had to draw Elroy behind the bar. It was their only chance.

'Peg of my heart

Peg of my heart!

"Shut the hell up!" Elroy screamed. BLAM! Another row of bottles exploded, raining glass and booze down on Earl, the booze stinging the scar tissue beneath his dark glasses. As he covered his head with his hands, the knife slipped from his sleeve.

Fearing the worst, Stella moved quickly to the edge of the bar immediately across from Elroy. Her left foot kicked the knife back beneath Earl. She had just put herself in the worst possible place, within arm's length of a maniac who seriously wanted her dead. She needed to make Elroy angry, so mad that he would more want to hurt her than kill her. At least for the moment. She remembered his attempted assault in the elevator and had a good idea which of his buttons to push. If she was wrong, she wouldn't get another chance. If she was wrong, he would kill Earl just to spite her, and she could not live with that. "The money is gone, you impotent sonofabitch." She spit in his face, then waved her hand wildly pointing. "It's all here, in the bar. I used the money to buy it. So, you're left with nothing. Nothing." She leaned forward, exposing her cleavage just enough to taunt him. "Nothing."

Elroy's hand shook as he pointed the pistol's barrel straight across the bar into her face. She could tell that he ached to pull the trigger.

Earl slid like an eel through sea grass across the floor, careful not to cause the glass to tinkle. How many marbles were on the floor he didn't know; he moved as many as he could in front of him. His hand held the knife closed in his fist. He could feel the sharp sting of liquor as he cut himself, holding the blade too tightly. Still he moved forward singing only to himself, "*O Peg of my heart...*"

"You haven't got the balls," Stella swore as she stared directly into the gun barrel. Her heart was thundering in her chest so hard she thought she might pass out.

Elroy lowered the gun just a little as he wiped the spittle from his face with his other hand. "Then I'll take what's mine another way." He let out a Woodpecker cackle as he bolted towards the bar service entry.

Ivory Burch had frozen just outside the door when he heard the first shot. He set his bag down and peered through the window. He knew immediately that Stella and Earl were in grave danger. He couldn't just rush in. Nevertheless, he slowly and quietly began to edge the door open.

Elroy was fast.

Earl readied the knife.

Elroy's cackle was cut short as he tumbled to the floor.

It wasn't the marbles that brought him down, it was Ivory pounding his fist into Elroy's head.

Stella had forgotten that Ivory was coming in. Now here he was, strong as a bull, a miracle out of nowhere, and more than an even match for Elroy.

Elroy had no idea who was on him or where he had come from. Whoever it was, he was strong and was beginning to get a choke-hold on him. In another moment he'd lose the gun. He twisted his wrist around just enough to get off what he hoped was a gut shot at his assailant.

Ivory lost his advantage as the bullet slammed into his wooden prosthetic, splintering off a section below the knee. The impact felt as if it had been torn free along with the scar tissue at the end of his stub. Until that moment he had a strong hold on Elroy's neck and was able to twist Elroy's arm back far enough to dislodge the gun. They fumbled for the gun.

Ivory saw Earl and rolled back, shouting, "Earl, now! I'm clear. He's at your 2100 — nine o'clock."

Earl lashed out with the knife, too late. Elroy seized it, rolled, and took aim at Earl's throat. It was the roll that gave Ivory his chance.

Elroy's scream became a sudden empty gasp as Ivory brought what was left of his artificial knee up hard into Elroy's groin. That was all it took.

Earl froze, not knowing which way to crawl.

Ivory now had Elroy pinned.

Elroy, helpless with pain, stopped struggling. "I've got him, Earl," Ivory said. He secured the gun and held it point-blank to Elroy's nose. "Stella call the cops. Earl are you okay?"

Earl nodded. "I've had better days."

"If you're good, see if there is any life left in that poor fella blocking the door. Watch out for the glass." Ivory never took his eyes off Elroy.

Earl rose, got his balance, and followed the edge of the bar until he reached Stella, who needed him to pass before she could get to the phone. She took his face in her hands. "I'm all right," he said as his free hand traced her cheek and caught a fading tear.

"Police," Stella said into the phone as she looked over at Earl who was kneeling beside Stub. "I need to report a murder."

"Not yet," she heard Earl say. "Stub is still breathing. He's going to need an ambulance right away." She listened for a moment to the officer on the other end of the line. "Yes, the attacker's name is Elroy Hawks. We have his gun pointed at him, where it can't miss. He's not going anywhere, but I suggest you get here before one of us uses that gun."

Earl was sitting out of harm's way at the piano when the police came and took Elroy away in handcuffs. Stub was loaded into an ambulance. Ivory was talking quietly to an officer who was taking notes on everything that had happened.

Earl was tempted to play something on the piano but continued to hold Stella's hand. "This here is a day to remember," he said. He turned on the piano stool towards where she was sitting next to him.

"Yes, it is," she said, still trying to grasp everything that had just happened.

"No, not that," he said as he found her face with his free hand. "This." He brought his fingers to her lips, found them, then brought his to hers for a long, lingering kiss. "Stella, will you marry me?"

Ivory stopped talking mid-sentence with the officer and turned towards the piano. "Well, I'll be damned..."

Stella kissed Earl, her tears falling on his cheeks.

The officer let out a low pleasant whistle.

Earl held her kiss, slipped his hand from hers, and turned back towards the piano. This time he sang as he never had before

'Since I heard your lilting laughter,

It's your Irish heart I'm after.

It's your Irish heart I'm after,

Peg of my heart.'

Stella said yes.